DARK STEEL

A MEDIEVAL ROMANCE

BY KATHRYN LE VEQUE

A DARK SONS NOVEL

Kathryn Le Veque Novels

Medieval Romance:

De Wolfe Pack Series:
Warwolfe
The Wolfe
Nighthawk
ShadowWolfe
DarkWolfe
A Joyous de Wolfe Christmas
Serpent
A Wolfe Among Dragons
Scorpion
Dark Destroyer
The Lion of the North
Walls of Babylon

The de Russe Legacy:
The Falls of Erith
Lord of War: Black Angel
The Iron Knight
Beast
The Dark One: Dark Knight
The White Lord of Wellesbourne
Dark Moon
Dark Steel

The de Lohr Dynasty:
While Angels Slept
Rise of the Defender
Steelheart
Shadowmoor
Silversword
Spectre of the Sword
Unending Love
Archangel

Lords of East Anglia:
While Angels Slept
Godspeed

Great Lords of le Bec:
Great Protector

House of de Royans:
Lord of Winter
To the Lady Born

Lords of Eire:
Echoes of Ancient Dreams
Blacksword
The Darkland

Ancient Kings of Anglecynn:
The Whispering Night
Netherworld

Battle Lords of de Velt:
The Dark Lord
Devil's Dominion
Bay of Fear

Reign of the House of de Winter:
Lespada
Swords and Shields

De Reyne Domination:
Guardian of Darkness
With Dreams
The Fallen One

House of d'Vant:
Tender is the Knight (House of d'Vant)
The Red Fury (House of d'Vant)

The Dragonblade Series:
Fragments of Grace
Dragonblade

Pirates of Britannia Series (with Eliza Knight):

Savage of the Sea by Eliza Knight

Leader of Titans by Kathryn Le Veque
The Sea Devil by Eliza Knight
Sea Wolfe by Kathryn Le Veque

<u>Note:</u> All Kathryn's novels are designed to be read as stand-alones, although many have cross-over characters or cross-over family groups. Novels that are grouped together have related characters or family groups. You will notice that some series have the same books; that is because they are cross-overs. A hero in one book may be the secondary character in another.

There is NO reading order except by chronology, but even in that case, you can still read the books as stand-alones. No novel is connected to another by a cliff hanger, and every book has an HEA.

Series are clearly marked. All series contain the same characters or family groups except the American Heroes Series, which is an anthology with unrelated characters.

For more information, find it in **A Reader's Guide to the Medieval World of Le Veque**.

TABLE OF CONTENTS

AUTHOR'S NOTE

Welcome to Dane Stoneley de Russe's story!

When I first wrote about Dane, it was as a secondary character, and the son of the heroine, in *THE DARK ONE: DARK KNIGHT*. Dane was a precocious but adorable seven year old, constantly getting himself (and others) into trouble. Therefore, I had to think about Dane before I started writing about him as an adult – what kind of man did he grow up to be?

The answer was: a good one.

With Remington as his mother, and Gaston as his stepfather, he couldn't help but grow up properly guided. He's grown up into a thoughtful, career-oriented knight. But Dane's problem? He's trusting. Sometimes too trusting.

While Dane's brother, Trenton (*Dark Moon*), grew up into a hardened assassin, Dane didn't go in that direction. He's a virtuous, chivalrous man, but he has a flaw – he lets his emotions get the better of him sometimes. Sometimes he acts before he thinks (and we saw that when he was a boy). He never outgrew it.

Enter Grier de Lara.

Smart, and rather naïve, she has the same trusting manner that Dane has, but she has a bitter streak in her as well. You'll discover that. It was such a joy to write about this pair and I hope that joy shows. Now, there are a few Welsh references in this book, as it's set on the Welsh Marches, so I've once again provided a pronunciation key to help as you go along:

Idloes: EEED-loys (much like the pronunciation of Eloi, from H.G.

Wells "The Time Machine")

Grier: Greer

Eolande: Yo-LAWND (her nickname is Landy, which is
    pronounced LAWNDY)

Moria (as in the Mother Abbess): Moriah/Mariah

That's about all of the "odd" pronunciations in this novel, so read on and hopefully enjoy Dane's story. It's a very fast and thrilling adventure, so hold on for a swift ride!

Love,

CHILDREN OF GASTON AND REMINGTON DE RUSSE

Trenton (Gaston's first marriage to Mari-Elle de Russe) married to Lysabel Wellesbourne

Dane (Remington's first marriage to Guy Stoneley) married to Grier de Lara

Adeliza (married, has issue)

Arica (married, has issue)

Cortland (Cort)

Matthieu (married, has issue)

Boden

Gage

Gilliana

The Shrewsbury (Salop) Battle Horn

(Folk song, author unknown, melody unknown.
Thought to have been composed in the 14th century)

In days gone by

A rallying cry,

Meant for one and all.

As brave men would fight,

Deep into the night,

For the safety of those at Salop.

Heeding this cry,

A devil's son,

Became a duke of Salop.

A man so true,

No who knew,

The pain he suffered through.

A lady fair,

No man would care,

To call upon her heart.

But the devil's duke,

Beyond rebuke,

Loved her as none would dare.

(chorus repeat)

In days gone by

A rallying cry,

Meant for one and all.

As brave men would fight,

Deep into the night,

For the safety of those at Salop.

For the lady and her Duke of Salop.

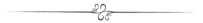

De Russe motto: *Et est spes est virtus*

"In Valor there is Hope"

Shrewsbury Motto: *Tantum in me, Deus, et rex fortis dominabitur*

"Only God and the King shall rule me"

PROLOGUE

1519 A.D., October
Battle of Erwood Castle
Welsh Marches

THE SHREWSBURY HORN had blared.

"Dane! Behind you!"

Sir Dane de Russe heard his brother's cry, bending in with the plaintive cry of the battle horn, and he ducked low and tried to spin away from whatever was coming up behind him. But he wasn't fast enough, nor was his body pressed low enough. A blow from a shield, the broadside shoved at him, caught him on the head and shoulder, and down he went over the side of the embankment.

Sliding, spinning, out of control, the weight from the armor he wore carried him down the side of the slippery slope. It was pouring buckets, the angry pewter sky above sending a deluge down to the earth as the Shrewsbury army and an angry Welsh army faced off at the base of Erwood Castle.

Water and mud ended up in Dane's mouth as, halfway down the slope, he finally rammed a dagger into the hillside like an anchor so he wouldn't slide all the way down into the moat. Down there, men were up to their waists in muck, struggling to not only stay alive, but struggling to kill the men who were trying to kill them in return.

It was sheer madness.

But it was worse up above. At the top of the embankment, where there was a partially destroyed wall, men were fighting with swords and pikes. But when they lost those, fists were flying. As a result, some of the battle had turned into a massive fist fight, and men were sliding down the slope and into the moat on a regular basis to the point that there was more fighting going on in the moat than on land. Dane didn't want to make it into that moat; once men went in, they were stuck.

They were dead.

Overhead, the sky lit up with thunder and lightning, creating a brilliant display, but in the mud lands of Erwood, no one noticed. They were all trying to keep alive, caught up in their own battles as the Duke of Shrewsbury's army tried to regain control of Erwood, a small but vital outpost along the Welsh Marches in the very southern fringes of Shrewsbury's territory that was disputed between the English and the Welsh. Shrewsbury claimed it, and had for decades, but a resurgence of Welsh rebellion, very unusual in this day and age, was trying to gain it back.

And that was why the English were here, sliding down slippery slopes and ending up in a moat of mud and blood. Dane had managed to avoid most of it so far. As he reached the top of the embankment, he paused, catching his breath and looking out over the great mass of fighting, dying men. It was beyond chaotic, and he found himself reflecting on how he'd come to this moment in time, fighting on the Welsh Marches for a slip of a castle that everyone wanted.

Truthfully, he didn't want to be here.

But he had little choice.

Dane had assumed control of one of his father's outposts along the Marches not quite a year ago, and what a glorious year it had been. Blackmore Castle had become his, along with the lordship, and for the first time in his life, Dane had been in complete control of something that was his very own.

Not that he minded serving his father, the Duke of Warminster. In fact, he'd loved serving his father as the captain of his army, but a man wanted more in life than to be subservient to a parent. His father knew that, as did his mother, so when Gaston de Russe had purchased Blackmore Castle from the king, he'd given it to Dane with the provision that Dane remain loyal to the Dukedom of Warminster.

That hadn't been a difficult task.

Taking a younger brother with him, Dane and Boden de Russe had set out for Blackmore Castle with four hundred de Russe troops and another knight, William Wellesbourne. It had been a great adventure for the de Russe brothers, and the Wellesbourne knight, but when they got to their destination, they'd discovered Blackmore Castle to be a rather dilapidated bunch of stones.

Still, it didn't matter; to Dane, it was the most beautiful thing he'd ever seen and a scant year later, Blackmore was mostly rebuilt thanks to hard work and de Russe money. Dane had built friendships and alliances among the border lords, including the elderly Duke of Shrewsbury, which was how he found himself here.

Aye... he remembered well how he got to Erwood.

Shrewsbury.

Old Garreth de Lara, Duke of Shrewsbury and Lord of the Trinity Castles, knew Dane's father and had taken an immediate liking to Dane. Shrewsbury wasn't far from Blackmore, only a half-day's ride, and Garreth came to visit Dane and Boden and William nearly every other week. He brought men with him, men he'd given to Dane to plump up his army of four hundred into an army of seven hundred, and he'd brought gifts and horses and food with him. He even brought his captain, Sir Dastan du Reims, a god of a man who had women falling all over him in spite of the fact that he was married. They would all sit together at night, feasting and telling stories. Garreth loved Dastan, but he loved Dane more. He showered the man with gifts.

It was as if Dane had a rich uncle who had suddenly died and left him everything.

Only Shrewsbury wasn't dead, and being that he was in good

health, he wasn't even close to meeting death. He was simply a lonely old man with no sons and an only daughter who was off in a convent somewhere. He took great delight in Dane and his brother, and in William Wellesbourne, whose family was so close to the House of de Russe that he was considered family, too.

Family...

That part of his family was here, fighting in this mess, and thoughts of William and Boden shook Dane from his reflections. Those two were around here, somewhere, as was the duke, and Dane was coming to think he needed to locate the pair sooner rather than later. With all of the chaos going on, he wanted to make sure they were well.

He wanted to make sure Garreth was well, too.

The old duke had no business in a battle but because it was his property, he had insisted on coming. Dastan had tried to stop him, as had Dane, but Garreth wouldn't be dissuaded. He had a contingent of bodyguards that he kept with him. But for Dane's own peace of mind, he wanted to make sure the old warrior was in one piece. The battle had been particularly brutal, especially with the Welsh involved, so something told him to find Garreth and ensure the man's safety even though he was fairly certain Dastan hadn't let the old duke out of his sight. Still, Dane might even be able to talk him into returning to camp, but something told him that wasn't a possibility.

Heaving himself up from the muddy slope, Dane went on the hunt. Almost immediately, he could see Boden over by the keep. His brother was whole and sound, shouting to some Shrewsbury men, so Dane didn't worry any more about him. Now, he turned his attention to the twin baileys, faced with a writhing mass of men.

One man found, two to go.

The castle, as a whole, was perched on the top of a hill, one that had been leveled off to build the structure, but the entire thing sloped downward, so as Dane walked from the inner to the outer bailey, he found himself slipping and sliding in the very wet mud as he went. By the time he'd reached the outer bailey, he'd slipped so much that he'd nearly fallen, twice, and with his broadsword in hand, he charged into the melee in the outer bailey.

Quickly, he spied William Wellesbourne, the fiery youngest son of Sir Matthew Wellesbourne. He was called Willie, or Dimwit, or anything else his family and friends could hurl at him because William had a wild and reckless streak in him a mile long. He'd come with Dane at Matthew's request – something about wanting his son to grow up – but so far, William hadn't done much growing up. He was still the same loveable, brilliant imp. He was too much fun to punish and too foolish to believe at times, but it was all part of the man's charm.

Dane spied William as he hacked away at a Welshman who wasn't very skilled, but who was very strong. He had a shield he kept up and William was slashing away at him. Dane suspected that the Welsh warrior was simply waiting for William to wear himself out so he could strike a deathblow, so Dane charged at the pair, the dark steel of his sword swinging at the Welshman and catching him off guard. Dane caught the man across the chest and shoulders with the sharp end of his blade, wounding him badly. As the Welshman fell away, William turned to Dane.

"What are you doing down here?" he demanded. "I thought you were going for the keep?"

Dane turned to the keep at the top of the rise, in the inner ward. "The Welsh have it," he said. "Boden is trying to organize a charge, but it's my sense that Shrewsbury is going to have to move some war machines in here if he wants to take the keep. The Welsh are dug in like rabbits in a hole. Where is Shrewsbury, anyway?"

William began to look around. "I saw him not too long ago with his personal guard," he said. "They were over by the bridge that crosses into the inner ward the last I saw. Didn't you come from that direction?"

"I did."

"And you did not see him in the inner ward?"

Dane shook his head. "Nay."

"Then you'd better look in the moat below the bridge," William said, warning in his tone. "The last I saw, Shrewsbury was right by the bridge."

"Where is du Reims? Isn't he with him?"

William shook his head. "Du Reims took a bad blow to his shoulder," he said. "He could not even lift his sword. He has been sent back to camp."

"So Shrewsbury is alone?"

William nodded ominously.

Somewhere up near the keep, the Shrewsbury battle horn sounded again, their rally cry. It was an alarm that the Shrewsbury army always carried with it, and always responded to. That horn was famous up and down the Marches. But Dane ignored the muted wail; he was feeling some trepidation now at William's words. So many men had fallen into that moat; not only did it surround the upper bailey, but the lower one as well. He couldn't imagine that an old man in armor would fare very well in it, so he motioned for William to follow him and, together, they made their way back up the slippery outer bailey towards the bridge that crossed into the inner bailey. It was a bridge that the English were trying to prevent the Welsh from actively destroying.

In fact, Dane sent William to the bridge to help the English fend off the Welsh, who had axes, and he could hear William yelling insults at the Welsh as Dane headed over to the moat to see if, in fact, Shrewsbury had ended up in it.

What he saw didn't help his anxiety.

Because of the slope of the hilltop, this portion of the moat was deeper than it was up towards the keep. Everything was draining downward, including men and guts and bodies. Down on this end of it, it was deeper and filled with far more muck than it was upslope.

And then, he saw it.

Two of Shrewsbury's personal guard, dead in the moat. As he ran to the edge of the pit, he could see two more trying to claw their way out, holding the limp, dazed duke between them.

Seized with panic, Dane ran to the edge of the moat, just where Shrewsbury guards were trying to lift out the duke, and he reached down, grabbing the old man by the arm and hauling him out of the moat. As the rain pounded and lightning lit up the sky, Dane ended up on his arse at the edge of the moat, clearing mud and debris from the old man's eyes and mouth. Shrewsbury coughed, beginning to come around.

"I have you, my lord," he said calmly. "You are safe now. I have you."

The old man was in a bad way, but he was so covered with filth that Dane couldn't see where he was injured.

"Dane?" he said feebly, trying to open his eyes. "Dane, is it you?"

"It is me, my lord."

"Are you injured?"

"Nay, my lord. Are you?"

Shrewsbury blinked, with eyes the color of the gray sky above. "My belly," he said. "They stuck a sword in my belly."

Dane looked at the man's midsection but he honestly couldn't see anything. He began to pull at the man's plate armor, trying to see what he was talking about. Shrewsbury had the latest in armor, and very expensive, so it fit together like pieces of a puzzle. Dane couldn't see where there were any gaps until he wiped away some mud near Shrewsbury's groin and saw a bright red river of blood burst forth. Then, he knew.

It was bad.

"My lord," he said, looking around to see if he could spy William. He needed help. "I shall find William and we shall remove you from this place."

He started to move, to shout at William, who was far enough away that he couldn't hear Dane's cries over the storm and roar of battle, but Shrewsbury stopped him. He grabbed at Dane, refusing to let him go.

"Nay," he rasped. "Dane, you must listen to me. It is important."

Dane didn't want to hear a dying confession. He was fond of the old man and the situation was dire. He had to get him out of there.

"My lord, if you will only…"

Shrewsbury cut him off. "*Listen*," he said. "I do not have much time, so I must tell you what I have done. I have done something terrible, Dane."

Dane sighed faintly, knowing he was going to hear a confession whether or not he wanted to. "I am sure it is not so bad," he muttered. "If it were Willie, I would believe it, but not you."

Shrewsbury smiled faintly. "You must trust that Willie will find his way someday," he said. "I have told you before. He will be a great knight."

"I will believe that when I see it."

Shrewsbury emitted a noise that sounded like something between a laugh and a groan. "You will," he muttered. "But I have done something to you, Dane, and I beg your forgiveness. Mayhap you will not be pleased about it, but I felt strongly for it."

Dane wiped more rain out of the old man's face. "What did you do?"

Shrewsbury's muddled gaze fixed on him. "My daughter," he muttered. "Grier. I have told you of her."

"You have, my lord."

"She is at St. Idloes Abbey, in Llandridod," he said. "You must go and bring her home."

"Me? Why not Dastan?"

"Because she belongs to you."

Dane blinked, registering surprise. "She *belongs* to me?"

Shrewsbury reached up an old, wrinkled hand, trembling because his strength was failing him. Everything was failing him. His watering eyes were intense on Dane.

"She is the last of my line," he rasped. "She is a great heiress, Dane. She will be a great prize for any man, but she is *your* prize. I made the decision some time ago that she should belong to you because, as the heiress to Shrewsbury, the dukedom goes with her. You shall be the

Duke of Shrewsbury when I am gone. Everything I have, I give to you. It is yours."

Dane couldn't keep the astonishment off his face. "*Me?*" he said. "But… I do not understand. You have nephews, my lord. You have told me this yourself."

Shrewsbury closed his eyes. "They are all very distant and very unworthy."

"But… but what of Dastan? He is most worthy and…"

"He is already married," the old man stressed. "Dane, only you are worthy of my daughter and my wealth. Accept this and let me die in peace, knowing that Shrewsbury shall be taken care of after I die."

It was too much for Dane to process. A wife, a dukedom… he was a simple knight, a son of a duke, but the truth was that he was the second son. In fact, Gaston de Russe wasn't even his blood father, only his adoptive one, so in that sense, Dane felt even less worthy.

Aye, that was the truth – he wasn't a real de Russe and everyone knew it. His real name was Stoneley and his father had been a vile excuse of a man. His history against the crown, against humanity, was something only whispered of by the brave.

It was something Dane had spent his whole life trying to live down.

"My lord," he said, taking a deep breath and trying to stay on an even keel. "You are most generous and you know that I am grateful, but I am not sure I can do this. I… I am no one of any great note, and certainly no one who should hold the Shrewsbury titles."

Shrewsbury's eyes opened again, but his lips were starting to turn blue, a sure sign that his blood was draining out of him, as was his life. Time was short.

"Your father disagrees," he said. "Warminster has accepted the offer of my daughter on your behalf."

Dane's jaw popped open at the mention of his father. So Gaston was in on this, was he? And just when did he, or Shrewsbury, plan to tell him this? It was clear that a mortal wound had pushed Shrewsbury's hand into revealing the truth out of necessity, but Dane couldn't help but feel both miffed and confused.

"My father *knows* of this?" he asked, incredulous.

Shrewsbury reached out a hand and Dane took it. The old man squeezed as hard as he could, which wasn't very hard considering his life was slipping away.

"He knows," he muttered. "He only wants the best for you, lad. My daughter is yours, Dane. Promise me you will take good care of her."

Dane didn't even know what to say. "But I…"

"*Promise* me."

Dane hesitated for a brief moment, knowing there was really nothing he could say other than the obvious. He felt as if he'd just lost a battle he hadn't even had the chance to fight. It was over and done with before he was even let in on it.

"I… I promise."

All of the concern seemed to leave Shrewsbury's features. "Then I am satisfied," he said. "Send word to your father right away to let him know of your new appointment. He will want to know. I know that you shall make me proud, Dane. I've always… known…"

Before Dane could respond, Shrewsbury's personal guard managed to make it out of the pit, and even as Dane sat beside the old duke, his men were picking him up, intending to take him to safety. Even though Dane knew the old man was beyond help, as the red river that ran from his groin and into the mud was heavy and dark, he waved the personal guard on, drawing his sword and providing protection as they carried the old man out of the fighting. Dane fought off many a Welshman, killing at least two, before Shrewsbury was clear of the fighting and carried off to camp.

And that was the last time Dane ever saw Shrewsbury alive.

CHAPTER ONE

St. Idloes Abbey
One month later

THEY COULDN'T MAKE her do it.

She had no intention of being married, not now, not ever. There was no way she was going to permit people she didn't know to push her into a marriage with a man she'd never even heard of. So many strangers attempting to control her destiny, and she wasn't going to have any of it.

She refused to cooperate.

Until the moment they'd arrived, it had been a day like any other day at St. Idloes Abbey – the day had dawned rather misty and damp. The bell had rung at Matins and the prayer candles had been lit. Nuns, novices, postulates, and oblates had been herded through the cloister and into the church, where they'd prayed before they'd eaten their simple oat gruel.

Once prayers were offered and the morning fast was broken, the women went about their daily chores. The Lady Grier Ysabel de Lara went to sew delicate lace shawls along with the other oblates, merchandise sold for profit to provide to the abbey, and supervised by Sister Agretha, who was a worse disciplinarian than any taskmaster alive. The woman was as hard as nails and twice as sharp; nothing missed her scrutiny. Therefore, Grier had learned to be perfect in her stitching and her behavior, lest Sister Agretha take her willow switch and smack her across the knuckles, among other places. She'd been struck in other places more times than she could count.

Ouch!

But the normal morning routine changed when the Mother Abbess, Mother Mary Moria, had come to pull Grier away from her sewing, giving her the message that men from Shrewsbury had come to deliver. Her father, Garreth, had been killed and, as his heiress, she was now being called forth to do her duty as the surviving child of the duke. She was to marry and take her place as the Duchess of Shrewsbury. A man had already been chosen for her husband.

But she wanted nothing to do with it.

In truth, Grier hadn't given her heiress position any thought over the years because being part of St. Idloes was simply a normal way of life. She had been very young when she had first come to the abbey following the death of her mother. Her father had been a kind man, but he had not been prepared to raise a child by himself. Therefore, the only option open to him was to send his young daughter to St. Idloes Abbey because the duke's sister had been a nun there, and she had died there, so the St. Idloes Abbey was part of the Shrewsbury blood.

Now it was part of Grier's blood.

But they were asking her to break that bond.

Quite honestly, she'd been shocked by the news, and by the expectations that had been so abruptly forced upon her. She didn't understand any of it; she'd been given over to the Benedictine order as an *oblate*, or someone who was to be raised as a nun with the intention of becoming one. Indeed, she was an heiress, but that had never been brought up as her obligation, not ever. Grier's father, in the limited communication she'd had with him over the years, had never mentioned it. Expectations had never been relayed.

But now, they were.

After delivering the news, the Mother Abbess had taken Grier from the sewing room, along with her friend and fellow oblate, Eolande ferch Madoc. Perhaps, the old nun had believed that Eolande would be of some comfort to her considering the girls had grown up together. Eolande was the closest thing Grier had to a sister, and even as they walked the cloister behind the old nun, the young women clung together. The Mother Abbess had taken both girls to a small room near the chapel and told them to wait.

But… for *what*?

For Grier, it was like waiting for a death sentence.

It was a chamber seldom used, smelling of dust and damp because of the packed-earth floor and old stone walls. There were two chairs there, rough-hewn and nothing fanciful. Once the door shut, Eolande took her seat in confused silence, but Grier remained near the door. She was frightened and bewildered with what the day had brought her, struggling to think clearly in the face of such rapid change, and it was in that small room where she decided that she wasn't going to cooperate. She was going to dig in, and if they forced her, then they would have a fight on their hands.

She wasn't going to be pushed into a marriage she didn't want.

"Are you afraid?" Eolande asked.

The softly-uttered question broke Grier from her thoughts of rebellion. Coming from a noble Welsh family, Eolande's English was heavily tinged with a Welsh accent, something that Grier had gotten used to over the years. In fact, Grier had picked up a hint of that Welsh accent herself.

She eyed her friend, a little woman with black hair and black eyes. Eolande tended to be rather wise in all things, but she also tended to be cautious. Grier did not have an ounce of caution in her, and she could be reckless at times, things that had her on the receiving end of religious beatings and scoldings from time to time. But she was as brilliant as a new day, and it was a brilliance that would not be silenced.

"Nay," she said. "I am not afraid. And I will not marry. I do not care who these men are. My father gave me over to St. Idloes to become a nun, and become I shall. I am not meant to be any man's wife."

Eolande heard the resistance in her voice, the defiance. That was normal with Grier. But that bravery could be misplaced, as she suspected it was now.

"*Who* has come for you?" she wondered aloud. "Mother Abbess says that your father's men have come, but I wonder if that is true."

Grier looked at her curiously. "What do you mean?"

Eolande's gaze moved over her friend; petite, with a curvy figure buried beneath the rough woolens. Grier had chestnut-colored hair to her knees and eyes the color of a sunset – shades of gold, of greens, and even yellow and dark orange. She had the face of an angel, with a bright smile and a quick wit. Eolande had seen other postulates and novices scorn her with their jealousies, even whispering about her when her back was turned.

She is too pretty, some would say. *She will lose her beauty when she gets older*, others would mutter. Hurtful words that were meant to wound, but Grier simply accepted them without complaint. Even when the Mother Abbess would punish the offenders, Grier took no pleasure in it. Eolande thought that the Mother Abbess had a soft spot for Grier, although the woman wouldn't admit it. But perhaps, that was why she looked so concerned when she'd delivered the news of Shrewsbury's death, concern over the young woman who had been her charge for many years.

A young woman who held the rich and vast Dukedom of Shrewsbury in her hands.

"What I mean to say is I wonder if these men are up to no good," Eolande elaborated after a moment. "They could be lying, you know."

Grier's eyes widened. "Lying?" she repeated. "Why should they want to do that?"

Eolande rose from her chair. "To take you away," she said simply, going to Grier and reaching out to take her hand. "What if they wish to abduct you and ransom you to your father?"

Grier's momentary shock became suspicion. "They'd not dare," she hissed. "Would men truly lie to the church? Do they realize how they can be punished?"

Eolande simply held Grier's hand, squeezing it tightly. "Mayhap, they do not care," she said. "Mayhap... mayhap, we should run to my brother for protection. He would save you!"

Grier smiled for the first time, a gentle gesture in the midst of such a serious subject. It was as if the bewildered nature of the conversation suddenly took a turn, one that caused Grier to soften at the mere suggestion. It was clear by her expression that Eolande's statement had touched her in some way that there was more to the words than the meaning they conveyed.

"Although your suggestion is noble, we both know it is not true," Grier said, a hint of sadness in her tone. "But I thank you all the same."

"But we can try!"

"You know that he would never help the woman whose family scorned him."

Those words brought the conversation to a halt because they were all too true. It was a tragic bit of history the two women shared, one that Grier's comment had stirred to the forefront. It wasn't something they discussed these days, but there had been a time when it was all they spoke of because it affected their lives nearly every day.

The tale of an unrequited love.

It was a sad story, truly. Eolande's brother, Davies, had visited the abbey quite a bit in years past, mostly to check on a younger sister who had been committed to the convent. He was rather fond of the girl, whose parents decided that she needed a religious education. But what Davies ap Madoc didn't count on was developing a sweet spot for his sister's friend, the young and lovely Grier, who was the daughter of an English duke. *An enemy.* He'd become so fond of her that he convinced his father to offer for the lass' hand, thereby linking the Welsh Lords of Godor to the Dukedom of Shrewsbury in marriage.

It had sounded reasonable enough, but Shrewsbury hadn't thought so. The request, politely delivered, had been summarily refused, and

Davies had nursed a broken heart and wounded pride for some time. Not that Grier ever did anything to encourage him; she hadn't. She was fond of him, as Eolande's brother, but that was where it ended. She'd never felt anything for him and never would, something Davies was well aware of. But still, he showed Grier kindness, at least as long as he could. A few months ago, he'd stopped coming to St. Idloes altogether.

There was no use in seeing a lass he was trying to forget.

Eolande, however, seemed to think that there was still something in her brother that would always have an affection for Grier. Knowing her brother as she did, she was convinced he would never stop loving the English lass, but she didn't bring it up to Grier any longer, for the woman couldn't help what she didn't feel. Moreover, her father wasn't about to turn the Shrewsbury dukedom over to a Welsh lord.

A tragic tale, indeed.

"Davies would not let men take you away," Eolande insisted after a moment, knowing she was on a sensitive subject. "If he knew men had come to abduct you, I know he would protect you to the death."

But Grier shook her head. "I would not let him lay down his life for me," she said, giving Eolande's hand a squeeze before letting go. "Besides, Mother Mary Moria can protect me far better than any Welsh warrior can. Once I tell her that I have no desire to be wed, and that I intend to take my vows, she will chase them away in spite of my father's wishes."

There was that confidence in her voice again, something that Eolande heard quite often. Grier was, if nothing else, a confident young woman in a world where that wasn't often seen. It was interpreted as defiance, or rebellion, but in Grier's case, neither was true. At least, it hadn't been until today.

Today, Eolande could sense a storm coming.

The door rattled before she could reply, sending her scurrying back to her chair as the panel swung open. While Eolande cowered, Grier faced the open door with the same courage as she faced everything else. She was cool and collected as the Mother Abbess appeared again, this time in the company of a very big knight.

The Mother Abbess snapped her fingers.

"Eolande," she hissed. "Come with me. *Now.*"

Eolande shot out of her chair, rushing to the Mother Abbess and trying not to crash into the knight in the process, who was stepping into the chamber just as she was coming out. He was so big, however, that it Eolande had to squeeze past him, brushing his arm, as the Mother Abbess extracted her from the chamber. Once she was clear of the door, the knight reached over to shut the panel behind them.

There was an odd silence in the chamber now. It was an uncomfortable one, and Grier eyed the man with dark eyes and copper curls down to his shoulders. She didn't back away from him but she certainly felt like it, wondering rather frantically why the Mother Abbess had left her alone with a stranger. Never one to shy away from a situation no matter how frightened she was, Grier spoke.

"Who are you?" she asked, not too politely. "What do you want?"

The knight bowed, his behavior courteous even if hers wasn't. "My lady," he said. "My name is Dastan du Reims. I was your father's captain at his death, and had been for the past seven years. May I extend my condolence at your father's passing?"

Grier studied the man. He was handsome, perhaps having seen little more than thirty years. He also had a somewhat genteel manner about him, which seemed rather odd considering he was dressed for battle. He looked as if he'd killed a man or two in his time.

"I did not know my father, my lord," she said honestly. "You may as well be speaking of a stranger."

The knight nodded faintly. "I know, my lady," he said. "As your father's captain, I can assure you that he expressed regret over the state of his relationship with you."

Grier was watching him with big eyes that missed nothing: a flicker of a brow, the twitch of a lip. She was watching him more closely than most because, in truth, she'd never really been this close to a knight before. Men were not allowed inside the abbey for the most part, and when there were male visitors, like Davies, they were kept outside in a sequestered area. That made this knight's presence here something of an anomaly and Grier's curiosity was natural.

But that curiosity didn't dampen the suspicion she felt at his appearance or in the message he bore, especially after what Eolande had said. *Perhaps, they have come to ransom you!* Although Grier didn't think that was the truth, it lingered on her mind. It kept her manner standoffish.

"He never expressed such a regret to me, my lord," she said with blunt honesty. "That he did to you I find rather curious. Were you with him when he died, then? Did he express these regrets to you on his death bed?"

Dastan shook his head. "He did not, my lady," he said. "He was wounded in battle, as was I. I was being tended to when your father was brought to the field surgeon. But by that time, he had already passed away. Your father was a kind and generous man, my lady. It was an honor to serve him and to carry out his wishes."

There was something in the way he said it that made her look at him in a knowing manner. "And that is why you are here," she said. "To carry out his wishes."

Dastan hesitated a moment before he nodded. "Aye, my lady."

Her gaze lingered on him. "Someone told me that you had come to abduct me and ransom me back to my father."

His dark eyebrows lifted. "I can assure you that is not the truth," he said. "Your father is dead. Should you wish confirmation from the priest who conducted his mass, I can produce him. It will take some time, but I can prove it."

Grier could have agreed with him and demanded he provide the priest, but she thought that a man with a guilty conscience would probably not have made such an offer. Perhaps she was naïve about it, but she believed him. Therefore, she put aside Eolande's conspiracy theory, hoping she wasn't wrong about it.

"There is no need to produce the priest, at least not at the moment," she said. "I will believe you for the time being. But let us return to the discussion of my father's commands. You have come here to carry out a specific command, have you not?"

"I have, my lady."

"And what will you do if I refuse?"

Dastan kept his polite manner in the face of what sounded like a challenge. "Is that what you intend to do, my lady?"

"It is."

He nodded as if in complete understanding. "I see," he said. "Then allow me to make this plain. You will do as you are told to do, and if you believe you have a choice in this situation, then you are sadly mistaken. You are your father's heiress; with you rests all of Shrewsbury, so your duty to you father and to your family is greater than your duty to God. In fact, you can do God more service with the Shrewsbury fortune than you could ever do within the confines of St. Idloes by wearing rough woolens and praying day and night. You will control a vast empire, my lady, and whether or not you assume that burden is not your choice. You will do as you ordered to do."

For a man who had been polite since the moment he entered the chamber, that firm statement showed Grier just how powerful and intimidating the knight could be. His features hardened and his voice growled. Grier had been plain and now he was being plain, as well.

But she still wasn't going to surrender.

"Then I shall take this to the archbishop," she said defiantly. "I was given over to St. Idloes as a child, to be raised by nuns and to take my vows when I came of age. That plan has not changed in spite of my father's death. You cannot force me to assume something I do not wish to do."

Dastan drew in a long, thoughtful breath. Crossing his arms casually, he pretended to consider her words. But the truth was that there *was* no consideration; he was going to let her know just how foolish her statement was.

"Actually, I can," he said. "Your father left provisions for a large donation to the abbey upon his death because he knew he would remove you from its walls and he wanted to compensate them for the years that they have fed and housed you. If they want the money, then they will have to turn you over, and if you think for one moment they are going to turn down such a large donation, then think again. You would be wrong."

That brought a reaction from Grier. Her eyes widened and she stiffened. "But...!"

Dastan threw up a hand to silence her. "At this moment, I have been sent to bring you to the chapel, where your new husband awaits," he said "We can do this one of two ways; either you can walk with me in a civilized fashion or, if you refuse, I will tie you up and carry you. I am bigger than you, and stronger, so you cannot overpower me. For the sake of your dignity alone, I should think you would walk with me, but I shall leave that up to you."

He sounded final. Grier's first reaction was to scold him, to chase him away. But looking into his square-jawed face, somehow, she knew that he wouldn't be chased. She may have been stubborn, but she wasn't stupid. She was starting to think that perhaps none of this was going to go the way she wanted it to and her composure began to crack.

"But... but this is cruel," she said, trying not to sound desperate. "My father sent me to St. Idloes and, until today, it was my belief that I should take my vows and live my life as a nun. That is what I wanted; it is what my father intimated would always take place. And now I am expected to marry and assume my position as the Duchess of Shrewsbury? I know nothing of such responsibilities. I would not even know where to start!"

Dastan wasn't unsympathetic. "I realize that," he said. "My lady, your father's death was unexpected and, to be truthful, never did he mention his plans for you to me. It was only after his death, when we found the missives to be read upon his death did we know of his plans. He had selected a husband for you and he wants the de Lara dynasty to continue. You are the last of your family, my lady. If you do not marry and procreate, hundreds of years of the de Lara legacy will die with you."

Somewhere in the back of her mind, Grier supposed she knew that. She'd always known it. But it was something she'd pushed aside and buried, digging such a deep hole that she hoped such an idea would never resurface. With a heavy sigh, she turned away.

She could feel the defeat creeping over her.

"I had a brother, you know," she said, glumly. "I was six when he was born. That was what killed my mother. My brother lived for an hour. A solid hour. And then he died and I was sent away, to live here at St. Idloes. I know I am the last of my family but my father never impressed upon me that I should continue his legacy. How can I? I am a woman."

"You are a woman with a great and honorable family name," Dastan reminded her firmly. "You are to be married into another family with a great and honorable family name. It will be the joining of two great lines and will ensure the Shrewsbury survival."

More defeat swamped her. Grier was coming to realize she wasn't going to talk her way out of it. She could be stubborn about it, or scream and run, but she would be caught. She could fight and kick, but men bigger and stronger than she was, as du Reims had pointed out, would subdue her.

Was that really what she wanted?

It wasn't. She was bold and mulish at times, but she wasn't a fool. And she most certainly didn't want to embarrass herself. So, this was to be her fate.

An unexpected and unwelcome fate.

"Then who is this man I am to marry?" she finally asked, clearly dreading the answer.

A flicker of smile licked Dastan's lips. He could hear how much she was hating all of this. She could hate it all she wanted so long as she didn't put up a fight, and he was secretly quite glad that she hadn't. He had no wish to wrestle the woman to the altar. Not that he blamed her for her position; he didn't. She'd been socked away in St. Idloes for years and, in spite of what he'd told her, the old duke had barely mentioned her. She had been an afterthought. Or, at least, Dastan thought so until he saw the documents that had been produced after de Lara's death. Then, it was clear she hadn't been an afterthought at all.

He'd been concerned with his legacy, and his daughter was the key.

The nun will carry on the de Lara name.

"He is waiting for you in the chapel," he said after a moment. "May I escort you to him, my lady?"

Grier wanted to deny him. Very badly, she wanted to. But she knew she couldn't

"If you must," she muttered.

"I must," came the quick reply.

A glance at the knight showed the man with a twinkle in his eyes and that only served to annoy her.

"If you take delight in this, I swear I will fight you all the way," she said.

The twinkle in his eyes was still there, but his jaw tightened and his lips stiffened. "I have no delight, my lady."

"Swear this to me."

"I do."

She wasn't sure she believed him. Something about the man told her that he was laughing at her and she hated it. Perhaps she'd embarrassed herself already and didn't know it or, worse, he knew something she didn't know. Maybe it was about her husband. Maybe he was the biggest joke of all.

God help me, she prayed silently.

She was about to find out.

CHAPTER TWO

"JUST GET IT over with and you can go about your life," William said. "Marry her and run. Or, better still, marry her and leave her at the abbey. Beget her with your heir and you need not think of her ever again!"

Dane knew William was trying to help in his own sloppy way. Leaning against the cold, stone wall of St. Idloes cavernous chapel on a dark, misty morning, Dane was slumped, looking at his feet, waiting for the arrival of the old duke's daughter.

My wife.

He sighed heavily.

"You know I cannot do that," he said.

"Why not?" William demanded.

Dane glanced up at him. "Must I explain this to you, Willie?" he asked. "She is the daughter of Lord Garreth. If I disrespect her, then I disrespect him. And I would not dream of showing the man any disrespect."

William knew that, or at least the reasonable part of him did. But there was an entire side to William Wellesbourne that was full of spit and madness, like the soul of an unruly five-year-old child existed in the body of a grown man. But there was another side to him that was oddly wise, brilliant, and a skilled fighter. William was a paradox that had him both frustrating and trustworthy all at the same time.

"You *know* why he sent her to the convent, don't you?" he asked.

Dane rolled his eyes. "I am certain you are going to tell me."

William began to tell his story with glee. "Because she is hideous," he said, bending over Dane and hissing at him. "She is a hideous beast, as ugly as sin, and he's tucked her away in the convent to hide her from the world. She's like Medusa, Dane – those who look upon her will be turned to stone."

Dane shook his head at William's theatrics. "Oh, shut up."

William grinned; any time he drew that reaction, it was like throwing fuel on a fire. "I can see her now," he said. "Eyes like a cesspool, hands like claws, and a face like a goat."

"She sounds delightful."

"Just your kind of woman!"

With that, William pulled at his jaw, making his face seem long and horrific. He even bleated like a goat, which made Dane turn away from him, afraid he was going to laugh at the man. If he did, and William saw him, then he would never stop. His harassment would go on and on until Dane grew annoyed enough to throw a punch.

"Think of it!" William followed his victim as he headed towards the chapel entry. "Your children will look like the spawns of Satan. There was a *reason* that girl was put in this convent, Dane. Run, man! Run as fast as you can away from here!"

They were passing near the entry to the chapel at this point, past Boden, who had been listening to William taunt his brother. Boden was a bit of a character himself and he didn't like it when William upstaged him, and he especially didn't like it when William went after his older brother. Therefore, as William walked past him, pestering Dane, Boden threw a punch that caught William in the belly. Dane heard the man grunt as air escaped his lips, turning with disinterest to see William bent over, holding his stomach, as Boden stood over him.

"Leave him alone," Boden growled at William. "He is nervous enough without you making a fool of yourself."

William was grossly unhappy that Boden had punched him. "Keep to yourself, little man," he said. "The conversation was between me and your brother."

But Boden wouldn't back down. "You will leave my brother alone. And, might I remind you, he is your liege since you came to Blackmore. You will show him all due respect."

William stood up, a frown on his face, and Dane could see there was going to be trouble. He hissed at the pair, holding out a big hand.

"Enough," he muttered. "William, keep your mouth shut and go see what is keeping the priest. Boden, keep watch beside the entry door. I would have this ceremony completed without having to worry about you two coming to blows."

Boden snarled at William, who pointed a finger at him even as he backed away. "Another time, Boring Boden," he taunted the man. "Another time!"

Boden's eyes narrowed dangerously but he didn't reply. The truth was that he and William adored each other for the most part, but there was a good deal of rivalry between them. They were both young and full of themselves, which put Dane in a bad position at times. Not that either man had failed him when it counted but, at times, it was like separating two rutting cats. As Dane tried to forget the tussling pair, another knight approached him.

"Should I keep Willie away from Boden, my lord?"

Dane turned to Sir Syler de Poyer, a knight who had served Shrewsbury but a knight he'd now inherited.

Syler was a cousin to Dastan's wife, from the Norman-Welsh de Poyer family. He was stocky, muscular, with enormous hands and big, brown eyes, and as loyal as a favorite dog. Dane never had to repeat a command to Syler. Everything he said was instantly attended to. Syler was no-nonsense and infinitely patient, especially when it came to William and Boden, who were constantly trying to outdo each other. Therefore, it was a relief to have both Syler and Dastan to balance the foolery of the other two, but Dane shook his head to the man's question.

"Just keep an eye on William," he muttered. "I will take care of Boden. If you see the two of them starting to go at it again, you have my permission to bash skulls."

"I will, my lord."

Dane knew he would, too, which gave him some comfort. Now, he could focus on what he needed to do without worrying over William and Boden scrapping.

It was a wait that was soon to be over.

As the sun began to sink low in the western sky, Dastan finally emerged from the cloister with a small figure next to him. Dane knew it was a woman because he could see the curve of her figure, even beneath the unflattering woolen garments. In truth, he hadn't honestly been nervous leading up to this day, he was merely resigned. But the moment he actually laid eyes upon the woman he was to marry, he could feel a twitching in his belly.

That twitching signified reluctance he'd kept buried.

Buried, indeed, because if he wanted the Shrewsbury titles, then he had to marry the heiress. That was a fact. He'd kept his displeasure hidden, focused instead on what he was set to inherit and pretending the means by which he would gain his new position didn't bother him in the least.

But it had.

The moments leading up to this significant point in time had been many. As Dane watched Dastan lead the woman towards him, it was as if the entire past month flashed before his eyes. It started with the duke's death and how he'd ridden with Dastan and Syler at the head of the Shrewsbury army to take Garreth home to be buried with his ancestors. Then he flashed forward to Shrewsbury's majordomo, a man with a strong Teutonic accent, as he read the missives he'd been entrusted with, only to be opened upon the duke's death.

When the missives were read, the majordomo left the castle to return to his home in Saxony, unwilling to serve the new duke. It was the general consensus among the knights that the old majordomo had maybe been expecting the dukedom for himself, or at least an abundance of riches that he did not get, so when he left, it was with Dane's good riddance.

He had enough to worry about.

Still, even though Dane had known the contents of the missives based on what Garreth had told him, he had been surprised to hear that everything the duke owned – and he'd meant everything – had been left to him, with some money going to Dastan, Syler, and even Boden and William to a certain degree. The duke had given the men money from his vast fortune to thank them for their loyalty and friendship, but Dane received the bulk of a very rich estate.

Provided he married the heiress.

So here he was, carrying out an old man's wishes, wondering if he shouldn't do just what William had said – marry the woman and leave her at the abbey. Dane had plans of his own, plans that didn't include a wife, but he was stuck. He would have been stupid to turn down the offer of Shrewsbury's dukedom, not that he could have, but when he returned to see his father now, it would be as the man's equal in station.

As he'd promised the old duke, he'd sent word to his father about the change in his status. Lord Blackmore was to become the Duke of Shrewsbury. That was a prideful thought, and one that had grown on him over the weeks. He couldn't even imagine what his mother, Remington, would say. That her eldest son should be given such a prestigious gift was probably more than she could have ever hoped for him.

But between him and this vast and great gift was the little matter of a marriage mass.

The closer it came, the more turmoil he felt.

Am I doing the right thing?

As Dastan and the woman closed in on him, Dane snapped out of his thoughts. Somewhere over to his right, William had managed to bring the priest around, and now men were taking positions in front of the door to the church, the traditional place where a marriage ceremony would begin. He felt Syler tug on his arm, also pulling him over to the archway, just as Dastan brought up the lady.

Now, two strangers were about to be married.

It couldn't have been more awkward.

Dane's attention turned to the priest, whom he noticed had been drinking. The man reeked of alcohol and was weaving a little, even as William stood next to him and tried to steady him. *That's all we need is a drunken priest*, Dane thought with annoyance. As if this situation wasn't uncomfortable enough, now they had a sauced priest. But at least the bride wasn't kicking or screaming, or giving in to fits of hysterics. That was something to be grateful for. But the truth was that even if she was so inclined, it would have been difficult with Dastan standing next to her, waiting to quell any such spells.

In truth, Dane felt a bit sorry for the girl. He didn't even know her, but he felt sorry for her. He could only imagine what a shock all of this must have been, and Dane wasn't heartless about it. Ambivalent, yes. Heartless, no. In fact, on their journey to St. Idloes, he'd even stopped in the Jewish section of Shrewsbury, at a goldsmith's stall, and selected two pieces of jewelry for the woman as gifts on the event of their marriage. One was a simple gold band for the third finger of her right hand, her wedding finger, and the second was a marriage brooch. The brooch was actually quite beautiful, with precious jewels inlaid into the shape of a hawk and on the back were these words:

A modest wife knows a chaste bed

Dane didn't think those words were particularly kind, or even pleasant, but it was the only thing the goldsmith had that was specifically designed for a marriage, so he bought it. With those two offerings tucked into the pocket of his tunic, he finally faced Garreth de Lara's daughter before the entry to the church.

Let's get this over with.

"My lord," Dastan said. "Be introduced to the Lady Grier Ysabel de Lara. My lady, this is your husband to be, Sir Dane de Russe, Lord

Blackmore. His father is the Duke of Warminster."

With those words, Dane found himself looking at the woman, who finally decided to lift her face to him. Until this moment, she'd had her head down and a kerchief over her hair, obscuring most her features. But when she finally looked at him and he got a good look at her face, he was in for a surprise – a round face and rosebud lips. Skin like cream. Big, bottomless eyes that were the most amazing color he'd ever seen – browns and greens and yellows, all mixed up together. She looked up at him, her eyes fixing on him, and Dane had to fight off an astonished reaction. He almost couldn't believe what he was seeing. Tendrils of chestnut-colored hair escaped her kerchief and he found himself staring at her – all of her.

This wasn't what he'd expected.

She was… *beautiful.*

"My lady," he finally greeted. "Your father was a dear friend. May I express my condolences on his passing?"

That didn't draw much of a reaction from her other than a brief nod of the head, but she seemed to be inspecting him much in the same way he was inspecting her. Did he read astonishment on her face, too? He couldn't tell. But one thing was for certain – William's words, of marrying her and leaving her behind, were suddenly something he wasn't inclined to consider. Not that he really had, but something told him he didn't want to leave her behind at all.

It was just a feeling he had.

Curiosity had the better of him.

But that curiosity would have to wait. The drunken priest began to speak and Dane tore his eyes off his bride to look at the man, watching as William had to keep pushing on the priest's shoulder to right him because he was tipping over. Time and time again, the man would start leaning and William was there to make sure he didn't fall over.

The process at the entry door was usual; the priest questioned the bride and groom as to their willingness to marry, making sure there was an agreement on both sides. There was an agreement of sorts, but it was clear from the couple that there was no excitement about it. When the questions were over, William paid the priest an allotted amount of coins for the wedding as Dane placed the plain gold band on the lady's finger and pinned the exquisite marriage brooch to her woolen garment. It looked terribly out of place. When that was finished, the group proceeded inside for the mass.

The chapel was very old, having been built centuries before, and it smelled like a tomb Cold, musty, and dusty. The priest began intoning the hastily-arranged marriage mass, joined by two small acolytes bearing candles, but there was little else by way of pomp and circum- stance It was all very simple, with heavily-armed knights surrounding one small and frightened oblate, who was now Lady de Russe, Duchess of Shrewsbury and Lady of the Trinity Castles.

And Dane was officially the duke.

It was the long-awaited title, but it didn't come with crashes of thunder or great beams of light from the heaven. A few words and it was his. Dane thought he would feel differently when he finally held the title, but that didn't happen. He felt no different. If anything, he felt the weight of the responsibility, something he'd never felt before and something quite unexpected. He glanced at his new wife once or twice, wondering if she felt the weight, too.

Wondering if she hated every minute of this, him included.

But her feelings didn't matter. There had been a task to complete and they'd completed it. When the mass was finished, the men began to move out and Dane took hold of his new wife, guiding her towards the chapel entry and thinking that the entire circumstance had passed in a blur. It was nearing noon at this point and the plan was to head back to Shrewsbury immediately. Dane wasn't entirely comfortable being so far into Wales without more of an army, so they planned to depart and make it to Welshpool before nightfall. There, they could spend the night and then continue on to Shrewsbury in the morning. If they traveled swiftly, they would make it by noon tomorrow.

Therefore, his thoughts weren't on his new wife at the moment.

They were on the return to England and making haste. Now that the marriage was completed, there was no reason to linger. The horses were brought around, including a palfrey they'd brought for the new wife, and Dane was all business. William, Boden, and Syler were ordering the escort mounted, all fifty men, as Dastan hung back with Dane and Lady de Russe in case something was needed.

The truth was that Dastan remained next to the new bride in case she decided to bolt now that everything was said and done. He knew how reluctant she was, given his initial conversation with her, but Dane didn't, which was why Dastan thought it was a good idea to remain at her side until she was mounted and heading out of St. Idloes.

Nothing like a runaway bride to spoil everyone's mood.

When the lady's palfrey was presented, it was Dastan who lifted the lady into the soft saddle as Dane mounted his enormous war horse, a beast the color of storm clouds with a fat, dappled arse. Dastan handed the reins to the lady's palfrey over to Dane because they certainly didn't want her directing her own horse. It was symbolic in the sense that Dane, now her husband, also had control of her. It was better that the lady learn that now, at least as far as Dastan was concerned. He didn't want her getting any bold ideas.

But Dastan was certain to remain close to her for the journey, just in case.

If Dane thought Dastan's hovering presence was odd, he didn't say so. He didn't even so much as glance in the man's direction. His men were moving, and he was moving, and that was all he seemed concerned with at the moment. Spurring the horses onward, the Shrewsbury men, complete with the new Duke and Duchess of Shrewsbury, headed north out of the small village of St. Idloes, away from the chapel and away from the convent.

There seemed to be an odd sense of urgency, leaving as quickly as they could, perhaps not giving the new duchess any time to linger over the life she was leaving, a life she had known for so many years and one that was so abruptly taken from her. Whatever the case, the wedding was completed and Dane had his dukedom. Heading off into the warm late-autumn day, the escort continued on for their destination of Welshpool.

What they did not see was Mother Mary Moria standing at the edge of the chapel, watching the Shrewsbury party as it headed off to the north. She'd watched the ceremony from the shadows, watching a young woman she'd raised being taken off by strangers. A father she never saw had dictated the terms of her young life, and there was something deeply unjust about that.

Unfair.

The Mother Abbess felt as if she'd lost a child, if she'd ever had one, as there was much the same grief in her heart. She knew that Grier didn't want to marry the English stranger; she had read that in the young woman's eyes. But she'd been powerless in the face of it and, perhaps, that was what grieved Mother Mary Moria most of all.

No choice had been given.

Returning to the chapel, she lit a candle for the new Duchess of Shrewsbury.

CHAPTER THREE

Welshpool
The Unicorn and The Griffin Inn

FIFTY MEN TAKING over a fairly large tavern on the eastern side of the Welsh Marches was an impressive sight.

Dane had sent men ahead to secure rooms in this particular inn, which was known all along the Marches for its food and entertainment. There was always something happening at The Unicorn and The Griffin, and since it was less than a day's ride from Shrewsbury, it was a popular destination for men with free time on their hands who wanted a good time.

William and Boden were a pair that knew the inn rather well, and it was that rambunctious duo that had ridden ahead to secure rooms. By the time Dane, Grier, Dastan, and Syler arrived, William and Boden had already polished off a pitcher of wine between them and were just tapping into another.

Dane knew this because he could hear them when they reined the horses to a halt just outside the inn. He could hear the music, and the singing, and he could hear William's booming voice above the dull roar of the patrons inside. Even out on the street, now dark as the sunset, Dane knew William's voice. He wasn't actually singing more than he was simply shouting. Dane grunted unhappily as he dismounted his

33

horse.

"Christ," he muttered. "There he goes."

Dastan heard him, too, as did Syler. While Dastan went to assist the lady, Syler went to Dane.

"Shall I take charge of him, my lord?" he asked.

Dane looked at Syler, a mixture of amusement and disbelief on his face. "Do you really think you can?" he asked, lifting a frustrated hand to the door. "Listen to them, Syler. When Willie and Boden reach that point, there is no taking charge of them and you know it. I remember my father repeatedly telling Boden and William and my youngest brother, Gage, to stay away from the taverns. He always told them that and I thought he was being too harsh with them, but this past year with that pair, now *I* know what my father knows about them."

Syler was trying not to grin. "And what is that, my lord?"

Dane threw up his hands. "That they are idiots," he said. Then, he flicked his wrist in the direction of the inn. "Go inside and see that they do not get themselves killed. Find out how much they have had to drink so I know when to cut them off."

Syler cleared his throat softly. "Forgive me, my lord, but the last time you cut them off, it did not end well."

Dane rolled his eyes. He knew what the knight was referring to. "That time in Shelton?"

"Aye, my lord."

Dane sighed heavily. "It is three against two this time," he said. "If we have to subdue that pair, then we can. But let us hope it does not come to that."

"The last time, if you recall, they broke furniture and threatened the barmaids."

"I remember."

"Do I have permission to bash heads, my lord?"

"If they do not bash yours first, aye."

Syler simply nodded, taking a deep breath to summon his courage as he headed into the tavern. As he moved away, Dastan approached with the lady in hand, and Dane turned to face them.

"My lord," Dastan said. "May I escort you and your lady wife to your chamber?"

Dane's gaze moved from Dastan to his new wife. He was coming to realize for the first time that Dastan had appointed himself what seemed to be the lady's protector. Dastan was a conscientious knight, no doubt, and he'd served the lady's father for years, so Dane didn't find it unusual that he should do such a thing. In fact, he was rather grateful for the man's thoughtfulness. But to his question, he shook his head.

"Nay," he said. "Go inside and help Syler with my brother and Willie. I can tend to the lady quite adequately."

Dastan nodded, but he hesitated a moment before speaking. "If I may have a word with you, my lord?"

Dane nodded, understanding that Dastan meant privately. As he moved away, he whistled to two nearby soldiers, pointing to the lady and indicating for them to keep an eye on her. Only when the soldiers moved forward to take positions near Lady de Russe did Dane move aside with Dastan.

"Now," Dane said. "What is it?"

"I wanted to have a moment to speak to you about the lady," Dastan said, lowering his voice. "We've not had the chance to speak privately since before your marriage and there is something I think you should know. When I first went to collect the lady, she was quite reluctant to be wed. I think she might have run away had she thought she might not be caught, so you should keep an eye on her. This is not a welcome situation for her."

Dane suspected as much. "Then she and I are of the same mindset," he muttered. "But thank you for telling me. I shall ensure she does not run away."

Dastan scratched at his neck. "Or stab you," he murmured. "I do not know just how resistant she is to this marriage, so it may do you good to at least talk to her and try to establish some communication.

You do not need to fear your wife trying to take a knife to you because she believes that will end the marriage before it begins, because if she is *that* adverse…"

Dane understood. "Point taken."

As Dastan nodded shortly and moved away, heading towards the entry to the inn, Dane turned his attention to the small woman standing in the gutter with the horses. Even though the day had been warm, the night was cool and dark. She was clutching something to her chest, something he was noticing for the first time. A satchel, perhaps? A sack? He had no idea. Truth be told, he hadn't paid too much attention to her since leaving St. Idloes.

That was something he was going to have to amend, out of duty more than anything else. Aye, the woman was beautiful, and she had him curious, but that was as far as it went at the moment. Dastan was right – it was time to talk to the woman and at least establish communication, if for no other reason than to prevent them from existing in awkward silence around each other.

Taking a deep breath, summoning his courage, he headed in her direction.

"My lady?" he said, holding out a hand. "If you will come with me, please."

She looked at him as if startled he'd addressed her but, quickly, she did as he asked. Dane ended up grasping her elbow and, together, they headed into the loud, warm inn, where William and Boden were still singing at the top of their lungs.

It was to be a night to remember for them all.

IT HAD ALL passed in a blur.

The marriage, the ride to the town, whatever the name of it was… all of it was a blur to Grier. She felt frightened and disoriented, now being pulled into a stale, warm inn that was stuffed to the rafters with loud, smelly people.

It was a struggle not to show that fear and not to run for her very life. From the silent, cold halls of St. Idloes to this madness, she swore she'd stepped into an entirely new world. It was hard to believe that both places – the abbey as well as the inn – existed in the same land. They were as different as night and day. It was so loud that she wanted to put her hands over her ears.

The man she'd married – the one who had hardly paid any attention to her from the onset – had her by the elbow. He'd dragged her into the inn and pulled her towards the sweaty innkeeper, who took them up a set of stairs at the back of the establishment, where it was much quieter, and directed them to a chamber at the very end of a narrow catwalk overlooking a courtyard of sorts.

There were barrels and other things belonging to the inn tucked into the recesses of the courtyard, and she'd been looking at all of the dried beef, stored in straw, when her new husband pulled her into the chamber he'd secured for the night. A chamber that was to become her chamber of horrors, she was certain.

She had no idea what to expect.

The room was pitch-black when they entered and she stood by the door as he ventured further in, finding a flint and stone and lighting at least three candles before he came back and shut the door and bolted it. Grier continued to stand by the door as he made his way over to the hearth, digging through the bucket of peat and wood, and placing stacks of it in the cold, dirty fireplace.

"Do you want to sit down?" he asked, looking in her direction. "You need not stand by the door, my lady. Sit and rest yourself. It has been an eventful day."

Grier was still clutching her possessions to her chest as she made her way over to a table and two chairs, placed near the bed. As she set the sack containing her possessions onto the tabletop, she noticed the bed. It wasn't like any bed she'd ever seen at the abbey; it was larger, and looked rather lumpy, and she went to it curiously, pushing at it and

realizing the mattress was stuffed with something soft. As she continued to poke at it, Dane spoke.

"Is it soft?" he asked. "If it is not, I will make them bring in their
finest bed. Sometimes these places stuff old straw into their mattresses,
which do not smell the best."

Grier looked at him. "Straw?" she repeated. "Why straw?"

It was the first time he'd heard her speak. She had a sweet voice, soft
and low, with a hint of a Welsh accent. Having spent so many years in
Wales, that was understandable.

"Because it is cheap and plentiful," he said. "Why? Have you never
seen a straw bed before?"

He asked in a way that made her feel foolish. "Nay," she admitted.
"We did not have mattresses of straw at the abbey."

Dane pondered her reply before shrugging. "It is good enough for
horses, so why not people?"

She hadn't thought of it that way. Returning her attention to the
bed, she pushed on it again. "This is not straw," she said. "It is something else, something soft."

With the fire starting to burn in the hearth, Dane stood up and
brushed off his hands as he made his way to the bed. He, too, pushed on
it.

"Feathers," he said, sounding impressed. "It seems that this establishment does not expect us to sleep on horse bedding. That is good."

"Feathers?" she said. "From chickens?"

"Chickens, ducks, geese. Any of those fowl. No feather beds at the
abbey, either?"

"Nay."

"Then you are in for a comfortable experience."

Grier turned to look at him as he came near, noting that he was
coming into view much better as the fire in the hearth gained in
intensity. It also reminded her of just how handsome the man was,
something that had caught her off guard when they'd first met.

The marriage mass may have passed in a blur, but she remembered her introduction to Dane de Russe quite clearly. She'd been struck by him in so many ways, not the least of which was the fact that he wasn't anything she had expected. She wasn't quite sure what she had been expecting, but a handsome man in his prime hadn't been it. He was, perhaps, nearing the fourth decade of his life, but he didn't look like any man she had ever seen. He looked as if a door to heaven had opened up and an angel had stepped through. Everything about him seemed to gleam, like the rays from the sun.

When she looked at him, all she wanted to do was stare.

He was a big man; not really tall, because he was only moderately tall, but he was broad-shouldered and the circumference of his arms was something truly astonishing to behold. He was, simply put, muscular and strong. He had glistening blond hair, cut short, but it looked as if the cut had been sloppy because his hair was growing out in several different directions, yet on him, it simply made him more handsome. His green eyes were big, and slightly tilted downwards at the ends, which gave him a very soulful and emotional appearance, as if those big eyes could look right through her. His nose was long and straight, and a hint of a reddish beard embraced his jaw and neck.

Nay, he wasn't anything she had expected.

Grier continued inspecting the man she had married when she suddenly realized that she should probably say something to him. He'd spoken to her and she hadn't answered, which had her thinking very hard of what he'd last said to her. Truthfully, it had gone in one ear and out the other because looking at him seemed to suck everything out of her brain. It was a very strange reaction. Struggling not to look like a fool, she replied.

"I did not know there were things such as this," she said, pushing on the mattress again. "I have never seen such a bed. At St. Idloes, we sleep on the ground."

Dane's brow furrowed as he thought on a woman sleeping on the cold ground. Actually, it was more than expressing displeasure at any woman sleeping on the ground, but Grier in particular. His gaze drifted over her. She was such a pretty thing, hidden away in that dusty convent all of these years and evidently living in primitive conditions. He rubbed at his stubbled chin.

"That will change," he said frankly. "As the Duchess of Shrewsbury, and my wife, you will never sleep on the floor again. You will only know comfort for the rest of your life. And speaking of comfort, I will send for a meal. You must be famished."

He promptly turned for the door, unbolting it and calling for a servant, whom he sent for food. When he closed the door and bolted it again, he turned to her only to note that she was looking at him with an odd expression on her face.

"I have eaten for the day, my lord," she insisted. "You need not send for more food."

His brow furrowed again, only more severe than before. First sleeping on the ground, and now a comment about a single meal? He thought to press her about it, but there were so many other questions in his head that he was jumbled with them. He pointed to the chair.

"Sit down, please," he said. "You and I have a few things to discuss. I think we should come to know each other, don't you?"

He seemed to be telling her more than asking her, and Grier scooted over to the chair and planted herself upon it as Dane stood a few feet away, his big fists resting on his hips. When she looked up at him expectantly, he continued.

"Now," he said. "This situation today has happened very quickly, so I suppose we are both a bit dazed by it. Would you say that is a fair statement?"

Grier nodded. "I would, my lord," she said. Then, she looked at the gold band on her finger, and the brooch still on her woolen garment. "I... I want to thank you for these gifts. But I am afraid I do not have a gift for you. I had no time to prepare one."

He shook his head. "I do not expect a gift," he said. "I have known about this betrothal longer than you have, so I have had the time to purchase something for you. You need not reciprocate."

"It was very kind of you, my lord."

His gaze lingered on her a moment, noting her stiff and slightly petrified manner. "I am your husband," he said, lowering his voice so he wouldn't come across as intimidating. "You do not have to address me formally when we are in private. In fact, I should like for you to call me Dane. Will you do that?"

She blinked as if surprised by the question. "If… if you wish it."

He nodded. "I do," he said. "May I call you Grier when we are in private?"

She bobbed her head up and down. "If it pleases you."

Now that they'd solved some of the personal protocols, Dane considered how to proceed. Pulling up a chair, he sat a foot or so away from her. Gazing into that lovely, doll-like face, he knew the best thing he could do was be honest with her.

At least, he hoped so.

"I realize that we are strangers, but I hope that we can be truthful with each other," he said. "All I will ever ask of you is that you be truthful with me."

Grier nodded, feeling some of the tension between them fade. "I will."

"Good," Dane said. Then, he paused a moment before speaking again. "I was told you did not wish to be married."

So much for the fading tension. It was back again and Grier's eyes widened, briefly, indicating her guilt in the matter. "I… I have been an oblate since I was six years of age," she said. "It was always my wish to take the veil. Never have I yearned to be a wife or mother."

It was the honest answer he'd asked for, given without emotion. "I can believe that," he said. "Your father told me you had been sent to St. Idloes after the death of your mother."

She nodded. "I was," she said. "My father never indicated to me that he wished for me to marry, not in all these years, so his wish that I should marry and assume my place as the Duchess of Shrewsbury is something of a surprise."

"An unwelcome one?"

She appeared to consider her answer. "As I said, I had always planned to take the veil. This is no reflection on you, my lord, so please do not think I am personally opposed to you."

Evidently, she still wasn't comfortable enough to call him by his given name, but it didn't bother Dane. With time, he hoped she would. He wanted her to.

"And you should know that I am not personally opposed to you, either," he said. "You are not the only one who did not wish to wed, but here we are, and we must make the best of it."

Her eyebrows lifted in surprise. "Is this true?" she said. "Then surely, my lord, you could have denied my father when he asked this of you."

Dane snorted, a rather rude sound. "Surely you jest," he said. "Your father made the request of me as he lay dying. I cannot deny a dying man. Besides, he had already made the offer to my father, unbeknownst to me, so I was your husband before I even knew of such a thing. Don't you see? Our fathers conspired against us to create this... this union."

His words were almost bitter, and the truth of the matter suddenly struck Grier. She knew why *she* was opposed to the union, but in those few sour words, she could tell that Dane was quite opposed to it, perhaps more deeply than she was. And she knew why – it was quite clear, at least in her view. He was a great man, the son of a duke, and deserved a lady that was equally as fine and cultured, one of equal status.

And that wasn't her.

She began to feel embarrassed.

"I am sorry for you, my lord, truly," she said sincerely. "I am not the kind of wife any man would want. I have been raised in a convent and I know nothing of the world in which you live. I do not own any fine dresses, and I know nothing of running a household, or of managing servants. I am terribly sorry that you were forced into it and if I could free you from these unsavory bonds, I surely would."

The expression on his face, once hard with irony, softened considerably as he looked at her.

"I did not mean that as an insult, Grier," he said. "I am sorry if it seemed that way. I simply meant that neither one of us was given any choice in the matter, but I do not hold it against you. In spite of the circumstances, I would hope that this marriage will be as pleasant as possible for us both."

His words were kind, but Grier still wasn't so sure about it. She remembered thinking once, when she'd first found out about the marriage, that she wouldn't let strangers control her destiny. She'd been adamant that she wouldn't accept this marriage, but she had. The rebellion had faded, at least for the moment. Grier was stubborn, but not stupid. She knew she was locked into this marriage for life, and all of the complaining and defiance wouldn't change that.

But in these few minutes with Dane, their first real conversation, she was coming to understand her new husband just a little. What was it that knight had said to her? *You are your father's heiress; with you rests all of Shrewsbury, so your duty to you father and to your family is greater than your duty to God.* Those words were rattling around in her head now, reminding her of her duty and reminding her that, like it or not, her life had changed forever.

And this man she'd married... handsome, powerful, unlike anything she could have ever hoped for or dreamt of. Never could she have imagined something as magnificent as him. It was true that he didn't seem too keen on the marriage, but it was also true that he was at least trying to be kind about it. She supposed she could hope for nothing more.

I would hope that this marriage will be as pleasant as possible for us both.

Having no other choice, she did, too.

"Mayhap, you will find a teacher who can teach me all I need to know about being a fine lady," she said. "I will learn quickly, I promise."

His lips flickered with a grin. "I am sure you will," he said. "I can teach you many things myself and what I cannot teach you, I will find the very best instructors. I would not worry overly of the things you do not know, because when you do learn them, no duchess will be able to come close to what you will be."

She wasn't quite following him. "And what will I be?"

"Magnificent."

Flattery. The only person who had ever remotely flattered her had been Davies, and that had been flattery that had only made her uncomfortable. Davies had made her feel ill at ease when he told her how lovely she was. But coming from Dane, the flattery wasn't uncomfortable. God's Bones, did she actually like it?

Her cheeks grew inexplicably hot.

"I am not certain that could ever be true, but I should at least like to not embarrass you," she said, averting her gaze because she could no longer look him in the eyes. "That is the hope, anyway."

Now, he grinned, full on, displaying a rather bright smile with straight teeth. "Have no fear," he said. "I am certain you will not. In fact, we shall have your first lesson now. When in a chamber with your husband, you shall ensure he has all he needs for a pleasant eve. That means plenty of wine and food. I am to be your utmost priority, even over yourself. Agreed?"

It was a foreign concept, but Grier nodded. "Agreed." She hesitated. "But what shall I do now? You have already ordered the food."

He laughed softly. "I know," he said. "The next time, you can do it."

She nodded, fighting off a grin because he was smiling so openly at her. "I hope I do it correctly," she said. "What do I do if they bring you the wrong food?"

"Beat them severely."

Her eyes widened. "Truly?"

He continued laughing. "If it pleases you," he said. "But not too much beating. You do not wish to gain a reputation as a brute."

Grier was about to reply to what she thought was a serious subject, but something told her that Dane was teasing her. She didn't know the man at all, but the twinkle in his pale eyes told her that, perhaps, he had a bit of mischief in him. Impish, even. Taking a chance, she played along.

"And why not?" she said. "Why should you not have a wife that all men fear? It would make you seem like quite the brave and bold man if you could stand up to my temper."

Dane looked at her, surprised she was teasing in return, but it made him warm to her faster than anything else could have. A woman with a sense of humor, or at least *his* sense of humor, was a rare thing, indeed.

"Good God, do you have a temper?" he said, pretending he was disgusted. "Why did no one tell me this? That settles the issue; I will have this marriage annulled tomorrow. No wife of mine shall have an unruly temper."

She leaned on the table, eyeing him. "Do you truly think the church will annul the union on those grounds?" she said. "By all means, let me throw a few things around and threaten you with a fork. Let us build a case, shall we?"

Dane began to laugh. "A fork? That is the best you can do?"

Grier bit her lip to keep from laughing. "A spoon?"

His laughter grew. "What do you intend to do? Scoop me to death?"

"I can but try, my lord."

He liked that answer but was prevented from replying when there was a knock on the door. He quickly moved to the panel and unbolted it, allowing two servant women in with trays of food and drink. When they set it all on the table and fled the chamber, Dane bolted the door back up again. He turned to find Grier sitting there with two spoons in her hands. When their eyes met, she held them both up.

"Well?" she said. "Shall I start scooping?"

He rubbed at his chin, chuckling. "Can we postpone this battle to the death until after we eat?"

Grier lowered the spoons, setting them both down. "As you wish," she said. Then, she seemed to sober a great deal, looking over the lavish affair on the table as if astonished by it all. "It was very kind of you to order the food. As I said, I have already eaten for the day, but it has been a long day and the ride was rather… taxing."

The jovial mood of the room eased as he went to sit at the table next to her. She was staring at the food but not touching any of it, as if fearful to. He picked one of the heavy metal spoons up and handed it to her.

"Eat to your heart's content," he said quietly. "You've mentioned twice that you have eaten for the day. To break your fast?"

"Aye."

"But what about supper?"

She shook her head. "There is no supper."

He frowned. "Were you only allowed one meal at St. Idloes, then?"

Grier cleared her throat softly as she took the spoon from him, watching as he took the cloths off the bowls that were on the tray. In addition to a hunk of boiled beef, there were beans and peas, carrots in brine, and bread with butter. She could smell it all and her mouth began to water.

"It was not that we were only allowed one meal," she said, "but sometimes there simply was not enough food to go around. St. Idloes is not a rich abbey."

Dane suspected there was more to it, a situation she spoke of with casual regard, as if it were nothing unusual. "And there were days that you did not eat at all?"

Grier hesitated before nodding her head, once. Then, to Dane's surprise, her eyes grew moist.

"I… I do not remember when I last had meat," she said, sounding choked up. "We have been existing on oat gruel for a very long time. Sometimes, we would eat berries that grew wild near the abbey, but our vegetable garden was ruined by a blight and the sacks of oats were given to us by another church in Newtown. Were it not for those oats, we would have starved."

Dane listened to her, feeling a good deal of pity for the woman. He would not have suspected such hardship at an abbey. Reaching out, he cut a big hunk of meat from the bone and put it on a trencher at the edge of the tray, the one closest to her.

"I thought St. Idloes was a wealthy parish," he said. "It is supported by Shrewsbury, after all."

She eyed the meat as if eyeing a pot of gold. "Nay," she said. "When my father sent me there, he forgot about me. If he sent them money whilst I was there, I did not know about it. But we did what we could to make money and sustain ourselves. I was taught to sew lace shawls that we would sell at market in Newtown and other villages, and it was some money coming in, but not enough. Not for what we really needed."

Dane's pity was deepening. He didn't want to ask her any more questions because he was fairly certain he wouldn't like the answers. She painted a bleak picture and he found himself wondering why Garreth hadn't supported his daughter. He couldn't imagine the old duke knew what she was going through. Surely if he had, he would have sent both food and money to sustain her. He wouldn't have let his daughter starve. At least, he hoped so, but that was a question he would never have an answer for now with the old man dead and buried. He pointed to the food.

"Go ahead," he said. "It should be cooled sufficiently."

Blinking away whatever tears she might be feeling, Grier reached out timidly and began to tear the stringy beef apart with her fingers. Timidly, she pushed it into her mouth and chewed once, twice, before realizing that it was very good.

Suddenly, her restraint was gone. More meat went into her mouth, followed by spoonfuls of peas. In fact, Dane didn't even eat. He found himself watching her as she ate with the fervor of a starving person, and he tore off a hunk of bread and put butter on it for her. When he handed it to her, she took it gratefully and shoved that into her mouth, too.

Dane had never seen anything like it. He poured her a cup of wine, placing it by her right hand, and she gulped it down, wiping her mouth with the back of her hand before plowing into the carrots. He thought to tell her to slow down, but he didn't have the heart, so he poured himself a cup of wine and let her eat her fill before even attempting to eat anything himself. He watched her stuff her mouth until it was so full that she could barely chew, and he seriously wondered if she was going to choke at some point. He'd never felt more pity in his life as he did whilst watching Grier her eat.

But then, the worst happened.

Grier had eaten more than half of her meat, and many spoonfuls of vegetables, when she suddenly came to a halt. Before Dane could ask her what was wrong, she put a hand over her mouth and tried to stand up when all of the food that she'd so ravenously eaten came back up as fast as it went down. Vomit spewed, and Dane grabbed the chamber pot to try and catch it. She ended up emptying the contents of her stomach into the air.

Still, he hadn't been fast enough. Most of it was on Grier's woolen clothing and once she finished expelling everything, she looked at him with such horror that he could feel the physical impact. Her shame was written all over her face and then some.

"My lord," she gasped. "I am so terribly sorry. I will clean this up, I swear it. I am so sorry."

She was trembling, upset and ill, and he reached out, grasping her by the arms to steady her.

"Not to worry," he said calmly, soothingly. "I will send for hot water and a servant woman to help you. Sit down, Grier. Everything will be okay."

Grier was shaking badly as he gently pushed her down into the chair. God, she looked so pathetic; there was vomit everywhere – her clothing, on the wedding brooch, her face and neck, her hands, the floor, and even part of the table leg. Quickly, Dane moved to the door and opened it again, grabbing the serving wench who was lurking down the catwalk and telling her what had happened.

As Dane sent the servant into a frenzy rushing to do his bidding, Grier sat on the chair and quivered, never more embarrassed or ashamed in her entire life. She could hear Dane as he spoke to someone else, demanding a tub and hot water to wash with, but she was wallowing in her own world of misery.

God's Bones... she'd been so hungry and the food had been delicious. Months of a gruel diet had made her stomach weak, only she hadn't realized it. Her belly couldn't handle the rich foods she'd so eagerly shoved into it, and the mess all over her was the result. If the floor could open up and swallow her, she would have been grateful.

All of this in front of the most handsome man she'd ever seen, her new husband.

It was a nightmare.

As Dane stood just outside the door and had a conversation with the innkeeper, Grier reached up a shaking hand and took a cloth from the table, gingerly wiping the vomit that had splashed onto her face because she'd put her hand over her mouth to futilely stop the retching. She looked down at herself, seeing the mess, and seeing that her lovely wedding brooch had been caught in the storm. Unpinning it, she wiped it off with the cloth, trying to clean it up. The tears came, no matter how much she tried to hold them back, and when Dane came back into the room, she kept her head down so he wouldn't see them.

"They are bringing a bath for you," he said kindly. "You shall be cleaned up and as good as new, so do not fret."

He sounded so nice and Grier felt all the more miserable about it. "But my clothing," she whispered tightly. "It is ruined. It must be washed."

He crouched down in front of her, which made her recoil. Here she was, covered with vomit, and he was putting himself close to her. She didn't want him close to her, a stark witness to her weakest moment.

"It will be," he said. "You can wear something else."

She looked up at him, then, her eyes glistening with tears. "It is all that I have."

He looked at her in surprise. "But you brought a satchel with you," he said. "There is no clothing in it?"

She shook her head, unsteadily. "I only have a spare shift, and a comb. Nothing more."

He stared at her. Then, he abruptly stood up. "Do you mean to tell me that your father supplied you with *nothing*?"

Grier could hear the anger in his voice and she was afraid. "As I said, St. Idloes was not a wealthy order," she said. "We took oaths of chastity and poverty. No one had any more clothing than what they wore. We kept it clean and mended."

Dane couldn't believe what he was hearing but he was prevented from replying by a knock on the door, which he quickly opened. There were two women standing there with steaming buckets of water, and he quickly ushered them in. As they both set the buckets down near the table, Dane pulled the older of the pair aside, practically yanking her from the chamber. When they were alone on the catwalk outside, he faced her.

"My lady has nothing else to wear," he said, his voice low. "I need clothing for her. Nothing fine, but something she can wear until I can get her to Shrewsbury. I shall pay handsomely for it. Do you know where I can get any clothing for a woman her size?"

The older woman with wild gray hair and yellowed teeth turned to look back into the chamber, where the younger servant girl was helping Grier wash off her face and hands.

"She looks like a nun, m'lord," she said. "That's a postulate's habit she's wearing."

Dane nodded impatiently. "We were married today," he said. "She was at St. Idloes for many years and that is all she has to wear. *Can* you help her?"

The woman's gaze lingered on Grier for a moment. "Aye, I think so," she said, gathering her skirts and turning for the stairs. "How much do ye want to spend?"

"Return with something for her to wear, and mayhap soap and other things a lady should need, and I will pay you handsomely."

The woman simply nodded and ran off, down the narrow catwalk and to the stairs that creaked under her weight. When she disappeared down below, Dane returned his attention to Grier as the servant wench continued to help her wash off.

He just stood there and looked at her for a moment. It was odd, really; he'd never felt such pity, for anyone, but it was more than that. Grier belonged to him now and she seemed so… helpless. Like a fish out of water, she was helpless outside of the convent that starved her and permitted her to live in dire conditions, and that realization made him feel extremely protective over her. She needed guidance, and help, and he was going to give it.

By the time the big copper tub was brought upstairs, Dane was already formulating what needed to be done. Leaving Grier in the capable hands of the young serving wench, he went on the hunt for the older serving woman.

He had some things to buy.

CHAPTER FOUR

IT WAS MORNING.

Grier knew that because a beam of bright light was hitting her right in the eye, so she squinted and rolled over in the feather bed that was like sleeping on a cloud. She'd never known such comfort. She closed her eyes again, so very weary, when abruptly, they popped open.

The events from the previous day came rolling over her and her head shot up, looking around the room as she oriented herself. Muddled from sleep, it took her a moment to filter through the cobwebs, recalling the day before in clarity, and recalling the night. That horrible, horrible night when she regurgitated her evening meal in front of her handsome new husband.

Embarrassment filled her.

Grier couldn't help but notice that she was quite alone in the chamber. Perhaps all of that vomiting and crude behavior had chased her husband away. In truth, she wouldn't have blamed him in the least. She wanted to run away, too, but there was nowhere for her to run.

Nowhere for her to go.

She was stuck.

With effort, she sat up in the bed, tossing back the coverlet and noticing the sleeping shift that she wore. It wasn't hers. A round serving woman with wild gray hair had given it to her to change in to once she'd finished bathing the vomit off of her, an event that had been another rarity. The nuns of St. Idloes believed that bathing was a sin, so the best the population of the convent could do was scrub parts of their body separately, which Grier had done religiously. They had crude soap, made at the convent, and she would scrub her face and arms and legs and body with it, separately of course, She'd never taken all of her clothes off at one time in her entire life until last night.

It had been an uncomfortable experience at first. She was so ashamed, about everything, but the serving wench had helped her out of her soiled clothing and had her sit in a big copper pot that was filled with hot water. Once she was submerged, holding on to the side of it for fear she might slip and drown, Grier realized that sitting in a tub of hot water wasn't such a bad thing. In fact, it had been a rather pleasant experience, especially when the serving girl began scrubbing her with a horsehair brush and soap that smelled of lemons.

Where the woman got the soap, Grier didn't know, but she surely didn't care. About ten minutes of scrubbing, including her hair, and she wondered why the nuns at St. Idloes had said bathing nude was such a terrible thing. It wasn't terrible at all. In fact, it had been a wonderful event. For the first time in her life, Grier was clean all over all at the same time.

And she smelled of lemons.

She loved it so much that she didn't want to get out of the tub, so she remained in the water until it cooled and she was forced to surrender. The serving girl had dried her off before the fire, including her hair, which she'd rubbed vigorously with a towel that quickly absorbed the water. Grier had never in her life had anyone help her bathe, or help her with her hair. Not even Eolande, who had been the closest to her, so it therefore made her very uncomfortable to have a stranger in the room with her when she was nude and vulnerable.

But the truth was that she didn't know her way around a bath, and she hadn't the faintest idea what to do with herself after she'd been washed, but the serving girl did. She combed her hair out before the fire, drying it, as Grier sat there wrapped up in bed linens to protect her modesty.

When her hair was nearly dry, the woman with the wild gray hair had appeared with a sleeping shift, which was worn but clean. Grier gratefully put it on, feeling the soft texture against her skin and marveling at it. She'd spent most of her life in rough wool, so the advent of something soft against her skin was as much of a miracle as the bed with feathers. She didn't know such things existed.

It would seem that her being married to Dane had opened a new world up to her, for many things.

But so far, they'd been good things. Once she'd put the shift on, the younger servant braided her dark hair into one long braid and forced her into bed. Grier climbed into the cloud-soft bed, astonished by something so fine and heavenly, and had fallen asleep nearly the moment her head hit the pillow.

And that was where she found herself now.

Grier had no idea if Dane had even returned to their chamber last night. She didn't even know if he'd slept in the same bed with her; surely she would have awoken when he climbed in but, then again, she was so exhausted, perhaps she slept right through it. All she knew was that he was gone, and she was alone in the chamber. She wondered seriously if she'd been alone all night, as her husband had been too repulsed by her to even sleep in the same room as her.

Not that she blamed him.

But wait...

The fire in the hearth caught her eye. Someone must have come in to stoke it and she hadn't even heard them. Over on the small table, which had carried that infamous meal, she saw a pitcher of something that had steam rising out of it. There was a cup next to it. Cautiously, she crawled out of bed and went to the pitcher, sniffing it; it smelled of wine and spices. Pouring herself a tiny measure, she took a sip of it; it was warm and spicy and sweet. Delicious. She poured herself a larger cup and drank it down, thirsty.

Just as she was licking her lips, wondering if the wine would come right back up again, there was a soft knock at the door. Startled, she rushed back over to the bed, realizing she was in the somewhat thin shift, so she pulled the coverlet of the bed in front of her, leaving everything but her neck and head visible.

"Come," she called hesitantly.

The door creaked open and Dane appeared.

It was like the sun had just come out from behind the clouds; everything seemed to instantly brighten in his presence, and Grier felt her heart skip a beat at the sight of him. In the light of morning, he looked like an angel. A big, powerful archangel. Surely he was what Michael and Gabriel looked like, with eyes that could see into her very soul.

But the truth was that she wasn't sure what to say to him. Should she apologize again for retching the meal he bought for her all over the floor? As she tried to work up another heartfelt apology, he spoke.

"Good morn to you, Lady de Russe," he said pleasantly. "Did you sleep well?"

Lady de Russe. It was the first time she'd heard her new title from his lips and there was a certain surprise to it. She was no longer just an oblate, or a woman in a sea of women that meant nothing. The marriage the day before hadn't been a dream. Now, she was officially Lady de Russe, Duchess of Shrewsbury, and that realization made her feel strangely proud. But to his question, she nodded unsteadily.

"Very well, my lord," she said. "This bed… it is as if I am sleeping on clouds."

He grinned. "It is, indeed."

Her eyes widened. "How do you know?"

He laughed softly and stepped into the room. It was then that she noticed he was carrying a big satchel in his hand, made of tanned leather. As he swung it up onto the table, he answered.

"Because I slept on it, too," he said. "I am not surprised that you did not feel me crawling in and out of bed. You were sleeping like the dead."

Grier wasn't sure what to say to that. She was fairly certain it was well past sunrise, and it was very unusual for her to sleep so late, so she suspected he was annoyed that she had been so lazy.

"It was a very busy day yesterday, but I assure you, I am ready to depart," she said. "If you could have the servants bring my clothing, I shall quickly dress. I am sorry to have kept you waiting."

He looked at her, the smile fading from his lips. "Is that what you think?" he said. "That you have kept me waiting? In fact, you have not. I have had a good deal of business to transact this morning, so if anyone has delayed our departure, it is me."

With that, he turned to the leather satchel on the table and began to untie it. Grier watched him, somewhat confused that he'd not called for the servants to bring her clothing.

"Do you know where my clothing is?" she asked. "You do not have to bother the servants. I am perfectly capable of going to retrieve them, if you can only tell me where they are."

"Your clothing is here." Dane whipped out a garment of some kind, made from pale yellow damask with gold buttons on it. He held it up in front of him as he turned to her, showing her the full scope of the magnificent gown. "Do you like it?"

Grier stared at it, shocked and confused. She pointed. "That," she stammered, "belongs to *me*?"

Dane's smile returned. "This is a large town and there is an entire street of merchants," he said. "The innkeeper knows the man who owns the largest stall in town, so he awoke him at dawn. I have spent the past hour with the merchant, his wife, and his daughter, who picked out an assortment of things that a duchess will need. Come and see what else I purchased for you."

Grier was stunned. He handed her the yellow gown, so fine and soft that it was like angel's wings. It was lined with even softer material and had long, flowing sleeves. As she was inspecting it, Dane began to pull forth other gowns; an emerald green silk, a red wool, and a flowing linen gown the color of eggshells.

"The merchant's daughter was about your size, mayhap a little taller, so these garments should fit well enough," he said. "If they are too long, we can have them altered when we reach Shrewsbury Castle. There are matching shoes for the gowns, but they are rather weak, so I purchased sturdy leather slippers for you as well. I noticed the ones you wear are terribly worn."

He was pulling out more merchandise than Grier had ever seen; matching shoes, several combs, things to wear on her head, scarves, hose, and shifts. All of it was ending up in a pile on the bed. Then he began to pull out little pouches, peering inside of them before setting them carefully upon the table.

"These are oils and balms," he said. "The merchant's wife said they were the latest things from France and Italy. Not knowing what you would like, I simply purchased all of them. You can look through them and see if they are to your satisfaction. If not, then I will take you to their stall and you can select what you wish."

Grier was staring at everything with her mouth hanging open. She was so overwhelmed that she simply plopped back onto the bed, having no idea what to even do with all of the new things he had bought her. When she looked up at him, there was distress in her features.

"I would not know if I liked them or not, my lord," she said. "And these dresses... the only time I have ever seen finery like this is when the local Welsh lords would bring their wives, and even then, they wore nothing even comparable to these dresses. Do you not understand? I have been living in a convent since I was six years of age. Sleeping on the floor and wearing woolen clothing is all that I know. I have never known anything else, so these things... I do not even know what to say."

He could hear the upset in her voice and he could clearly see it on her face. He hadn't meant to upset her, but he feared that's what he had done.

"I do understand that," he said quietly. "I suppose... I suppose this is my clumsy way of introducing you into the world you live in now.

You shall never sleep on the floor again, you shall never know hunger, and the only garments touching your skin will be the finest money can buy. Do *you* not understand, Grier? You are no longer an oblate. You are a duchess, and it is time to become part of the world."

Grier sighed heavily, looking to the yellow damask that was laid out beside her. "I never wanted to be part of the world," she said. "This was forced upon me, as it was forced upon you. But for me… it is different. Forgive me, but it will take me some time to become accustomed to all of this and if I appear ungrateful, then I apologize. I am simply overwhelmed."

Dane understood, for the most part. He'd been sensing her reluctance, her fear, since the onset, and that was why he'd shopped for her this morning. The woman had nothing, but something inside of him wanted to give her everything. *She* had given him everything by marrying him, by making him the duke. It was only right that he return the favor and show his gratitude.

"I will try to make it a smooth transition for you," he said. "But if I come on too forcefully, you will tell me, won't you? Remember what I said yesterday – all I will ever ask is that you are honest with me, and that means with everything. Agreed?"

Grier looked up at him and there was some relief in her expression. "Agreed."

"Have I come on too forcefully bringing you these things? You had no clothing at all and, as my wife, I should like for you to be well dressed. It would honor me."

Grier's gaze lingered on him. "Even after what happened last night," she said. "Even after that… you still want to have me at your side?"

"Why wouldn't I?"

"Because I made a horrible fool of myself. I should think you would want to send me straight back to the abbey."

He shook his head. "What happened was my fault," he said. "I should have realized you'd not had much to eat and I could have stopped you, but I did not. Will you forgive me?"

Grier was astonished that he should take the responsibility for her projectile vomiting. She shook her head.

"It was not your fault, but mine," she insisted. "It will not happen again, I promise. I will be more careful."

He nodded. "I am glad you said that," he said. "I have ordered a meal for you – gruel and bread. Mayhap, you can try to eat again without becoming ill. We shall introduce meat to you gradually, once your belly can tolerate bread and other foods like that. There is a very good cook at Shrewsbury, in fact. I am sure she will take great delight in making you many delicacies."

Grier couldn't even imagine such a thing. "I have never had delicacies," she said. "Like what?"

He lifted his shoulders. "Sweets, cakes, puddings," he said. "Anything you wish. But for now, let us take it slowly so you are not spraying the walls again. The last time I saw something like that, my brothers had become so drunk that it took them three days to become sober. It was as if they'd painted the walls with wine-smelling vomit and my mother was furious."

He said it with some humor, so she wasn't offended. In fact, it was the same humor she'd seen from him the night before and she liked it, very much. It made her feel comforted and she was willing to believe that he truly wasn't angry with her, after all.

"You have brothers?" she asked. "How many?"

He smiled as he reflected on his contingent of brothers. "I have five," he said. "You will meet them all soon enough. But we shall discuss them later; right now, you must dress so that we can depart for Shrewsbury within the hour. I will send the servant women up to help you."

Grier sensed his urgency so she didn't ask him any more questions. But she was becoming increasingly comfortable with him and questions were natural. He'd gone out of his way to put her at ease since last night and she appreciated it very much. Dane de Russe was endearing himself to her, whether or not he realized it. He'd been so kind that she surely couldn't feel anything else towards him.

"I have never had anyone help me dress before," she said, standing up from the bed and looking at the garments slung across it. "But I suppose I should. I will admit that I am unfamiliar with garments such as these."

He turned for the door. "You will learn," he said. Then, he paused, his hand on the latch as he looked at her. "If you are wondering what gown to wear, I am partial to the yellow."

She turned to look at him, only to see him wink at her as he quit the chamber. When the door shut softly behind him, Grier couldn't help the smile that spread across her lips. She genuinely had no idea why, only that Dane was kind and handsome, and she thought she might come to like him. Perhaps it was a foolish thought, but she didn't think so. Something about the man was easy to like.

When the serving women arrived a short while later, the three of them rifled through the goods Dane had purchased, pulling together the lady's dress for the day. Grier didn't have much of an opinion about it except she wanted to wear the yellow brocade because her husband had requested it.

The serving women were more than happy to comply.

"How is your wife this morning?"

Dane heard William's question and he knew exactly what the man meant. There was a lewd hint in his tone.

He'd found his men down in the common room of the inn, breaking their fast for the morning with warmed beef and fresh bread. The room itself was cold, smelling of smoke and unwashed bodies, and the innkeeper was trying to clear out the blocked chimney before starting the fire for the day.

Men were sleeping around the perimeter of the room, now awakening as the innkeeper's wife began to open up the shutters. Sunlight streamed into the dark room as Dane took a seat at the end of a dilapidated table, ignoring William's leering question for the most part.

"She is dressing," he said. His attention moved to Dastan, seated on his right, as the man handed him a cup of watered wine. "Are the men being mustered?"

Dastan nodded. "Syler and Boden are outside, organizing the escort," he said. "William and I were waiting for you. We heard something interesting earlier this morning that you will want to hear."

Dane took a hunk of the warmed meat for himself. "Oh?" he said. "From whom?"

Dastan looked over his shoulder to the corner of the tavern where three men were sitting, off in the shadows, eating a meal in the early morning hour.

"That group over there," he said. "They came in at dawn, when you were off at the merchant's stall."

"What about them?"

Dastan turned back to his drink. "They are from a place called Caereinion," he said. "It is to the south of the lands ruled by the Lords of Godor. Have you heard of them?"

Dane shook his head. "Should I?"

Dastan shrugged. "Godor is a Welsh lordship that once belonged to Dafydd ap Gruffydd," he said. "The lords that rule over it are minor Welsh royalty, but they still hold some power with their people in the north. Their lands butt against the northern portion of Shrewsbury lands."

Dane shoveled beef into his mouth. "Has Shrewsbury had hostilities with them?"

Dastan shook his head. "Not really," he said. "We stay on our side of the Marches and they stay on theirs, unlike those fools to the south near Erwood Castle. But what those men told us of the Lords of Godor was... interesting."

"Why?"

Dastan glanced at William, who had also spoken to the Welshmen.

He was rather surprised young William wasn't mouthing off about it but, then again, there were times when William showed some control in a situation. Far and few between, but always when it mattered, at least for the most part. William caught Dastan's look and leaned forward, speaking quietly to Dane.

"Those men serve the Lords of Godor," he said. "They serve the son of the great lord in particular, a man named Davies ap Madoc. It would seem that Davies made an offer for the Shrewsbury heiress some time ago but was denied."

Dane looked at William in mild surprise. "And why would they tell you this?"

William threw a thumb over his shoulder, in the direction of the street outside. "Because they saw the Shrewsbury standards," he said. "They came in here and when they saw us sitting here, eating, they struck up a conversation. They wanted to know why the Duke of Shrewsbury was in Welshpool, and if he was going to visit his daughter at St. Idloes. One thing led to another, and they told us about ap Madoc's marriage proposal."

Dane stopped chewing. Then, he swallowed the bite in his mouth and took a big gulp of the watered wine. "And what did you tell them?"

Dastan grunted, a sound of regret, and lowered his head as William continued. "I told them that the old duke was dead, and that there was a new duke," he said. "I am sorry, Dane. I probably should not have said that, but I didn't think. But I did not tell them that the old duke's daughter married and that we had come for the wedding."

Dane sighed faintly. "I see," he said. He looked over Dastan's shoulder at the three men huddled back in the corner. "So the Lords of Godor offered for Grier's hand, did they? Undoubtedly to control the dukedom, I would say. The news of Garreth's death will get back to them now."

"I am sorry, Dane," William said again. "I did not even think not to tell them."

Dane could see that William was genuinely contrite, a rare state for the overconfident knight. He put his hand on the man's shoulder.

"If you had not told them, someone else would have," he said. "It is no secret that Garreth is dead, so I would not worry overly. But I am interested to know if they will offer marriage to Grier again, knowing her father is dead. Did you know any of this, Dastan?"

Dastan nodded. "I did," he said. "It was about two years ago. Davies ap Madoc sent his father to Shrewsbury to plead on his son's behalf. It seems that Davies' sister was also at St. Idloes, and that is how he knew of Grier."

"And Garreth refused him?"

"Flatly. He did not want his daughter married to a Welsh warlord. As you say, the Welsh would control Shrewsbury if Davies married her, and that would bode badly for the English along the Marches. Besides… Henry would not have allowed it."

Dane thought it all rather interesting information. "Then I suspect I may have another visit on behalf of Davies ap Madoc," he said. "We should be prepared for some hostilities when ap Madoc is told Lady Grier is already married."

Dastan couldn't disagree. "The Lords of Godor control quite a bit of the mountainous area from Buttington up to Oswestry."

"And they wanted Shrewsbury, too."

"Indeed."

"You do not think Godor had anything to do with the battle at Erwood last month?"

Dastan shook his head. "Not at all," he said. "Godor to the north, and the warlords further to the south, are not on good terms as far as we know. I am sure he had nothing to do with it."

Dane pondered that. "Other than a few small skirmishes, Wales has been quiet for over one hundred years," he said. "Ever since the death of Owain Glyndŵr. I do not expect we are in for another round of rebellion, although you never know. The Welsh nobility is rebellious by nature, and greedy, as evidenced by the attempt on Erwood and also by the proposal to marry Shrewsbury's heiress, so we must be vigilant. We cannot let our guard down with those bastards for one moment."

It was a fair statement. As William quit the table to go outside and help with the men, Dane and Dastan sat there in silence, each man to his own thoughts. A serving wench brought around more food and warmed wine, and they took it gratefully, stuffing their bellies for the journey home. As Dane began his second cup of watered down wine, Dastan spoke.

"How is your lady wife?" he asked. "I'd heard she'd been ill last night."

Dane wiped at his mouth. "She was, but she is better this morning," he said. He hesitated a moment before continuing. "Dastan, did Garreth pay any attention to his daughter all those years she was in the convent? What I mean is did he ever visit her to see how she was faring?"

It was an answer that Dastan was clearly reluctant to answer. Perhaps he had even known that, at some point, Dane would ask, because the reluctance was evidenced on his face.

"I am sorry to say that he did not," he said. "But not because he did not care about the woman. I think it was self-preservation."

"What do you mean?"

Dastan shrugged. "I think she reminded him of his wife," he said honestly. "Lady Grier was a young child when the duke's wife died in childbirth with a son. I never knew his wife, but some of the old soldiers have told me about her. She was very young compared to the duke's advanced years but, somehow, the marriage was a good one in spite of their age differences. Her name was Grier also, you know. Your wife is named for her."

"It seems like an odd name, I must say."

Dastan picked up his cup. "Scottish," he said. "Lord Garreth told me that his wife was the only child of a Scottish earl. Cairngorm, I think. His name was Gregor, and she was named for him."

Dane nodded his head. "Interesting," he said. "I suppose any bit of information helps where it pertains to Lady de Russe. I know very little about her except for the fact that she has been kept at a convent for the past fourteen years and, in that time, she has known great hardship and poverty. Do you know why she became ill last night? Because she has been starving. She said that those at St. Idloes have been existing on oat gruel for quite some time. When the beef was presented last night, she stuffed herself and then promptly vomited it all up again. Dastan, I have to believe that Garreth did not know the hardships she had suffered but, in the same breath, I cannot believe that he did not. I cannot believe that he would ignore his flesh and blood so."

Dastan understood a great deal in that rather intense statement. "As I said, I think he stayed away because she reminded him of his dead wife," he said quietly. "From what Lord Garreth said, his daughter looks just like his wife. I believe he stayed away because of the memories, not because he harbored some resentment towards her."

Dane shook his head. "Then that is just as bad," he said. "That poor woman was starving. She has absolutely nothing to her name, living in poverty like the lowliest serf. How can you not call that neglect?"

Dastan didn't have an answer. "I cannot, Dane."

Dane was verging on disparaging Garreth, but he stopped himself. He knew that Dastan had adored the old man. In fact, all of his men had, so he wasn't going to speak ill of the dead. But what he had seen from the lady did not sit well with him. Taking a deep breath, he returned to his cup and drained it.

"Well," he said, wiping his mouth again. "That is in the past. What matters now is the future, and the lady will be well-tended. I would like to think that would make Garreth happy."

"It would," Dastan agreed. "My wife is prepared to help Lady de Russe settle in to her new role at Shrewsbury, so at least she will have a woman for a companion. That should help her a great deal."

Dane looked at him, suddenly remembering the man's wife. Lady Charlisa du Reims was a vivacious blond who had her husband completely enamored. In the brief time that Dane had been at Shrewsbury Castle, he had seen it for himself. It never even occurred to him that Lady du Reims would become his wife's companion, but it was the truth. He felt better knowing she would have some guidance.

"I'd nearly forgotten," he admitted. "I do believe your wife shall be a great comfort to Lady de Russe simply because the convent taught her nothing of daily life in a castle. She admitted that to me and she is quite distressed about it. Dastan, it is as if that woman has been living in a cave somewhere, shut off from the world for all of those years. She is going to depend on all of us to teach her what she needs to know."

"It will be a pleasure."

Dane opened his mouth to reply when Dastan suddenly caught sight of something behind him. Dane turned to see what had Dastan's attention, only to see Grier emerging from the corridor that led to the rear courtyard, where their chamber had been.

What he saw astonished him.

It was as if he wasn't looking at the same woman.

As the gray-haired serving woman stood behind Grier and beamed, Dane rose to his feet. He swore that an angel had just walked into his midst because he'd never seen anything finer. She was wearing the yellow damask, which clung to her curvy figure and dragged out behind her in a sweeping train. Her hair had been braided and pinned, with a hair net he'd purchased held it in place, and the wedding brooch was back on her chest, shined and cleaned. She was brushed and scrubbed, looking for all the world like a duchess.

Dane could hardly believe it.

"My God," he said as he approached her. "You are a glorious creature. I see that I was correct; the gown fits you."

Grier's cheeks flushed pink. She was in a whole new world, completely out of her element, but the expression on Dane's face told her how pleased he was. Truth be told, she was self-conscious about how the dress fit her, being that it was a snug fit and showing off her figure lines, but if Dane liked it, then she would force herself to become accustomed to it. She so wanted to please him.

"It does," she agreed. "It is a bit long, as you suspected, but it seems to fit me."

Dane shook his head in awe. "You are beautiful," he said. "Do you like it?"

She gave him a half-smile, an embarrassed one, and looked down at herself. "It is very soft," she said. "Softer and more beautiful than anything I have ever worn."

He couldn't help but notice she mostly avoided his question. "But you do not like it?"

Her cheeks turned a shade of red as she looked down at herself, the way her breasts were embraced by the dress, the way the swell of her bosom was exposed. She smoothed at the garment.

"I... I do like it," she said, keeping her head down.

Dane bent over her, his head very close to hers. "But... what? You are not thrilled with it?"

Grier was terribly embarrassed to admit the truth. "I... well, there is a good deal of flesh showing and..."

She trailed off and he grinned. "And you do not look chaste enough," he finished quietly. "Not to worry; I purchased scarves for you. Cover up your shoulders and neck if it pleases you."

She grinned at him, timidly, the first real smile he'd ever seen from her, and it was enchanting. "You do not mind?"

He scowled at her, but it was lightly done. "Not at all," he said. "You must do what you feel comfortable with, but know that you look absolutely stunning. I have never seen a more beautiful woman."

Grier's smile grew, now a flattered one. From the corner of her eye she caught sight of the old serving woman, and she stepped aside, indicating the woman to Dane.

"This is Euphemia," she said. "She has helped me since I have been here, both last night and this morning. I know it is asking quite a bit, but do you think she can come with me to Shrewsbury? She has been so very helpful and I should like to have her with me."

Dane looked at the old woman, the same one who had helped him bring clothing to Grier last night. She looked like she had a gray-colored haystack on her head, and she was a little rough around the edges, but she had, indeed, been quite helpful and he didn't want to deny Grier her first real request of him. He nodded.

"If it pleases you," he said. "In fact, the first thing she has to do is ensure your baggage is packed and bring it to the escort. I will send Dastan to secure a mount for her."

Grier turned to Euphemia, smiling that the old woman would be accompanying her, and the servant woman fled to do Dane's bidding.

But Dane wasn't watching her; he was watching Grier as Grier watched the old woman. He still couldn't believe that the timid little oblate was now this lovely woman before him. The curiosity he'd always had towards her, since the moment he laid eyes on her, was now turning to something else.

It was turning into interest.

"Come," he told her. "While Euphemia is gathering your things, come and sit. I will have gruel and bread brought to you."

Grier nodded, taking a step as he took her elbow and promptly stepping on the hem of her dress. She would have tripped had Dane not grabbed her, and she smiled up at him with that embarrassed little smile he was coming to recognize.

"How clumsy of me," she said, gathering her skirt and holding it up so she could walk. "I fear that wearing fine clothing is going to take some practice."

Dane smiled in return, holding tight to her elbow. "Not to worry," he said. "You'll catch on."

"Do you think so?"

He simply nodded, a knowing smile playing on his lips. It was a gesture that sent Grier's smile blooming. As he carefully led her over to the table where Dastan greeted her politely, he couldn't help but think that if all went well and according to plan, that he would have a magnificent wife on his hands when all was said and done.

For the first time since he was told of the betrothal to Lady Grier de Lara, he was actually happy about it. He wasn't going to have to kill his father, after all, for getting him into this situation.

But he prayed, quite seriously, that the happiness wasn't fleeting.

He rather liked the feeling he got when he looked at Grier.

CHAPTER FIVE

St. Idloes

EOLANDE WAS HEADING for the common area next to the chapel, the one that was outside the cloister and away from the dorter where the nuns slept. She was moving swiftly, and with a purpose, as Mother Mary Moria had just come to her as she worked in the chamber where the oblates sewed their lace shawls.

Your brother is here, Mother Mary Moria had told her. *See to him at once.*

It was later in the day, the same day that Grier had been taken away, as Eolande made her way through the damp cloister, through the lay gate that led to the yard behind the chapel. It was an open area where male visitors were kept, one that her brother always used when he came to visit her. It was the same place they used for travelers, permitting them to camp in the area, so it was a well-used space. As Eolande came through the great iron gate, she immediately spied Davies standing near the chapel.

Dressed in a heavy tunic to his knees, breeches, and boots, and with a dark green cloak resting upon his shoulders, Davies ap Madoc turned to see his sister coming towards him across the muddy yard. A tall man, sinewy, with black hair and black eyes, he quickly made his way towards her.

"Is it true?" he demanded.

Eolande's movements slowed. She knew exactly what he meant and her heart sank. "Is what true?"

"About Grier. Is she gone?"

"Who told you?"

Davies reached her. "It does not matter who told me," he said. "Is it true?"

When he reached out to grab her, she yanked her arm away. "It matters, Davies," she said, suspicious and unhappy. "You always know what is happening here. You are paying someone to send you information. Well? Who is it? If you do not tell me, I'll not tell you anything at all."

Davies stood his ground, but he knew that butting heads with Eolande would come to no good. It never had. She was stubborn, his little sister, so he eased his stance. If he wanted the information he'd come for, then arguing with her wasn't going to help.

He had to treat her carefully.

"I pay local men to watch the comings and goings of the abbey, and relay to me any information of note," he said. "There is nothing wrong with that. I would be foolish not to know what was happening in my own lands."

It was more than that, and they both knew it. "Then if you already know what has happened, why are you asking me?"

She was being annoying about it and Davies struggled to keep his temper in check.

"I was told that early this morning, a large contingent from Shrewsbury came and took Grier away," he said. "Well? Why did her father take her away?"

So he doesn't know all of it, Eolande thought with surprise. *He only knows that Grier was removed, but not why.* Even so, there was no use in keeping any of it from him, because he'd find out eventually. Davies was the nosy sort and he always had been. As he'd said, he paid men to watch the abbey for him. He had men all over the area watching roads, or towns, and reporting back to him. And as he'd reminded her, these were his lands. At some point, he'd probably try to find out why Grier was taken back to Shrewsbury simply because he'd been obsessed with Shrewsbury's heiress since nearly the first time he'd met her.

Therefore, for her brother's sake, Eolande knew she had to tell him the truth.

"It was not her father who came to take her away, Davies," she said, reining in her snappish manner. "It was the new duke. Her husband."

Davies' eyes widened in an instant. "Her husband?" he sputtered. "She *married*?"

Eolande nodded. "Her father died last month," she said. "He betrothed her to a man of his choosing, although I do not know who he is. All I know is that he came to St. Idloes and married Grier this morning. Then, he took her away."

Davies stared at her, clearly stunned. For several long seconds, he simply looked at her as if unable to comprehend what he'd been told. But in that shocked expression were hints of grief and anger. The woman he wanted for his own had been taken by another.

He could hardly believe it.

"Married," he muttered again. "She is married."

Eolande nodded, knowing her brother was shaken by the news. She could see it in his eyes; the light that was often there, that light of spirit and vibrancy, was dulled. In spite of Grier's father refusing Davies' proposal of marriage, she knew he still held out hope that he would have her someday. But that hope was now ended.

She felt pity for him.

"She is," she said, more gently. "Davies, you must forget about Grier. She was never meant for you. Now that she is married, you must forget her. You must find another wife, someone worthy of the Lords of Godor."

He looked at her, but it was a look of displeasure. "You think I can forget about her so easily?" he asked. "I have tried, Landy. Why do you think I stopped coming to visit you? It was because I could no longer bear to see Grier. God knows I tried to forget about her, but I cannot."

It was starting to mist now, a faint sheen of water coming out of the sky and blanketing the land. Wearing her woolen garments, Eolande wrapped her arms around her slender body, trying to stay warm as she faced her devastated brother.

"You must," she insisted softly. "Whoever Grier is married to now is the Duke of Shrewsbury and commands a bigger army than anything Godor can muster. He will not take kindly to a man pining over his wife, and would you truly shame the woman so by challenging her marriage? Papa would not let you do that."

That was true. Madoc ap Iowerth was the Lord of Godor, a powerful Welsh warlord, but a man who had grown soft in his old age. It was Davies who kept their vassals in line, or who made decisions that would affect them all. Davies had grown up admiring his father but since that fateful day when he went to Shrewsbury to plead for Grier's hand, all Davies could feel was disappointment in the man. When Davies had needed him most, he'd failed him.

It was something he'd not forgotten.

"If you are referring to that weak man who fathered us, then he has no say in what I do," he said grimly. "All he does is sit before the fire these days and complain that his bones are cold. Beyond that, he does nothing that would bring honor to the lordship of Godor."

"And you do?" Eolande fired back softly. "Do you think challenging the Duke of Shrewsbury for his wife is honorable? He will destroy you, Davies, and rightly so."

Davies wiped the water out his eyes. "Who said anything about challenging her marriage?" he said. "But I will go to Shrewsbury to see who she has wed. If she did not wed me, then I must satisfy my curiosity that she married a worthy man."

But Eolande shook her head. "It is a terrible intention," she said. "Nothing good can come of it. Why would you torture yourself? It will only hurt you."

Davies could hear the concern in her voice. Little Eolande, his beloved sister. It was that concern that caused him to second guess his intentions, but his obsession with Grier would not be sated. It had long surpassed attraction; obsession was exactly what it was these days. Grier consumed him and had for a long time. He looked at his sister.

"Dear Eolande," he said, the twinkle of vitality back in his dark eyes as he looked at her. "You have always been concerned for me."

She nodded eagerly. "Of course I am."

He smiled sadly, putting a hand to the side of her head. "As I am concerned for you," he said. "Even these days as St. Idloes knows only poverty, there is not much I can do for you, although I wish there was. Everyone is suffering from famine in these lands. So many crops have been blighted, and even Papa and our men suffer from hunger. It is as if we are all cursed these days."

Eolande shrugged. "At least we have grains," she said. "We are able to eat, but our bellies are not full because there are many mouths to feed. And you? How are *you* faring, Davies? I have not seen you in some time."

Davies dropped his hand from her head. "I am well enough," he said, his gaze moving across the gray landscape. "But there is a restlessness among the men. They are tired of being hungry. The want food and they want to fill the bellies of their families. There has been talk of raiding villages on the *Saesneg* side of the Marches, and I know for a fact that some have already tried. Our people are hungry, Eolande."

She could sense something in his words, something ominous. "What are you saying?" she asked. "The Marches have been mostly quiet for one hundred years, Davies. Will starvation motivate our people to go to war against the *Saesneg* again?"

He lifted his shoulders. "Possibly," he said. "We have little money; how are we to buy food? I fear we must take what we can for our own survival, and Shrewsbury is the largest town this far north. They have a market center and trading."

Eolande frowned. "It is also where Grier is."

"A coincidence."

Her frown grew. "Is it? You sound as if you have already decided to raid Shrewsbury. Mayhap to punish them for taking Grier away from you?"

Davies looked at her. "I do not know for certain that we shall raid Shrewsbury," he said honestly, "but I do know that Grier is there. For my own sake, I must see this man she has married. I must see who took the woman I wanted. Mayhap that is my only business in Shrewsbury, but mayhap not. That is for me to decide."

Eolande shook her head. She didn't think any of this was a good idea. Not only was Davies obsessed with Grier, he was also thinking on raiding Shrewsbury because the vassals of Godor were starving. It was adding up to a very bad situation.

"Davies," she said quietly. "I can see that you will not listen to me when I tell you to stay away from Shrewsbury, so all I will say is be cautious. Whatever you do, take great care. I should not wish to lose you."

"You will not," he said, kissing her on the forehead. "I will come to see you again, very soon. But before I go… tell me one thing, Landy."

"What?"

"Did Grier ever speak fondly of me? Was I on her mind as much as she was on mine?"

Eolande didn't want to hurt him, but she thought that if she told him the truth, he might stop obsessing over Grier. Perhaps, it would be enough to discourage him and even keep him away from Shrewsbury. Somehow, she didn't think so, but she had to try.

"Nay," she said after a moment. "She never gave you a thought."

Davies face fell and the glimmer in his eyes dimmed. It had been a difficult truth for him to hear.

"I see," he said, turning away from her. "Thank you for telling me."

Eolande watched him walk away. "That would make going to Shrewsbury to see her a waste of your time, Davies," she called after him. "She would not care."

Davies kept walking, but he lifted a hand to acknowledge that he heard her. But still, he kept walking, disappearing around the side of the chapel.

When he was out of sight, Eolande turned for the lay gate that led back into the cloister. Truly, she hated to hurt his feelings, but it was for the best. He needed to know that whatever he felt for Grier was unrequited. She'd thought he'd already understood that, but evidently not. Davies was prideful and stubborn; perhaps, he still believed there was a chance. No man liked to face a rejection of the heart.

Opening the old iron gate and listening to it creak on its hinges, all Eolande could think about was her foolish brother and her dearest friend, wondering if Davies would truly be foolish enough to go to Shrewsbury. If it was for a raid, or if it was to see Grier, either reason was dangerous.

She only had one brother.

She didn't want to lose him.

CHAPTER SIX

Shrewsbury

SHREWSBURY WAS A very big city.

The noise, the smell, the people… everything about it was overwhelming. As the Duke of Shrewsbury's escort entered from the south side of town, Grier was struck by all of the sights and smells of the bustling burgh. At first, she was curious about the city and the people, but as the situation overtook her, that curiosity faded into fear and distress.

Memories she'd long forgotten began to seep back into her mind.

Crossing a bridge that spanned over the murky, green waterway of the River Severn, the party ended up on a sloped street called St. John's Hill. It was a busy avenue, full of people moving in both directions, and Grier clung to her palfrey as the little animal scooted after the bigger war horses. She was surrounded by soldiers and knights, and Dane was slightly ahead of her, so there were men everywhere who were there to protect her. She was the center of a sea of armored men.

But she'd never felt so alone in her entire life.

It was odd to think that this was her town, where she was born. Memories of her mother and father, things she'd long pushed aside, returned at the sight of the familiar red city walls. She remembered her mother's warmth, her father's detachment, and a carefree life of a happy child until her mother died.

After that, her life had changed so quickly. Her mother had been pregnant with a son. *A brother*, they'd told her. Then the child had died alongside her mother and both were swiftly put in the cold ground. Grier had hardly come to grips with her mother's death when her father had sent her off to Wales. Surrounded by people she didn't know, and a nun who liked to take a switch to their backs when they disobeyed, she remembered how much she'd cried during her first years at St. Idloes.

And how much she'd hated her father for it.

Odd, she'd forgotten about the weeping and sorrow of those early years until now. Perhaps, she'd simply blocked it all out. But, God, there was a terrible hatred for her father, something deep-rooted into the recesses of her mind that she'd never completely let go of. She thought she had, but feeling it bubble up again, she realized she hadn't. It was those red walls of Shrewsbury reminding her, with every step the escort took, how much she'd hated him. Even when she'd been told of her father's death, she hadn't remembered the hatred. But those red walls had been the trigger.

It was ugly, black sludge that filled her heart.

Along the sides of the road, people were stopping to watch the duke's procession move through with the big blue, gold, and red bird of prey standards that announced Shrewsbury. People were looking at the soldiers, and at her. Grier put aside the hatred roiling in her gut because she realized that she was increasingly uncomfortable with the attention of the crowds. All of those eyes, staring. Because of her nerves, the grip she had on her palfrey turned her knuckles white. As if holding on to that little horse gave her some measure of safety, something to hang on to in an unfamiliar world that was swallowing her up.

Proceeding up the road, buildings rose on either side, the wattle and daub construction, with wooden beams and whitewashed walls. Windows opened and people began hanging out of them, looking at the procession from overhead, and Grier found herself looking up into what she thought were unfriendly faces. The new Duke and Duchess of

Shrewsbury were a curiosity, and all the world seemed to be turning out for them. Grier finally gave up looking around and simply focused straight ahead; seeing all of those people made her feel nauseous.

In truth, this wasn't the city she remembered. It was an unsavory, dirty place. She could hear people calling to her, shouting and then laughing, but she didn't look at them. She kept her eyes ahead, noticing when Dane turned around, casually, to see how she was handling the noise and the excitement. When their eyes met, he smiled encouragingly, but she couldn't smile in return. It would have been a lie because there was nothing around her that she felt like smiling about. Therefore, seeing his kindness in this sea of chaos made her want to cry.

Mercifully, the shouting and crowds and buildings faded away and a massive wall built of the same red sandstone that comprised the city walls rose up in their place. Grier dared to look at it now that she was away from the people. The wall towered over them and, ahead, she could see a gatehouse with a great yawning mouth. There were two portcullises, both of them raised, and Grier found her curiosity returning as she inspected the big walls and the ceiling of the gatehouse as they passed through it.

The gatehouse opened up into a vast outer bailey that sloped to the northeast, with many outbuildings, including a two-storied great hall. It was the biggest building in the outer bailey, surrounding by housing for the men and the stables tucked back against the north wall. The escort finally came to a halt and men began dismounting, including Dane, who headed directly for her.

"Welcome home, Lady Shrewsbury," he said. "I cannot imagine you would remember much of this place, but from what I am told, you were born here."

Reaching up, he lifted her off of the palfrey and for the first time since they'd met, Grier felt his arms around her. He had big muscles and big hands, lifting her as if she weighed no more than a child. It was enough to cause her heart to skip a beat, and she was embarrassed for it. But once he set her to her feet, she found herself sorry that he'd let her go.

"I was," she said, looking around the bailey. She remembered it, but not very clearly, and the dark hatred for her father threatened again. This place had his stench all over it. "But you are correct; I do not remember very much of it. Only impressions, really."

Dane held out an elbow to her, to politely escort her, but she looked at his elbow as if she had no idea what to do with it. His smile broadened as he took her left hand and tucked it into the crook of his elbow.

"When a man gives you his arm, you are meant to take it," he said softly. "To refuse is to insult him. Would you insult me?"

She looked mortified. "Nay," she said. "I would not knowingly, I swear it."

He chuckled. "I believe you," he said. "Now that you are holding my arm, hold tight. I intend to show you this place that you and I are to rule over."

That was an immense thought in a day that had already been full of them, and Grier was reluctant to go with him but she had little choice. She looked around as they began to head towards the gate that led to the inner bailey and the red-stoned keep that she could see rising in the middle of it. The day was a little cloudy, perhaps a little murky, and the towering keep was impressive against the gray sky.

The keep, she thought. *The last place I saw my mother alive.*

Oh, but the memories were difficult now that she was here. Her stomach was in knots because of it but she didn't want to let on to Dane. She hardly knew the man, and their beginning had been rough enough without her lamenting her hatred for her father and the terrible memories coming back to Shrewsbury had brought her. It wasn't his fault, after all. Perhaps, it was best to keep her feelings to herself.

Hopefully, she would learn to forget them again.

"I will admit that this is all rather frightening," she said, trying to distract herself. "I am returning to a place I thought I would never see again, and I'm now expected to do something I never thought I would do."

"I know."

"I hope you will teach me how to rule alongside you."

Dane nodded, his pale eyes glimmering. "Of course I will," he said. "You shall be the best chatelaine Shrewsbury has ever seen. In fact…"

He never got to finish, as suddenly, a lady thundered across the bridge that spanned a small moat surrounding the inner bailey. Her skirts were held up as she ran, squealing all the way as she blew past Dane and Grier, rushing into the bailey and then throwing herself at Dastan, who barely had time to brace himself.

Grier watched the woman with surprise. She had come to a halt, watching the excited reunion with some fascination.

"*Who* is that?" she asked.

Dane shook his head at the overenthusiastic wife who didn't even stop to greet her liege. "That is Lady Charlisa du Reims," he said. "Clearly, she is mad about her husband, so do not take the fact that she ignored us as an insult. She simply has eyes only for him."

Grier didn't take it as an insult at all but, as she watched, Dastan grabbed his wife by the arm and began dragging her in their direction. He was obviously peeved at her behavior and as he came near Dane and Grier, he grunted, a sound of great annoyance.

"My wife did not mean to be rude, my lord, when she ran past you," he said. Then, his gazed moved to Grier. "My lady, this is my wife, Charlisa. She has been very eager to make your acquaintance."

Grier thought that was a rather absurd statement considering that that woman nearly mowed her down in her haste to reach her husband. She couldn't help but chuckle.

"I could see that by the way she darted past me," she said, her gaze moving to Charlisa, who was looking genuinely mortified. "Lady du Reims, it is an honor to meet you."

Charlisa dropped into a practiced curtsy. She was quite lovely, with pretty blond hair and big blue eyes. Even as she curtsied, she looked up at Grier, a smile playing on her lips.

"I was overeager to see my husband, Lady de Russe," she said. "I am sure you can understand that, having a handsome husband of your own, but please forgive my bad manners. It shall not happen again."

Grier didn't believe that for a moment. "At least not until the next time he returns home from a long journey."

It was lightly said and Charlisa giggled, giving a bit of a nod. At least she was honest when confronted. Already, there was some warmth between the ladies as Grier and Charlisa took a good look at each other. Truly, Grier wasn't offended and Charlisa seemed to have the charm of a kitten, so there was no anger. Only open curiosity at that point. Dastan merely rolled his eyes at his silly wife, but a smile played on his lips as well.

"May we accompany you on your tour of Shrewsbury, Lady de Russe?" he asked. "I may be able to answer any questions you may have since I have been here for several years. I knew your father well, and I know Shrewsbury well. I may be of service."

Grier nodded, looking to Dane. "I do not mind if you do not."

Dane shook his head. "He and his frenzied wife are most welcome," he said as he began to walk. "I was just about to show Lady de Russe around the outer bailey. Dastan, you may take charge of the tour if you wish."

Dastan stepped forward. "Thank you, my lord," he said, his twinkling gaze on Grier. "You were born here, my lady, in that very keep, and you lived here until you were six years of age. Do you recall your life here?"

There was that question. *Do you recall your life here?* Words of bitterness immediately came to her lips, but she swallowed them. What she felt, the intense feelings she'd shelved, belonged to her and her alone. She thought Dastan's question was a rather personal one, and one that she really had no intention of answering. Dastan and Dane were trying very hard to be kind to her, to introduce her back into life at Shrewsbury, and she didn't want to talk about her feelings.

After a moment, she simply shook her head.

"Not very much," she said. "My lord and I were just only speaking of it. I remember mostly impressions. Of my mother, who had a sweet voice and was very beautiful, and of my father, who did not spend much time with me."

Dane was listening to her as she spoke, watching her manner. The ride to Shrewsbury on this day had been uneventful for the most part, and he'd been able to ride with Grier for some of the way. But the moment they drew near the city, he'd gone to the front of the escort, leaving her buried in the men behind him.

And something in her manner had changed.

The moment they'd entered the city, something about her changed entirely. He wasn't sure what it was, but even now, there was something in her eyes – perhaps even the lack of eye contact – that told him she was, perhaps, feeling more than she was letting on. He wondered if she remembered more than she'd told him – and simply didn't wish to speak of it.

Dane wasn't going to push her into anything, of course, but over the past couple of days, he'd found himself increasingly interested in the woman he'd married. He was hoping that, someday, she might put enough trust in him to speak of the thoughts on her mind. His parents, Gaston and Remington, had shared a wonderful and loving marriage over the past thirty years, and there was some part of Dane that envied what they had. Perhaps he wished for it, also.

But perhaps, that was a fool's wish.

In any case, Grier's answer to Dastan's question brought about a conversation he'd had with Dastan when he'd learned how starved and neglected Grier had been. It made Dane think yet again that Garreth had intentionally ignored his daughter in all ways and, given that thought, he couldn't imagine that this homecoming was all that pleasant for her.

Perhaps that was the change in her demeanor he'd seen.

"Your father and mother are buried in Shrewsbury's chapel over there," he said after a moment, pointing to the building over near the hall. It was long and slender, with a rounded wall at the end that had lancet windows cut into it. "One of your father's de Lara ancestors built it next to the hall and you will see carvings on the door that show men going straight from the hall with cups of wine in their hands and then into the chapel to pray. I am assuming it was a hint to the degenerates in the hall who drank or cursed too much."

Grier grinned as she shielded her eyes from the sun as she looked over at the red-stoned chapel. It was the same color as the keep and walls. "I do remember it, a little," she said. "I remember my mother being buried there. It was shortly thereafter that I was sent to St. Idloes. Would… would you mind if I visited the graves of my mother and father? Now that I am here, I feel as if it should be the very first thing I do."

Dane nodded. "Of course," he said. "I will take you there."

With a pause in their tour, Dane and Grier left Dastan and Charlisa standing near the gate to the inner bailey as Dane took her down the slope to the chapel. His pace was slower because Grier was having trouble with the overlong gown. She kept stepping on the hem. Finally, they reached the chapel, but before he could accompany her inside, she turned to him.

"I would like to go in alone," she said. "If you do not mind."

He shook his head. "Not at all," he said. "I shall wait for you here."

With a forced smile, Grier headed into the chapel, but not before looking at the elaborately carved doors with scenes of drunks spilling out of the hall and heading straight into the chapel to pray for their drunken habits. It was a lesson in woodcarving, and she timidly pushed the enormous doors open, emerging into the dank innards of the chapel.

The smell…

Like damp, moldy earth. She remembered that smell and, in a rush, all of the memories of the last time she was here came tumbling back on her. She could hear the priests praying the funeral mass as her father wept over the bodies of her mother and infant brother. It had all been scary and overwhelming, and she had stood with her father as the bodies were put in the ground in a stone-lined grave and covered with a massive stone that a stonemason had hastily carved. Her mother had been covered with a funeral pall of expensive blue silk, and that was the last memory Grier had of her.

A corpse in blue.

Slowly, she began to head towards the front of the chapel where she knew her parents were buried. The light from the lancet windows was streaming in, so the visibility towards the front of the chapel was much better than it was to the rear. Immediately, she saw her mother's grave right in front of the altar and the freshly-turned earth right next to it showed her where her father was buried.

Grier came to within a few feet of the graves, gazing down on them, reconciling herself with what she was seeing. The light that streamed in through the lancet windows hit her mother's grave head on, but missed her father's.

She thought that was rather appropriate.

All of the hatred she'd been feeling, and trying to suppress, since entering the city was now coming forward, full force, like the rush of the tide. But along with the hatred was something more; it was a horrific sense of longing as she gazed at her mother's grave.

Grier Eleanor Gordon de Lara

and infant Garreth de Lara

May Angels embrace them

Grier stared at it, feeling grief that she hadn't felt since the day they'd buried the woman. She missed her so very much. All of that fear and sadness of a young girl swamped her, and tears stung her eyes.

"I'm home, Mama," she whispered as she went to the edge of the grave, gazing down at it. "I've been gone a very long time and I just returned. Father sent me to a convent when you died. Did he tell you that? He did. He could not stand to look at me, I am certain. But here I am. I've been brought home again by a new duke."

Her whispered words echoed off the walls of the chapel, for it was a vast and empty space. Nothing to break up the sound. A tear escape from Grier's eye and she flicked it away.

"I wanted to tell you how much I have missed you," she said. "I did not know how much until I came here. Now that I see your grave... I still do not know how you can be gone, even after all of these years. You were so young and strong and alive. I remember running with you in the fields outside of the castle and playing by the fish pond. Do you remember? We would stick long blades of grass into the water to try and lure the fish. I did not know how much I missed those days until now. I miss them so much."

Unable to stop herself, Grier broke down into quiet tears. But she was angry at the tears, angry that after all of these years, the tears were back again.

"It was not fair what happened to you," she wept. "I held your hand whilst you were laboring with the baby and you told me everything would be fine. But it was not – you lied to me. You lied to me and you left me behind, and Father sent me away with strangers who beat me. Did you know that? Because I wept and because I was little, and I did not know how to do anything, they beat me. You were gone, Father did not care, and there was no one to help me. No one!"

The last words were spoken angrily as she wept, wiping at her face to wipe away the tears and mucus, but the more she wiped the more the tears fell. Her legs gave way and she plopped forward, her knees on the edge of her mother's grave. She put her hands on the stone, feeling the cold hardness of it but, even so, she was touching her mother beneath. She closed her eyes, imagining that she was touching her soft, warm flesh.

"I was so young," she sobbed. "When they were not beating me, they were starving me. Fourteen years of being beaten and starved, all in the name of God. It wasn't fair. *It wasn't fair!*"

With that, her gaze moved to the freshly turned earth on the other side of her mother's grave, and the sorrow she was feeling made way for the black sludge of hatred that had been filling her heart.

"And you," she hissed. "You did that to me. You sent me away like rubbish, like something disgusting and unwanted. I was your *child*, you unspeakable bastard. I was your daughter and you threw me away. God, I hated you for it. I still hate you for it. You sent me to that horrible place and you left me to the mercy of people who had no compassion. It was a hatred that I kept with me for years, but those years faded, and I forgot. I have not thought of you in years until your men came to tell me that you expected me to assume my place as your heiress. I thought I was over my hatred of you, but I am not. I hate everything about you and I always will."

Rising on unsteady feet, she walked around her mother's grave, respectfully, only to stand at the edge of her father's grave and look down upon it. Her weeping had lessened and she wiped at her face, wiping away the moisture. Her focus upon Garreth's grave was full of contempt.

"Do you know what I learned at St. Idloes, Father?" she muttered hoarsely. "I learned how to survive. I learned that God is cruel, and that there is hardly any love and kindness in the world, for I have seen very little of it. The only person who ever showed me any measure of it was my friend, Eolande, and the new Mother Abbess, Mary Moria. She came from another abbey when the old Mother Abbess died, the old witch who would beat young girls until they bled or force them to stand all night in the darkness because they had not learned their verses properly. Only from those two did I see any hint of kindness, and they made it so I never wanted to leave St. Idloes. But then you made me come back here. I am glad only in the sense that I am able to tell you what I think of you. I hope there is a special place in hell for what you did to me."

With that, she spit on his grave and turned away, feeling liberated and free in a sense that she was able to speak of her feelings, but she was also feeling alone and devastated and lost. There was a whole world out there, and she had a great position in it, but it was something she still wasn't sure she wanted. Even with a handsome husband to help her along.

A handsome husband she was now bound to, for better or for worse, until death.

She had to forge ahead with her new life.

DANE HAD HEARD her.

He hadn't meant to, at least, not at first. He'd simply gone to close the big doors behind her because she'd left them open and he didn't want anyone interrupting her. So he went to close the heavy carved doors when he heard her soft voice as she began to talk to her mother.

He knew he shouldn't have listened, but he was innately curious. He didn't know her well, but he wanted to, and with her change in manner since reaching Shrewsbury, he was genuinely concerned that something might be amiss, something she was afraid to speak of. So, he did what he shouldn't have done and listened to her.

And he got more than he bargained for.

Grier's words to her mother had been sweet and sad, and he'd felt a good deal of pity for the woman. But when she began to speak to her father, that was where things changed. The venom was palpable, and when she began to speak of her treatment at St. Idloes, he understood a great deal more about her life there. It wasn't just the starvation; she'd also been abused, and all of the rage and pain she was feeling was directed at the man who had sent her there.

It was difficult to hear, and Dane felt guilty for listening, but not enough to stop. It made him understand so much more about her in ways he couldn't have imagined. *I learned to survive,* she said. The little oblate he'd picked up from St. Idloes evidently had a will of iron, because the woman he heard cursing her father was stronger than he could have ever guessed. But it also underscored his suspicion that Garreth had been quite cruel to his only surviving child.

And she hated him for it.

It was an interesting and unpleasant secret about the old duke that all of the men seemed to love. With the men, Garreth had been kind and generous, but with his only child, he'd been a fiend. It was information that Dane wasn't sure he ever wanted to share with anyone, like Dastan or Syler or even William or Boden, but it certainly gave him a new perspective on the old fellow.

He was certain that he didn't like it.

At some point, Grier stopped talking and Dane began to hear footsteps coming towards the door, so he darted away, far enough away so that when she emerged, he was standing a goodly distance from the doors. When he saw her, he headed in her direction.

"I hope your visit with your parents was satisfactory," he said pleasantly. "If you need more time, please do not feel as if you must rush. We have all the time in the world."

Grier's eyes were red-rimmed. It was clear she'd been crying and she kept her head lowered so he wouldn't notice too much.

"It is not necessary," she said. "I have completed my visit."

It sounded rather final so he didn't push. Instead, he held his elbow out to her, jabbing it at her when she didn't immediately take it. When she looked up and saw what he was doing, she smiled weakly and slipped her hand into the crook of his elbow again.

"My apologies," she said. "I fear I am unaccustomed to proprieties."

He patted her hand. "Not for long. Soon, it will become second nature."

Grier wondered if that was true. At the moment, her mood was somber and she didn't care much about anything. They were walking towards Dastan and Charlisa, who were still waiting where they'd left them, but Grier didn't feel much like socializing. In fact, she was weary and emotional, and very much wanted to be alone. She looked up at Dane.

"Would it be too inconvenient to tour Shrewsbury at another time?" she asked. "I fear that I am more exhausted than I thought I was.

I would very much like to rest."

Dane looked at her with an expression suggesting he'd been quite insensitive. "Of course it would not be inconvenient," he said. "I should have been more considerate. I will take you to our chamber right away. Shall I send Euphemia to you?"

Grier nodded. "She can help me with this devil of a dress," she said, pulling at it once again as she nearly tripped on it. "I fear I have nearly ruined it, stepping on it as I have."

He smiled at her. "Not to worry," he said. "I am sure it can be fixed. And you are still quite beautiful in it. You made a handsome duchess for the town to see."

Grier smiled at him, somewhat reluctantly, and he winked at her. She could feel her cheeks flush. Patting her hand again, Dane called out to Dastan and informed the man of their change in plans, and he also sent Dastan for the old serving woman who was still down with the escort. Charlisa offered to go with Grier, but Dane politely declined, stating that Lady de Russe simply wished to rest without an audience.

Dane thought he saw gratitude on Grier's face after that, and it was probably not something she expressed often. From what he'd heard, she had very little to be grateful for. But he was going to make sure that changed. From now on, the woman who survived the hell of St. Idloes was going to know nothing but a pleasant existence. Dane was going to ensure she had all the food and comfort she wanted, because that protective instinct he'd started to feel for her had just blossomed into something firm and strong. He didn't know why, because he hardly knew the woman, but what he did know of her, he liked. He respected her.

And he wanted to ensure she knew it.

CHAPTER SEVEN

IT WAS HER first big feast.

After an afternoon that saw her sleep for several hours, Grier had been awakened by Euphemia because Dane had come to tell her that a feast in her honor was soon to be held. Groggy, but wanting to do what was expected of her, Grier had climbed out of the very large bed that belonged to Dane to prepare for the evening meal.

It was an event that Dane had known was coming and he'd tried to prepare her for it. Because of what had happened the night before at the inn, he'd seen that she ate frequently throughout the day, explaining that might help her fragile belly if she kept it full with something light. The gruel in the morning had been followed by soft bread a few hours later, and an apple after that, and then more apples and cheese. He'd ridden with her most of the time, handing her food, and making conversation.

In fact, nearly the entire ride to Shrewsbury, Grier had been chewing on one thing or another, but sparingly, and it had all stayed down. Therefore, in spite of the emotional and exhausting day, the lure of a real feast had her interest.

So did spending more time with Dane.

As she staggered out of bed, a real bed that she hardly wanted to leave, Euphemia was already in motion. She was a woman who knew how to get things done, at an inn or in a castle, and she knew how to boss the servants around, and how to get hot water and a tub sent up to her lady's chamber immediately. As Grier stood in the dented copper tub and yawned, Euphemia cleaned her up with warm water and rags that had been rubbed with more lemon-smelling soap.

Grier had never bathed so much in her entire life as she had in the past two days, but it was something she very quickly became accustomed to. She also became accustomed to being without her clothes on, a fear that had evaporated at an alarming rate with the lure of a hot bath. This new world she found herself part of may have been overwhelming and, at times, uncomfortable but a hot water on her body was something she quickly came to like. With her hair piled on top of her head, Euphemia scrubbed and rubbed, but when it came to Grier's back, she slowed her enthusiasm.

"Does it hurt ye when I scrub, my lady?" the old woman asked.

Grier wasn't sure what she meant. "Nay, it does not hurt," she said. "You've not hurt me at all."

The servant could see that she didn't know what she meant and she gingerly touched the scars on the lady's back.

"Here, my lady," she said quietly. "The scars on yer backside – do they hurt ye?"

Grier sobered dramatically as she realized what the old woman meant. Much like her hatred for her father, the damage to her back was something she kept buried and forgotten. Although she'd never actually seen it, Eolande had told her that the scars were terrible, scars that had come from the many beatings when she'd first arrived at St. Idloes as a frightened six-year-old girl. After all of these years, they'd simply become a part of her. Out of sight, out of mind.

She didn't even think about them anymore.

"Nay," she said after a moment. "They do not hurt me."

Euphemia continued with the rag and the soap, but it was with far less force than she had with the rest of Grier's body. Grier simply stood there, feeling the rubbing and the buffing, feeling the warm water pour over her as it rinsed her clean.

Those scars...

She wished the old woman hadn't reminded her of them.

"What has yer husband said about them, my lady?" Euphemia cut into her thoughts.

Grier watched a bird as it flew past the chamber window. "He has said nothing because he has not seen them."

Euphemia came around front, wrapping a big linen towel around her. "He's not *seen* them?" she repeated, surprised. "But... but he's yer husband. He is supposed to see all of ye."

Grier looked at the old woman, thinking that she was probably right. But the truth was that she knew nothing about a marriage, or about a relationship between a man and a woman. She was so very ignorant, raised in an isolated convent, but she suspected that if Euphemia knew that a husband should see all of her, then she probably knew even more than that about the ways of men and women. It wasn't as if the nuns could teach her anything, and she'd had no one to ask. As Euphemia pulled her out of the tub and had her sit down, Grier turned to the old woman.

"I am sure you are correct when you say that he has a right to see all of me, but he has not," she said. "Euphemia, I have spent nearly my entire life surrounded by nuns. My marriage to the duke was both unexpected and unwelcome, at least at first. But I have come to see that he is a kind man and he is trying hard to please me. I want to please him, too, but I am forced to admit that I know virtually nothing about marriage. Are you married?"

Euphemia was drying her skin about the neck and shoulders. "I was, once," she said. "One of those big, strong, redheaded men. He had a temper to match."

"Was he cruel?"

The old woman smiled faintly. "Not much, my lady," he said. "Oh, I'm sure I deserved his anger, when he was angry at me. It 'twas that anger that caused his heart to give out a few years ago. Men like my

Bodell aren't meant to be sane and rational."

Grier looked at her. "But you *did* marry him," she said, trying to find the correct words to ask what was a very embarrassing question. "The duke and I have married, but nothing more. What I mean to say is that we've not... we've not done what it is that men and women do to have children."

Euphemia understood, grinning with her yellowed teeth on display. "Ah," she said. "Do ye not know what to do when ye take a man to yer bed, then?"

Grier's cheeks were flaming already with the subject, made worse by that question. "Nay," she admitted. "I... I have seen dogs mate. We had dogs around the convent, but you must understand I lived with women who did not... there were no men around to speak of. I do not believe anyone knew what to do in a man's bed. If they did, they never spoke of it to me."

Euphemia finished drying her arms and pulled out a small phial of oil that Dane had purchased in Welshpool. It smelled of flowers and she put a sparing amount on her hands, rubbing them together and them smoothing them onto Grier's skin.

"Then I shall tell ye," she said confidently. "First, yer husband is to kiss ye. Has he done that yet?"

Grier was feeling freakish and humiliated. "Not yet."

Euphemia gave her a rather sympathetic look and continued. "Well," she said, "when he does, what follows is important. A man comes to yer bed and the fleshy sword betwixt his legs becomes long and hard. He takes it and stabs it into yer body."

Grier's eyes widened at the shock of that mental image. "Where does he stab it?"

"Anywhere he pleases," Euphemia said, as if such a thing was completely normal. "If he wants to put it in yer mouth, then ye let him. If he wants to put it anywhere else, ye'll *still* let him. But if ye want a child, then he stabs it betwixt yer legs."

That caused Grier's eyes to widen even more. "Be... between my legs?"

Euphemia nodded. "That's why God gave ye a fleshy flower, my lady," she said. "Ye bleed monthly, don't ye?"

Oh, what a horrifying subject they were on, but in the interest of learning what was expected of her, Grier nodded. "Aye," she said hesitantly. "Why?"

Euphemia merely nodded, not feeling the same horror about the conversation that Grier was. It was a subject she had no reservations on speaking about.

"Because that blood means ye can bear a child," she said. "Yer husband will stab ye with his fleshy sword, but the first time he does it, there will be some pain. Ye must be prepared for it, but don't cry out. Don't make a fuss. He'll stab ye a few more times with it and then the fleshy sword spits right into yer womb. And then, in time, the bleeding will stop and a baby will come."

It all sounded shocking and vulgar to Grier, and certainly something to be feared. In fact, she was quite repulsed by what she was told, but she was also grateful that at least someone was telling her what she should know. In all of the years she spent at St. Idloes, the subject had never been discussed because it was purely taboo. The ways of men and women were never brought up. Now, Grier knew why, and she had to wonder why women married at all if this was what they had to go through.

She was soon to find out for herself.

"I see," she said, pondering the idea of spitting fleshy swords. "Thank you for telling me."

Euphemia patted her on the shoulder. "Ye'll do fine, lass," she said. "Not to worry. Yer husband seems to be the kind sort, so I'm sure he'll be careful with ye. Now, what dress do ye want to wear tonight?"

Off of one subject and on to another, so swiftly that the old woman had to ask twice before Grier could focus. Even as she selected the emerald silk, her mind was still on what she'd been told about the mating of a man and a woman. It sounded violent, messy, and painful.

She wasn't looking forward to it.

As Euphemia finished dressing her, Grier's thoughts were wrapped up in the situation in general and, truthfully, the future. She worried over what Dane would think of her, being as ignorant as she was about the ways of men and women, but she also worried about the scarring on her back that Euphemia had mentioned. Surely the man would find that extremely distasteful, so she knew she was going to have to make sure he couldn't see it. She would simply lay on her back for whatever fleshy sword stabbing had to take place. It began to occur to her just how ignorant she really was when it came to the world at large.

But she was ready to learn.

She had to.

By the time she was dressed in the green silk, with her hair braided and pinned, the sun had set completely and the smells of the cooking fires wafted in through the arched windows. Euphemia was putting more perfumed oil on her shoulders, and it was then that Grier caught a glimpse of something shiny in the woman's hand. When she turned to look to see what it was, Euphemia held it up in her face.

"There, now," the old woman said with satisfaction. "Take a look at yerself, my lady."

Grier found herself looking into a glass hand mirror, and the reflection she saw was the first time she'd ever seen a clear reflection of herself. Stunned, Grier slapped a hand over her mouth to stifle the gasp as pale skin, hazel eyes, and a sweet face came into view. Tears stung her eyes.

"That… that is me?" she asked hoarsely.

Euphemia smiled. "It 'tis, love," she said, touched at the girl's reaction. "Do ye like it, then?"

Grier nodded, blinking away the tears. Then, she took the mirror from the old woman and just looked at herself, studying the lines of her face, the color of her hair. She'd never seen herself in such detail before and it was truly an astonishing moment.

"I… I have never seen myself like this," she murmured, turning her head from side to side.

Euphemia watched her. "Ye're a lovely lass," she said with confidence. "Ye make a fine duchess."

Grier's hand moved from her mouth to her hair, touching it carefully. "Where did you learn to do this?"

Euphemia shrugged. "I know a thing or two about fine women," she said. "I've seen them come through the inn and there were times when I helped them. Also, I have daughters, who are grown now. I used to tend them when they were younger."

Grier turned to catch a glimpse of the hair net that was covering the braided bun at the nape of her neck. It was such a pivotal moment, in truth; having never really seen herself clearly, and having spent most of her life cold and dirty and clad in rough woolens, Grier had ceased to think of herself as a woman. Merely an oblate, meant for God, and that wasn't a creature that was particularly womanly. But at this moment, she saw a woman before her.

Nay, a *beautiful* woman.

It was something she'd never imagined she would see, and for the first time in her life, Grier was caught up in her appearance. She was still looking at herself when there was a knock on the door and Euphemia went to answer it.

Dane stood in the doorway. With the burning torches in the corridor behind him, his big frame was silhouetted against the darkness as he stepped into the chamber. Immediately, his gaze found Grier, who was standing in the middle of the chamber with a mirror in her hand.

"Now," he said, his voice full of quiet satisfaction, "you look like a duchess."

Grier lowered the mirror and looked at him, a timid smile spreading across her lips. "Euphemia dressed my hair," she said. "Do you like it?"

Dane was smiling as he stepped closer, getting a good look at her. "I do."

She nodded, hand still to her hair. "I do."

His smile grew. "When I found you at the abbey, you were like a rosebud," he said. "You were small and pristine, but not yet unfurled. Now, the flower is blooming and I like it very much."

Grier honestly had no idea what to say to him. She wasn't any good with flattery, or sweet words, so she simply kept her mouth shut and smiled that embarrassed smile Dane was becoming familiar with. Seeing that she was tongue-tied, he laughed low in his throat and pulled her towards the door.

"Come along," he said. "There is a fine feast waiting for you in the great hall. Your father's men are anxious to meet the de Lara heiress."

Grier's good mood faded at the mention of her father. A fine moment spoiled as the subject of Garreth de Lara come forth. As Dane took her out into the corridor and towards the mural stairs that led to the floor below, she spoke softly.

"I do not know why they should be," she said. "I am sure most of them did not even know there was an heiress."

Her words were bitter. Given what Dane had heard earlier whilst she'd been in the chapel, he proceeded carefully. He'd been thinking about it all afternoon, even as he went about his duties and she rested after an arduous day.

At first, he thought he should simply leave well enough alone, hoping she would speak honestly of her feelings towards her father in time. But the more he thought on it, the more he thought it best to have her speak on her trouble with her father now rather than later. Keeping it suppressed wouldn't be good for either of them, not when they were trying to establish a relationship left to them by the very man she hated. He didn't want any secrets between them. That, more than anything, would bother him. He had told Grier in the beginning that all he would ever expect from her was honesty.

He meant it.

"It is possible," he said after a moment. "It is unfortunate that you did not have a relationship with your father, but it is certainly not your doing. He sent you away quite young. I, however, did have a relationship with your father, as did his men, and he is much respected and admired here at Shrewsbury. The men want to respect and admire you also."

They were nearly to the bottom of the stairs, with the entry spread out before them and the door that led outside. Oddly enough, for the size of the keep, it was a very small door, but quite elaborately carved, like the doors on the chapel.

But Grier wasn't thinking about the doors as she came off the stairs. She was thinking about Dane's comment and wondering just how much she should say about it. After her outburst that afternoon in the privacy of the dim chapel, she felt somewhat better, but bringing her father up again and again would only reopen old wounds. She was coming to think that if Dane knew of her true feelings towards her father, then perhaps he would not speak of the man so often.

Perhaps, he would give her a chance to forget about him again.

"You have expressed to me that all you expect from me is honesty," she said. They reached the entry door and she came to a halt, facing him. "Then mayhap, I should be honest with you about my feelings for my father. I have told you that I did not know him. He cast me off like an unwanted shoe, sending a very small girl to live with strangers at a convent. I will be honest with you, then, and tell you that I hold a great deal of resentment towards my father. It is something I have pushed aside, and forgotten even, but returning to Shrewsbury this morning brought it all back. I do not know what kind of man you knew as my father, but I only knew cruelty and neglect. That does not make me fond of him, so if men want to speak of their fondness and respect for my father, I would prefer they not speak it to me."

Dane was deeply pleased that she had enough faith in him to tell him the truth. He was pleased that she hadn't tried to skirt the issue or, worse, lie about it because she thought that was what he wanted to hear. A bond of trust was building between them already, something he'd hoped for but hadn't really expected, at least not so soon.

"Thank you for telling me the truth of the matter," he said quietly.

"I will do my best to ensure no man offends you with his fondness for your father, but you know that will be difficult. They do not know the man from your perspective."

Grier was rather relieved that he didn't become angry at her for her opinion. "I realize that," she said. "I am coming to understand that my father treated his men far better than his own flesh and blood."

Dane couldn't disagree with her and he wasn't unsympathetic. "And for that, I am sorry," he said. "Though I cannot change the past, I will promise you that the future will not be so bleak. I will do all I can to make sure of it. But your father's men… you will have to be tolerant. They do not know what you know, and it would be best, for the sake of morale, that you did not tell them. I fear it will only upset and confuse them, and it might even make them less than willing to be loyal to a duchess who speaks poorly of her father."

Grier nodded. "I understand," she said. "I have been concerned for that very thing. My thoughts on my father are my own. But do not expect me to weep at his grave."

Dane simply lifted his eyebrows, a gesture of understanding and agreement, and Grier felt that he, at least, respected her position. He didn't try to talk her into reforming it. Extending his elbow to her, he did not have to prompt her this time to take it. She did it without hesitation and held it tightly.

There was confidence in that grip.

Together, they headed out into the dark English night.

CHAPTER EIGHT

"THE SHREWSBURY PARTY arrived earlier in the day, Davies." A man with shaggy dark hair, wrapped up in a dirty brown cloak, had slipped into the doorway near the city gates where Davies and a few of his men were lingering. "They came right up through town from this very gate and into the castle."

"And the lady?" Davies asked.

"She was sighted."

Even though Davies knew that would be the case, still, it was difficult to hear. The woman he loved, the one he'd wanted to marry, was now married to another. He looked at the faces of the four men with him, his *teulu*, or the personal guard of a Welsh lord. They were with him for better or for worse and, in this case, they were with him on a very large undertaking.

On the ride to Shrewsbury, he'd had time to think. Davies had told Eolande that their people were starving and, perhaps, Shrewsbury might be the only source of food for them. But Eolande had seen through his farce; she knew that he was going to Shrewsbury to wreak havoc upon the new duke, the one who had married Grier and take her away from him. Perhaps that was the truth, but Davies wouldn't admit it to his little sister. She'd been right, in every way.

Now, all Davies could think about was that the woman he loved had been married to the man for two days. Two long days for the man to do anything he wanted to her. Even now, as night fell on the second day, Davies was crushed to think that Grier would be warming the bed of the man she married.

Davies should have been that man.

He'd tried to lie to Eolande about his true purpose in going to Shrewsbury, but she had known his heart. She'd known why he intended to roust the town, but she didn't know all of it. Perhaps, he hadn't even known all of it himself until the ride to Shrewsbury. During that ride, with his heart full of hurt and anger, Davies had made plans.

Plans to kill Grier's new husband.

And now, here he was, ready to carry out those plans. He'd brought men with him from Godor, a gang of at least fifty Welshmen, all ready and willing to carry out his commands. They were gathered outside of the walls, in the forests in the distance, awaiting Davies' command, but for them, it was a different purpose. Davies had given them permission to raid for food and valuables. They thought they were here only for that, which was why they'd come so eagerly when summoned late last night.

Only Davies was here to kill.

Only his *teulu* knew the truth.

"So, she is here," Davies said, his eyes moving about in the darkness to make sure no one was listening. "When the gates open before dawn, we shall summon our men and we shall ride straight into the market. That will bring out Shrewsbury's army."

Davies' *teulu* glanced at each other nervously; these were not the fighters their ancestors had been. There hadn't been the need. With an uneasy peace between England and Wales for so many years, men weren't particularly bred these days to battle against armored knights. Many of them had become farmers and tradesmen. There was a warrior class, but it was small and not particularly well armed but for their spears and crossbows. They had horses that were swift, however, and in that swiftness was their saving grace. The heavily-armored war horses of the *Saesneg* didn't move quickly, and that was what they would be up against.

But a full-blown raid into a major city along the Marches? They were fairly certain Davies had lost his mind.

"There will be soldiers on the southern gate, Davies." A man named Efor spoke quietly. Dressed in a dark green woolen cloak, he had it pulled tightly around him to ward off the evening's chill. "They will close the gates before we can escape!"

Davies shook his head. "We have the best archers in all the land," he said. "We will position them so they can take out the sentries at the gatehouse, but we must leave quickly before the gates close for the night. Come, now, we have little time to waste."

The five of them moved from the shadowed doorway and out into the street, with the last strains of the day fading overhead. They'd spent most of the day scouting out the city, finding the marketplace, locating the gates, and now that their reconnaissance was finished, it was imperative they make it back to the men waiting in the distant trees.

A mist was beginning to fall as the sun went down, filling the streets and creating more of a shield for their escape from the city. Citizens were coming out to light the street torches for the night, to illuminate the darkness, and the last few travelers were coming in through the open gate for the night just as Davies and his men slipped out. The sentries on duty were too busy worrying about who was coming in to pay any attention to who was going out.

In the darkness, they slipped away into the trees and towards the Welsh who were bundled up in their woolens against the night, since a fire would have alerted those on night watch to their presence. No fires, no warm food, only cold and damp, as men waited for dawn to come so they could charge in and take what food they could before the castle was alerted. As they sat in the darkness and clung to each other for warmth, it was all they could speak of.

Soon, their bellies would be full.

If Davies felt any guilt in using his men's hunger to suit his own purposes, he refused to acknowledge it. For him, he was doing what needed to be done. With the old duke dead and, hopefully, the new duke soon to follow, he would go to Shrewsbury and propose marriage yet again to Grier, now a lone woman in charge of a vast empire. He didn't care about the empire so much as he did for the lady. It was her he wanted; the Shrewsbury entitlement was secondary, but it was one that would make his spineless father rather happy.

In the end, Davies would have what he wanted, and his father would have what he wanted.

Tomorrow would be the day.

CHAPTER NINE

"YOU ARE AS weak as a woman!" William cried, trying to wrestle Boden to the ground with one arm. "A Wellesbourne can always beat a de Russe!"

Boden grunted, both in effort and in pain. "Only you would think so," he said. "I will show you otherwise."

With that, they doubled their efforts, each man trying to send the other to the ground. There was a great deal of gambling and drinking and shouting going on inside the great hall of Shrewsbury this night, a massive place with an enormous pitched ceiling, two stories tall, with a roof covered in thatching.

Nights here were usually the same. There was a vast open firepit in the middle of the hall, almost always with a roaring fire in it, and the smoke went up into the soaring roof, finding an outlet in the many holes that were in the eaves for that very purpose. The hall had been built in the Saxon fashion three hundred years earlier, and the building was still holding up quite nicely. As always, it was full of food and drink, and men having a good time.

Tonight was no exception.

William was seriously trying to break Boden's arm as Dastan and Syler stood by and watched. Charlisa was on the dais, speaking to her young cousin who happened to be Syler's sister.

Charlisa's father and Syler's father were brothers, and two months ago, Syler's youngest sister had arrived to serve Charlisa and learn something of the world. She was a little old to foster at fifteen years of age, but Charlisa was happy to take the girl under her wing. Young Laria de Poyer had the dark de Poyer eyes and a head full of curly dark hair. She was a pretty girl, but a little silly, something Charlisa suffered from as well, and she only had eyes for William Wellesbourne.

But William soundly ignored her, as he was doing now by trying to snap Boden's arm in two. Men were betting on who was going to win.

"Well?" William yelled as he tried to twist Boden's arm. "Who are the men betting on?"

He was yelling at one man in particular, the older sergeant who had a good grasp of command with the men. He'd been with Shrewsbury nearly forty years, and he and the old duke had known each other well. With a grin, the old sergeant checked on the two soldiers who were the bookmakers for the event, and nearly every other event held in the great hall. They were busy organizing the pot, and one man muttered a name to the old sergeant. His smile grew.

"Sir Boden, my lord," he said. "They are betting on the bigger man."

William didn't like that at all. With a shout, he elbowed Boden in the ribs, causing the man to falter. When he did, William jump on him and the two collapsed onto the ground. After that, it was part wrestling match, part fist fight. As Dastan and Syler watched the goings-on, Dastan shook his head.

"Those two are exhausting," he said. "If they were not such good knights, they would be positively worthless."

"Agreed, my lord," Syler said grimly.

Dastan was torn between disgust and amusement as he watched William and Boden throw punches. "Do you know that Dane has three more brothers just like Boden?" he said. "Well, I'm not entirely sure if they are all *just* like him, but he has at least two that fall into that category. There is a younger brother, Gage, and then an older one, Cort. I have seen them together and they all behave like this."

Syler was trying not to laugh. "I have no brothers," he said. "Only sisters, and they do not wrestle like this."

"Thank God."

"Should we stop this? Lord Dane will be arriving with the new duchess any moment."

But Dastan shook his head. "Nay," he said flatly. "Let the woman see the rowdy family she has married in to. Better she become accustomed to it because I suspect this is what she can expect at her family reunions."

Syler did laugh at that, turning away from the fighting, as Dastan did, and they made their way back to the dais where the ladies were. They had barely made it to the table when Dane and Grier entered through the enormous front entry.

The women at the table caught sight of the couple first because they were facing the door. Charlisa pointed towards the entry, and Dastan turned to see Dane and Grier making their way across the floor as the crowd of men in the hall parted the way for them.

The fact that Grier was beautifully dressed was not lost on them. Resplendent in the green silk, she was washed and rested, looking nothing like the rather dirty little waif they were acquainted with. Her cheeks were rosy, her hair carefully pinned, and she had a certain grace about her that they hadn't seen before. It was something that couldn't be taught, perhaps the innate sense of her bloodlines finally showing its elegance. In any case, the transformation was rather shocking.

"*That* is the woman we collected from St. Idloes?" Syler asked, awe in his tone.

Dastan nodded. "Indeed, it is," he said. "God's Bones, it looks as if she has the making of a duchess, after all. I will admit that I had my doubts."

Syler nodded in agreement, taking a second look at the woman as Dane brought her to the table. His face was rather prideful as he indicated the exquisite creature next to him.

"My lords," he said, "my ladies, may I present Grier de Lara de

Russe, Duchess of Shrewsbury and Lady of the Trinity Castles. Make her feel welcome in her own hall."

Charlisa was on her feet, rushing to Grier as her cousin tagged after her. "Lady de Russe," she greeted. "I was hoping you would feel well enough to attend the feast. It is in your honor, after all. We are very glad to have you."

Grier smiled into Charlisa's rosy, beaming face. It was difficult to be standoffish when the lady was so open in her manner. Not that she wanted to be standoffish, but Charlisa made her feel like she wasn't a stranger at all. Having that kind of instant acceptance of another person, especially another female, was an admirable quality.

"Thank you," she said, looking at the beautifully set table. "Have you been waiting for me? If you were, my apologies. I did not realize."

Charlisa shook her head, indicating the cushioned chairs in the center of the table. "Nay, we have not been waiting on you," she said. "But please be seated. I am sure you are famished."

Grier headed for the indicated chairs with Dane coming along behind her. "Lady du Reims has been acting as my chatelaine before your arrival," he told Grier. "She has been quite competent."

Grier was struggling with the skirt of her green gown; she wasn't used to the volume and she struggled to move it aside so that she could sit.

"Then I hope she will teach me everything I need to know," she said, finally pushing it aside. "I am sorry to say that I do not know much about managing a house and hold."

Charlisa was moving eagerly behind her, taking a seat at Grier's left hand. "It would be my pleasure, my lady," she said. "I can help you with anything you wish to know. I fostered at some of the finest homes in England, including Castle Questing. Have you heard of it?"

Grier shook her head, reluctantly. "I am afraid not," she said. "Where is it?"

"Far to the north," Charlisa said. "It is the seat of the Earls of Warenton, the de Wolfe family. Surely you have heard of de Wolfe."

As Grier thought about the name, which she was fairly certain she had never heard before, she caught sight of Charlisa looking past her, over her shoulder. There was someone, or something, greatly annoying her from the look on her face. Whatever it was seemed to be directly down the table, behind Grier. As she turned to see what had the woman irritated, Charlisa spoke.

"My lady, this is my cousin, Lady Laria de Poyer," she said. "She has only come to Shrewsbury recently to foster under my tutelage. She is Sir Syler's younger sister."

Grier quickly noticed the dark-eyed lass who was sitting down at the end of the table, a few seats from Dane. She was a young, little thing who lifted a timid hand to wave when she saw that she had Grier's attention, and nearly everyone else at the table. Grier smiled at her.

"Greetings, Lady Laria," she said before returning her attention to Charlisa. "It looks as if you will have two women to tutor. I hope you are patient."

She said it with a rather foreboding wriggle of the eyebrows and Charlisa giggled her charming little snicker. But ever the dutiful lady, who knew her role in the hall, she quickly lifted her hand to the servants standing on the fringes of the room, near the dais, and they suddenly began to move. Almost immediately, trenchers and bowls of food were being brought to the table, a lavish feast for the eyes as well as for the palate.

The guest of honor had arrived, and the feast had begun.

It was an army of people, moving forward with food and drink as the diners settled down to their meals. Terrified of a repeat of the night before at the inn, Grier was much more timid this time around as food was placed before her. A large trencher with a great hunk of beef was the crown of the meal, surrounded by beans and boiled carrots.

Being that the beef didn't sit well with her the night before, she didn't try to grab at it and shove it in her mouth. She simply looked at it, rather fearfully. As she sat there and wondered if she should try to eat it, Dane reached over and took it off of her trencher, putting it on his own.

"Better to remove the temptation," he said quietly. "We do not want history to repeat itself."

Grier shook her head quickly, and gratefully, as Dane instructed the servants to give her white bread and butter, and a fruit stew of apples and pears and honey. There was also something called May Eggs, which were eggs that had been partially boiled, the yolks removed and mixed with spices, and then the yolks returned to the eggs and cooked all the way through. They were quite delicious, but Grier only took one even when Charlisa encouraged her to take another. She begged off politely, even though it was more food than she'd ever seen in one place in her lifetime. She honestly never knew there could be so much food.

Everything smelled and tasted delicious. There wasn't much conversation while the meal went on, mostly Syler talking about the home in Wales where he was born, Netherworld Castle, and Laria chiming in once in a while. Dastan seemed to be watching William and Boden, still wrestling and knocking over chairs, while Dane and Charlisa were focused on Grier to ensure that she had enough to eat.

After her tasty egg, bread and butter, and a few carrots, Grier wanted another egg so she took one, taking small bites from it so she wouldn't overwhelm her tender stomach. A servant also brought out fried turnip slices, hot from the kitchen, which were liberally sprinkled with precious salt from the salt stores. They were crunchy and tasty. She must have had too many because, before she realized it, Dane was leaning in her direction.

"Easy, my lady," he said quietly. "You've been quite liberal with the turnip crisps."

Grier had one halfway to her mouth. Sheepishly, she set it down. "I have not been keeping track," she admitted. "They are very good."

Dane smiled at her. "They are," he said. "But they have also been fried in fat and it may not settle well with your belly. You do not want to overdo it. Here, have some ale."

He picked up a pitcher from the table and poured a measure into her cup. Grier picked it up, looking at the milky liquid.

"I have not had ale," she said.

"Never?" he said, interested.

"Not that I can recall. What is in it?"

He shrugged. "I am not an ale wife, but I believe it is made from barley and honey and a little yeast."

"Is it sweet?"

"Not really," he said. "The honey is just for flavor. Ales all taste differently depending on the ingredients and who is making it. All ale wives have their own recipes; I have had ale that tasted of lemon, and others of roses. It just depends. What did you drink at the abbey?"

She cocked her head thoughtfully. "Wine," she said. "But very bad wine. Sometimes we had boiled apple juice, or sometimes just boiled oat water."

Dane thought boiled oat water sounded terrible, but he didn't comment. It was just one more distasteful thing about her life at St. Idloes. Instead, he lifted his cup to her.

"No more boiled oat water," he said. "From now on, you shall only have the finest in your cup. Welcome to Shrewsbury, Lady de Russe. It sounds odd to say that, and probably odder still for you to hear it. To me, Lady de Russe was always my mother. It never occurred to me that it would also be my wife someday."

Grier smiled faintly as she lifted the heavy pewter cup to him. "It never occurred to me that it would be my name, either."

He chuckled as he took a healthy swallow of ale. Grier did, too, nearly choking on it as she swallowed it down. It was a strong ale with the distinctive taste of roasted nuts. Dane grinned as he patted her on the back as she coughed.

"Too strong?" he asked.

She stopped coughing, clearing her throat instead. "Nay," she said. "It is simply… different. It seems thick."

Dane took another swallow. "You will become accustomed to it. I prefer it over wine."

Grier wasn't sure if she did, but she took another drink because he was. She didn't want him to think she was being rude. As she choked down another swallow, William and Boden appeared in front of the table.

They were sweaty, smiling, and moderately drunk, which wasn't unusual with them. Red-haired William had his hair plastered to his face with moisture as he picked up another pitcher of ale on the table and held it up.

"Welcome, Lady de Russe," he said loudly. "We are very glad to see you within these old walls, and I am sure the men are comforted to know that a de Lara is at the helm again. Do you have a few words to say to your loyal men, my lady?"

Grier was mortified at the sudden attention on her. She looked around the hall, and most of the men had come to a halt and were now looking at her as William announced her welcome. She looked at Dane, wordlessly asking the man what she should do, but he took it as a cry for help.

"The lady is exhausted from her journey today, as you can imagine," he said loudly to the men who were expecting something from her. "She will be more than willing to speak with you at another time, but not tonight. You must be mindful of her frail female constitution."

Grier was watching the faces of the men as he spoke and she could see the disappointment. Not wanting to make a bad impression on her vassals, and given that she'd never had vassals before, she thought she should say something. She put her hand on Dane's wrist.

"I will say something," she said quickly. "Will you allow it?"

He looked at her. "Are you sure? You do not have to, you know. They can wait."

She nodded, grateful that he was looking out for her. But it was more than that... he was being protective and kind, the same qualities she'd seen from the man since the beginning of their association. Even though their marriage had been unwanted to them both, he'd never made her feel unwelcome or unwanted. She felt as if she owed the man something for that, for certainly, she had been very fortunate to have married such an agreeable man.

A man she was coming to appreciate more by the hour.

"I am certain," she said. Hesitantly, she stood up, facing the expectant throng and lifting her voice. "Thank you for your kind attention and your warm welcome. I hope in the days to come that we may come to know one another, and you shall think me worthy to be your lady."

It was a tidy little speech and the men began to cheer. William, who still had the pitcher of ale in his hand, held it up again.

"A toast to Lady de Russe!" he said.

The men shouted in response, downing whatever was in their cups. At the table, Dane and Dastan and Syler stood up, also saluting their new lady with a toast of honor. Dane still had his cup to his mouth when he gently tugged at Grier's arm.

"Drink," he said. "That is what they want – to share a drink with you."

Quickly, Grier collected her cup and choked down more of the thick ale. As she tried not to cough, Boden stepped forward, his cup lifted to the room.

"The House of de Russe is greatly honored to be joined with the House of de Lara," he shouted. "We will drink to the success of this union."

More drinking. Dane lifted his cup and so did Grier. She ended up draining it, thinking that it wasn't so bad now that she'd had a few swallows. It was strong, and thick, but she thought she might be able to become accustomed to the taste. As she set her empty cup to the table, William rushed forward with his half-empty pitcher and poured her a full cup.

"We shall drink to the House of de Lara," he said loudly. "God rest the soul of Lord Garreth!"

More drinking all the way around as men drank to the memory of their beloved duke. Dane drank, and so did Grier, without coughing this time. It was going down a little smoother now. But she had just managed to swallow the burning drink when one of the men back in the hall held up his cup and began to shout.

"A drink to Lord Garreth's daughter!" he said. "May she make her father proud, and may we make him proud by honoring her!"

That had the entire room drinking yet again, men pouring ale down their gullets and enjoying every last drop. Dane glanced at Grier, who was now swallowing down her fifth gulp of the strong ale. She looked a little pale, but she didn't want to disappoint the men. He admired that. Thinking she might need a break from the continual toasts, he held up his cup and spoke loudly,

"Lord Garreth is already proud of you for accepting his daughter with great warmth," he said, wondering how long he was going to be able to talk before someone made another toast that they couldn't refuse. "You have served her father well and I know that you will serve me well, also. I am already proud to know you and to have your fealty. The House of de Russe has a long and important legacy in England, and I am proud to merge that legacy with the great de Lara name."

"A drink to Lord Dane!" someone shouted.

The entire room lifted their cups again and Dane gave a sigh of regret, turning to Grier and wondering how the poor woman was going to down yet another big drink of ale. Much to her credit, she wasn't going to insult the men by not accepting their toast. In fact, as he watched, she downed the entire cup and licked her lips.

It was then that Dane knew there was going to be trouble.

"Truly, you do not have to drink anymore," he muttered to her. "The ale is strong and if you are not used to it, it might make you ill."

She was looking at him with a rather earnest expression. "I feel well enough," she insisted. "And I do not want them to think me rude."

"They will not."

"But I want for them to like me, as they liked my father."

"They will," Dane said, pulling the cup from her hand. "Give them time. For now, sit down and I will turn the men back to their food and games. You have had enough to drink."

Grier did as she was told. Plopping back in the chair, she wasn't feeling terrible at all. In fact, she was feeling rather good. The stuffed eggs were near her and she reached out, taking another one and pushing the entire thing into her mouth because it was so delicious. Her stomach was well enough, so she saw no reason not to eat a whole egg. But that egg was followed by another dish on the table, an apple and raisin and almond pudding, and she put her spoon into it, tasting it. It was quite good with honey and cinnamon, so she pulled the bowl over to her and began to eat it.

Meanwhile, there was more drinking going on.

Men were calling to her to have another drink with them and William went so far as to fill up her cup before Dane could stop him. The food was excellent, and Grier was feeling quite good now, so she took another drink with the men and they cheered. She rather liked that feeling, when they all cheered her on, so she took still another drink with them before Dane thanked the men and encouraged them to turn back to their food. He took her cup away from her for a second time.

Grier was well into the raisin and apple pudding by then. She didn't even notice that Dane had removed her drink. As he sat there and watched her, wondering what all of that ale was going to do to her, Charlisa struck up a conversation.

"The men like you already, my lady," she said to Grier. "That is a very good sign. Your days will be those of joy here, I am certain."

Grier looked at Charlisa, wondering why the room tipped sideways as she moved. "Do you think so?" she asked. "I hope so. I did not wish to come, you know. I wanted to stay at the abbey. But I think I shall like it here."

Charlisa grinned. "You will," she said. "I like it here very much. I have since Dastan and I were married, but I have been lonely for want of a lady friend. That is why I was so excited for you to come. I do hope we can be friends."

Grier smiled at her, a rather open gesture as the ale began to fuel her actions. "Of course we can," she said. "You have been very kind to me already. You remind me of my friend, Eolande."

"Who is that? Is she another nun?"

Grier both nodded and shook her head at the same time, which threw her off balance. "She is not a nun," she said as she gripped the table to keep from falling. "She is an oblate. Do you know what that is? It means that her parents gave her over to the abbey with the intention that she should take the veil. That is what I was, you know – an oblate. Now, I am a wife, but I do not feel like a wife."

Charlisa looked concerned. "Why not?"

Grier leaned in to her as if to tell her a secret. "Because I have not been stabbed yet."

Charlisa had no idea what she was talking about. "Stabbed? By what?"

Grier's reactions were those of a drunkard by this point. The ale had flooded her veins and was beginning to do its damage. She looked at Charlisa in surprise, but it was in an odd, exaggerated gesture.

"You *know*," she insisted. "A man's fleshy sword. I do not think my husband is very pleased with me, because he has not stabbed me with it yet."

Over her shoulder, Dane had been listening to the conversation and when she said that, he spit out the ale that he'd just put in his mouth. It went spraying out onto the table, enough so that both Grier and Charlisa turned to him in concern. Grier knew immediately that it had been because of her, that she had said something wrong.

"I am sorry," she said quickly. "I do not know why I said such a thing. But… but it is true. Euphemia says that men and women make a child when his stabs her with his fleshy sword!"

Dane's eyes widened and it took every bit of self-control he had not to burst out laughing. He didn't think it would be well-met. But he could quickly see one thing; the ale had gone straight to Grier's head and she was, in fact, quite tipsy. He could see it in everything about her, and much more quickly than he would have expected. It would probably only grow worse, so he thought it might be a good idea to remove her from the feast immediately. God only knew what else she would say now that the alcohol had loosened her tongue.

He didn't want to wait around and find out.

"It is time for us to retire," he said, standing up and reaching out to pull Grier from her seat. "Lady du Reims, you will excuse us."

Charlisa had a wide-eyed, shocked look as Dane pulled Grier to her feet. She simply nodded as Dane took his wife and led her away from the table, to the edges of the room where he could slip her from the hall through the servant's entrance. He knew if he took her to the entry doors that there were hundreds of men who would see them, and quite possibly stop them for more drinking, and he didn't think it would be good for her to engage in any manner of conversation or drinking right now. At least, not with anyone other than her husband and his fleshy sword...

Biting his lip to keep from laughing, he managed to remove Grier through the servant's entrance, out into the cold night beyond.

"You are displeased with me," Grier said, hiccupping as she tripped over her too-long hemline. "I am very sorry. I do not know why I said that."

Dane had her by the arm, holding fast so she wouldn't fall. "I am not displeased," he said. "But you have had too much to drink and it would be better if we retire for the night."

Grier frowned. Then, her eyes filled with a pool of tears. "That... that *ale*," she said, unhappy. "I did not want to be rude. Do you not understand? I *had* to drink it."

Dane put his left arm around her slender shoulders, holding on to her right arm with his right hand to brace her up because she was weaving all over the place.

"I know you did," he said. "It was very accommodating of you. It made the men happy."

She sniffled as she looked up at him. "Did it?" she said. "Do you think they will like me?"

"I am sure they will."

"Do you?"

"I do."

"Then why have you not stabbed me with your fleshy sword?"

Dane could hardly hold back the smile. It was becoming more and more difficult. "Because I did not feel as if last night would have been the best time to do it," he said. "Do you even know what you are asking, Grier?"

She nodded, but that threw her off balance terribly, so he bent down and swept her into his arms. Grier yelped, throwing her arms around his neck, and quickly realized that their heads were very close now. She found herself looking at his stubbled jaw and the shape of his lips. That reminded her of something else that Euphemia has said.

Has yer husband kissed ye?

"Is a husband not expected to kiss a wife?" she asked.

Dane eyed her as they neared the keep entry. "Of course he is."

"Then why have you not kissed me, either?"

Dane couldn't help the grin then, but it was a weak one. He wasn't sure he could explain all of this to her in a way she would understand given her drunken state. Therefore, he simply tried to placate her.

"I will," he said. "You needn't worry about that."

"But *when*?"

"Will you at least let me do it in private? When I return you to our chamber?"

Grier didn't have anything to say to that. She was still contemplating everything Euphemia had told her but in her drunken state, it was all rather confusing.

"You will kiss me in private first," she said, "and then stab me with your fleshy sword?"

He was carrying her up the mural stairs to the floor above with little effort. "Who told you about a fleshy sword?"

"Euphemia."

He grunted, perhaps in disapproval. "I see," he said. "You should not repeat that, Grier."

"Why not?"

"Because it is something only whores call a man's member. It is not something fine ladies speak of."

Her eyes widened. "Euphemia is a whore?"

Dane didn't know, but he didn't want to speculate. "It does not matter if she is or not," he said. "But what you are speaking of is not something fine ladies mention. Do you understand?"

Perhaps she did, perhaps she didn't. There was really no way to tell. They arrived at the big master's chamber and Dane kicked the door open, charging into the room.

Euphemia was on her knees in front of the hearth, stirring a small pot that was brewing over the gentle fire. When she saw Grier aloft in Dane's arms, she lurched to her feet, her eyes wide.

"What is it, my lord?" she cried. "What has happened to the lady?"

All Dane could think of when he looked at her was fleshy sword. *Because she is drunk and speaking with your whore's tongue for all to hear!* It was a struggle not to scold her for it.

"Nothing," he said. "Get out."

Euphemia fled. As the door slammed behind her, Dane put Grier upon the mattress and, leaving her there, went to bolt the door. By the time he returned, Grier was trying to slither off of the bed.

"Where are you going?" Dane asked. "It is time for you to sleep."

She was still moving off of the bed. "But I cannot sleep in this dress," she said. "It will ruin it. Can you help me remove it?"

That was perhaps the best invitation Dane had in a very long while. He could have easily called for Euphemia for help but, somehow, he didn't want to. Besides, he'd just kicked her out of the chamber. Grier was his wife and, perhaps, this was the best time of all to get to know her on a more intimate level.

He couldn't think of a better opportunity.

This was the first time he'd had a wife, after all.

Unlike his older brother, Trenton, who had been married four times, Dane had never been married once. It wasn't because he hadn't met women he might have taken as a wife; he'd met a few. He'd even had a couple that he'd called on, but none that he'd seriously courted. He'd spent his life living as a knight, and that meant he ate, slept, and breathed warfare. He had been the captain of the Duke of Warminster's army for several years until his appointment to Blackmore Castle, which still belonged to him, only now it was part of his Shrewsbury properties.

His ambition and dedication to duty had prevented him from taking a wife, and he'd only married Grier because he'd been given no choice. Had he not been forced to do it, he'd probably still be a bachelor knight. True, the marriage to Grier had been unwanted but, as the days passed, he was coming to think it wasn't unwanted any longer. He rather liked having a beautiful young woman he could call his own.

He liked it a great deal.

Therefore, Grier's request for him to help her undress was met by an inclination to do it on his part. Grier belonged to him, and she was horribly naïve, so it was up to him to indoctrinate her into the world of men and women.

Of man and wife.

He was ready.

"Aye, I'll help you," he said after a moment, pulling her all the way off the bed and turning her away from him. He inspected it, looking for the obvious way to get her out of it. "How did Euphemia get you into this bloody dress?"

Grier lifted up her arms. "Something on the side," she said. "Do you see the fastens?"

He did. Quickly, he unfastened the ties and the dress loosened up dramatically, but when Grier tried to pull it over her head, she ended up pitching forward onto the bed, tangled up in the green silk. Dane had to unravel her from her garment and pull it the rest of the way over her head as Grier sat up on the bed and smoothed at her mussed hair.

"You saved me, my lord," she said, puffing out her cheeks. "I thought I was doomed."

He grinned as he tossed the dress over a chair. "I am good for many things," he said. "Saving women from their murderous garments is one of them."

Grier continued to smooth her hair back. "Have you saved many, then?"

He shook his head. "Actually, you are my first."

Grier wanted to look up at him but tipping her head back made her feel as if she wanted to fall over, so she kept her head level. "As you are my first," she murmured. "Husband, I mean. God's Bones, I never thought I would say those words. May I ask you a question?"

"Of course."

"You introduced me earlier as Lady of the Trinity Castles," she said. "I have not heard that title before."

He smiled faintly. "The Trinity Castles are a very old de Lara lordship," he said. "It goes back more than three hundred years, according to your father. He told me about them, once, in one of the many conversations we had before his death. The Trinity Castles are Hyssington, Trelystan, and Caradoc Castles along the Welsh Marches. That was the original de Lara holding. Shrewsbury came later."

Her mouth formed an "O" shape as she understood what he meant. "I do remember hearing those names when I was younger," she said. "I'd forgotten until you mentioned them."

"I will take you with me when I go to visit them. I've not seen them yet."

Grier was touched by the fact that he would think enough of her to take her with him when he went to visit the rest of his holdings. He was treating her like she were truly a part of all of this, which she was.

"I would be happy to go with you," she said, pausing a moment before continuing. "Truthfully, part of me wonders if this is all a dream and I shall soon wake from it, sleeping on the cold earth next to Eolande."

"Eolande? Who is that?"

"She was my friend at St. Idloes. We have been friends since we were small."

Eolande. That reminded Dane of what he'd heard in Welshpool, about the Welsh warlord who had asked for Grier's hand. The man had a sister at St. Idloes, which is how he knew about Grier. Dane wondered if this Eolande was that sister, but he didn't ask. Now was not the time, with her head swimming with drink.

Besides, none of it really mattered; even if Davies ap Madoc had offered for Grier's hand, Dane had been the one to actually marry her. He'd gotten the prize. But in the same breath, he wondered if Grier had wanted to marry ap Madoc. Had she been fond of the Welshman who had offered for her? That question didn't settle so well with him. The thought of Grier being fond of another man made him feel tight inside, as if something was wrong with his belly.

Nay, he didn't like that thought in the least.

"I see," he said belatedly, his thoughts lingering on Eolande and Davies, and Grier's affection for one or both. "To answer your speculation, this is no dream, I promise. You are my wife, and you are the Duchess of Shrewsbury. In the days to come, you will grow accustomed to that."

Grier dared to look up at the man, as he was standing over her, but the gesture caused her to tip right back onto the bed.

"I cannot sit up straight," she said sadly. "Forgive me for being so foolish, my lord. I am very sorry."

"Dane. You promised to call me Dane in private. A few times you have addressed me formally and I have ignored it, but in our bedchamber, I will not ignore it. Say my name."

A smile spread across her lips with unnatural speed. "Dane."

He laughed softly as she murmured it in her low, sweet voice. "Good," he said. "I wanted to make sure you knew it."

"I do, indeed, know it."

He looked at her, lying flat on her back on the bed, and he couldn't help but think how beautiful she was. By the light of the fire and the few candles that were burning about the room, she had an angelic glow about her. She was clad only in a fine shift and as she lay there, he could see the outline of her breasts and hips.

His thoughts turned to pleasures of the flesh.

Drunk or not, she was his wife. He hadn't consummated the marriage the night before because, given her state at the time, it simply wouldn't have been a good situation for either of them. It was his right, and he knew it, but he wasn't so demanding or selfish that he was going to demand his husbandly rights regardless of her physical condition. But tonight... tonight, things were different.

It was time to get down to business.

Reaching down, he pulled her up into a sitting position.

"Can you remove your shift yourself or do you need help?" he asked.

A little woozy, Grier looked down at the fine garment she was wearing. "I can remove it, I think."

Dane nodded. "Good," he said. "Remove it and get into bed."

She blinked as if she didn't quite understand the order. "Why?"

"Do you want your husband to kiss you?"

That was all she needed to hear. Staggering up from the bed, she fumbled with the shift as Dane moved towards the hearth and turned his back. He gave her some privacy, pretending to stoke the fire as he listened to the sounds of a struggle behind him. Something hit the floor. He thought it might have been her and he turned slightly to see that she was getting to her feet from a position on her knees.

Dane had to smile at the woman's inebriation. Perhaps, he should wait and consummate the marriage when she wasn't so tipsy. But he thought that, perhaps, it was a good thing she was a little drunk. Perhaps, she wouldn't be so fearful about it; she certainly didn't seem fearful. He wanted her to be relaxed, so this was as good an opportunity as any.

A few minutes passed and he could hear the bed give as she climbed into it. Taking that as his cue, he realized that his stomach was twitching with anticipation as he approached the bed. As he moved, he blew out one of the iron candle sconces as he walked by; melted tallow dripped from the iron onto the floor, creating big white splotches.

Dane's gaze remained on the bed, where Grier was now laying, the heavy coverlet pulled up to her neck. But as he looked at her, he also noticed the table next to her side of the bed where the marriage brooch he'd given her had been placed. She'd worn it almost constantly since he'd give it to her.

A modest wife knows a chaste bed.

They were finally coming to the meat of that statement. Smiling at Grier's anxious face, he sat down on the bed to remove his boots.

"If you have any questions about what we are about to do, I would be happy to answer them," he said. "Or did Euphemia tell you everything already?"

He had a smirk on his face, one that Grier could see in the darkness. "How do you know she told me anything?"

"You said she told you about the fleshy sword. I will assume she told you everything."

Grier seemed a bit sheepish. "I… I did not wish to seem too ignorant."

"You have spent your life in a convent. You are supposed to be ignorant."

"Are you angry that I asked Euphemia about the ways of men and women?"

He shook his head, tossing his boots against the wall. He went to work on unfastening his breeches.

"Of course not," he said. "And you should have a woman to talk to, which is why I allowed Euphemia to accompany you to Shrewsbury. But you can talk to Charlisa, too. She might be a better source of information when it comes to how to please a husband. And you can always ask me. I will tell you the truth."

He turned to look at her, to see her reaction, and he was met by a wide-eyed gaze. When he smiled at her, faintly, the wide-eyed gaze became thoughtful.

"When I was told that I was to marry, I never expected someone like you," she said. "I am not sure what I expected; mayhap, someone old and gruff. Mayhap, a foolish man with no hair. I really do not know. But you… I never expected *you*."

He gave her a lopsided smile. "I am assuming that is a good thing?"

She nodded, or at least she tried to. "You are handsome and kind," she said. "You are like the knights from the stories mother used to tell me."

"You remember your mother's stories?"

"I do," she said firmly. "She would tell me of strong knights, men who were handsome and virtuous, and how they saved their ladies fair. You are like those knights from my mother's stories – you are handsome and virtuous and compassionate."

Leaning over, he blew out the taper next to the bed and, in the darkness, pulled off his breeches. They ended up in a pile next to the bed as he climbed in, pulling the coverlet up.

"My father is a great knight," he said. "I learned everything I know from him."

"The Duke of Warminster?"

"Aye. Did someone tell you that?"

She turned her head to look at him, lying next to her in the bed even though he was at least an arm's length away from her.

"Sir Dastan did," she said. She was quiet for a moment before speaking again. "You love your father a great deal, don't you?"

He turned his head to look at her, her haunting beauty in the darkness. "What makes you say that?"

Her gaze lingered on him a moment before she laid her head back and looked up at the ceiling.

"There was something in your expression when I spoke of my feelings towards my own father," she said. "It is difficult to describe, but I saw both understanding and sorrow. As if you completely understood, yet you felt pity for me."

Dane pondered what he considered a perceptive observation. "I understand your feelings because the man I call my father, the Duke of Warminster, is not my actual father," he said. "My father, the man whose blood I carry, died many years ago. He was a beast of a man, a vile piece of humanity, and I hated him. I do not speak of him, but I will this once so you understand what it means to me. It is your right, as my wife. My father by blood was a man named Guy Stoneley. He was a powerful warlord in Yorkshire. When he died, my mother married Warminster and it is his name I carry, by choice."

Grier was looking at him again, surprised by the confession. "Then you *do* understand my feelings about my father."

"I do, indeed," he said. "But I also know what it means to have a father to love. I love Gaston de Russe very much. He is my father, regardless of the fact that there is not a drop of de Russe blood in me. I am his son."

"I look forward to meeting him."

"And I look forward to introducing you."

"Do you think he will like me?"

"I am certain of it."

Grier appreciated his candor, but her alcohol-hazed mind was easily distracted. She was in bed, without a stitch of clothing on, and from what she saw with Dane, so was he. She didn't want to talk about fathers any longer – the promise of husbandly kisses was of more interest to her at the moment. Laying her head back on the pillow, she found herself staring up at the ceiling once again.

"Have you forgotten already?" she asked.

He looked at her, curiously. "What do you mean?"

"You said you were going to kiss me if I removed my shift and got into bed. I do not wish to talk about fathers anymore."

He fought off a grin. "Nay, I have not forgotten," he said. "I would very much like to kiss you. May I?"

Grier simply nodded. "Aye," she said. "And... and do you intend to stab me, too?"

"We'll get to that."

Anticipation and fear welled up in Grier's heart. She kept the coverlet up around her neck, staring up at the ceiling and waiting for him to make the first move. Dane finally rolled onto his side so he could look at her; every woman he had ever bedded had taken the aggressive role with him and he'd simply gone along for the ride. Given that Grier had never done this before, he was going to have to be the aggressor.

It was a role he was more than willing to take.

Leaning over, he kissed her naked shoulder, the only thing that was peering out from the top of the coverlet other than her head. Her skin was warm and soft, and she smelled faintly of lemons. Then, a big hand snaked under the covers and cupped her left breast, feeling her jump with surprise at his action.

"That is *not* a kiss!" she gasped.

He laughed low in his throat, moving closer to her. "That is coming. Be patient."

Beneath his hand, he could feel her tremble, but she didn't pull away. Her breast was warm and soft, and he was instantly and madly aroused as he fondled her. From one breast to the other, he squeezed gently and caressed, pinching her nipples and feeling her quiver in response. It excited him so much that he buried his head beneath the coverlet, which was still pulled up to her neck, and began suckling her nipples.

His hot, wet mouth on her breasts caused Grier to gasp, first in shock but then in pleasure. She could never have imagined a sensation like this, something that made her entire body quiver and bolts of lightning race through her limbs. His mouth was aggressive, moving from breast to breast as his hand kneaded the tender flesh of her belly. His roving hand seemed to be everywhere as he nursed against them hungrily.

It was quite a first kiss.

In truth, Dane was having difficulty controlling himself. He knew she was virgin, but her soft skin and sweet body had his blood boiling with need. The moment he touched her, he could feel it. The flame of passion had been turned into a wildfire. He continued to suckle her breasts, his hand finally moving to the junction between her legs. The moment he touched the dark curls there, she started violently and tried to move away from him, but he wouldn't let her.

Holding her fast, he gently parted her thighs.

A big finger began to stroke the outside of her woman's center and Grier put her hand over her mouth because she was startled, embarrassed, and aroused all at the same time. Her head was swimming with ale, but what Dane was doing to her caused it to spin wildly out of control. When the finger that had been stroking her invaded her private folds, gently but firmly, she drew her knees up, gasping in response.

Her hissing reaction was all Dane needed to roll is big body on top of hers, his head coming out from beneath the coverlet and his mouth fusing to her lips. It was the kiss Grier had been waiting for, and he kissed her passionately, his tongue forcing her teeth apart to lick the pink interior of her mouth. The finger that had wormed its way inside her body was still there, now joined by a second finger, thrusting into her, making her wet and heated as it mimicked the lovemaking they would soon be engaging in. Dane was still kissing her deeply when he placed his manhood against her swollen, wet folds and thrust into her virginal body.

It was a sharp and startling action, and Grier tore her mouth away from his, gasping with the shock of it. She barely had time to draw another breath when he thrust again, and then again, finally seating himself fully in her tender, trembling body.

Finally, it was done.

It was an overwhelming and painful act, and Grier squirmed beneath him, unaccustomed to a man's body inside of hers. But Dane's senses were heightened, his sense of passion and lust boiling over, and as Grier continue to twitch beneath him, he began the ancient primal rhythm of mating.

His thrusts were firm and measured. Unaccustomed as she was,

Grier grunted with every thrust, struggling not to gasp at the sensual intrusion. Dane's lips had moved to her neck, her shoulders again, nibbling on her flesh and causing bolts of excitement to race through her body. But the more he thrust, the more she relaxed, and before she realized it, she was even coming to respond to him.

Her hands reached for him, timidly, feeling the naked flesh of his body for the first time. He was warm with a fine dark mat of blond hair covering his chest. She liked it very much. But as she moved to touch him, she ended up touching herself as well, which brought about an unexpected result. Her hand brushed against her right nipple and the moment she touched herself she could feel a wild explosion in her loins that caused her entire body to seize. The sensations were heightened as Dane impaled her on his manhood repeatedly. It was like nothing she had ever experienced in her life, causing her eyes to roll back in her head and her breathing to come in shrieking gasps. The more Dane pounded into her, the more heightened the exquisite sensation.

It seemed as if it went on forever when, in fact, it was only a few seconds because the moment Dane realized that she had found her release, there was nothing to hold back his own pleasure. Feeling her body draw at him brought about the greatest climax he had ever experienced. He spilled himself deep, feeling his hot seed as it made her very slick and very wet. He liked the feel of what he had put inside her as he finally marked her as his own.

It was the sweetest thing he had ever experienced.

When the tremors faded away and Dane lay on top of Grier, it took very little time for the still-tipsy, exhausted, and satisfied lady to pass out. Dane realized it when she began snoring softly against him, and he didn't even try to wake her. He simply shifted so his weight wasn't on her, wrapped her up in his arms, and settled in for the night.

And what a night it had been.

Lady de Russe had finally been stabbed with her husband's fleshy sword… and liked it.

CHAPTER TEN

THE ALARM AT dawn woke Dane up out of a dead sleep.

He could hear the Shrewsbury horn on the battlements, its mournful cry rousing men to battle, and he threw back the coverlet and leapt out of bed. His breeches, in a pile next to the bed where he had left them, were quickly on and he snatched his boots, yanking them on his feet as Grier, groggy and hungover, sat up in bed.

"What is happening?" she asked, rubbing her eyes. "What is that noise?"

Dane hardly had time to explain. With his boots on, he grabbed his tunic and bent over the bed, kissing Grier on the top of the head.

"An alarm," he said. "Stay here and bolt the door. You will not open it except for me or any of the knights. Is that clear?"

Fearfully, Grier nodded. "An alarm?" she repeated. "Is the castle being attacked?"

Dane yanked his tunic over his head as he made his way to the door. "I do not know," he said. "Bolt this door when I go."

As Dane rushed to the stairs, he heard the bolt as Grier threw it across the chamber door. Taking the steps quickly, perhaps too quickly, he was just hitting the entry when Boden burst in through the entry door and headed for his brother. The pair came together somewhere in the middle of the foyer.

"What is happening?" Dane demanded.

"A raid on the market street," Boden said. "Syler and Dastan are already mounted, riding out to stop it."

Dane didn't like the idea of his men fighting a battle without him. "Bring my horse to the gatehouse," he said. "I will be there in a few minutes. Where is William?"

"He is preparing to ride out after Dastan and Syler."

Dane came to a halt. "We cannot all ride out to fight," he said, irritated. "Boden, you remain here. I will ride out with Willie. Tell him to wait for me, do you hear?"

Boden rolled his eyes. "You know he will not listen to me."

"If he does not, then I send him home to Wellesbourne and tell his father that he has shamed the Wellesbourne name." He jabbed a finger at his brother. "Tell him that, Boden. I will not hesitate to do it."

Boden knew it was the truth. As he headed back out to the gatehouse to have Dane's horse brought around, Dane ran with him, stopping at the western tower of the inner gatehouse because the armory was there. His armor, his weaponry, had been taken there after they'd returned yesterday to be cleaned by the small army of squires and pages they had serving at Shrewsbury.

And that small army had an entire story behind it.

Garreth de Lara was generous in that he accepted young men and boys from noble families who were perhaps not too well off so that the lads could learn the vocation of the knighthood. The problem was that Garreth never denied a truly willing and eager family, so there were literally dozens of young men at Shrewsbury, willing and able to complete any task asked of them.

That was never more evident than it was when Dane dashed into the armory only to find it full of boys and young men, all working furiously on the racks and stacks of weaponry and armor that were there. When they saw Dane, the new duke, they rushed him, bringing his armor and weapons and anything else they thought he needed, and Dane had to settle the boys down so he could properly dress. It had been like a rush of eager puppies the moment he walked through the door. There were two older squires there, young men who had seen sixteen or seventeen years, and they were quite efficient in holding off the throng of young men as they helped Dane dress.

It was heavy plate armor, made for great protection, and Dane had them fasten on the chest and back plates, and the protection for his arms and shoulders. Time was growing short, so he forewent most of the plate on his legs. He had a mail coat on, that hung to his knees, and with his boots on, he was nearly fully dressed, but time was passing swiftly and he didn't want to delay any longer. With one of the older squires running after him, carrying his shield, he ran all the way to the bailey where his horse was just being brought around.

As he'd hoped, but not really expected, William was impatiently waiting for him. Astride his excitable war horse, William rallied the other soldiers astride their steeds and formed a protective barrier around Dane as the patrol raced from the main gatehouse of Shrewsbury. It was an impressive formation organized by William and meant to protect Dane. The trouble was, it also singled him out, which Dane didn't like. He broke from the formation and charged towards the marketplace in the center of town with his contingent thundering after him.

They deeper they went into town, the more panic they saw. People were running in their direction, screaming in terror. Dane tried not to mow them down, but it was difficult because they were all fleeing in terror. Dane was finally forced to slow his horse and as he drew closer to the market area of town, a high-pitched wail suddenly filled the air.

Knowing immediately what it was, Dane threw himself off of his horse just in time for the arrow, launched from a crossbow at high speed, to sail overhead and hit the soldier behind him. Hit squarely in the chest, the man grunted and fell backwards off of his horse.

"Get down!" Dane bellowed, and men began falling from their horses. "Find cover!"

Everyone was scattering, rushing into doorways and alleys, trying to stay clear of the arrows, which were flying in their direction. Several more were launched as Dane and William took shelter in the doorway of a large house.

"Where are they coming from?" William demanded, trying to stick his head out. "Did you see?"

Dane pressed himself up against the door as another arrow sailed in their general direction, hitting the house on the eaves above them.

"Nay," he said. "But they are coming from the general direction of the marketplace, which concerns me. *Where* are Dastan and Syler? They rode out ahead of us, didn't they?"

William nodded. He dropped to his hands and knees, peering out into the street beyond. "I can see the merchant houses that line the marketplace, but this is the rear of them," he said. "The front faces out into the market street. I cannot see any movement."

Dane thought quickly. "We need the army, not just small patrols," he said. "Someone needs to make it back to the castle to muster a few hundred men."

"I'll go," William said confidently. "If I can move to this row of homes behind us, I can make it to the castle without being seen."

"Then go," Dane commanded quietly. "Hurry, now, and stay low. I am concerned for Dastan and Syler. We must find them."

William was gone, using stealth to make his way to the row of residences several dozen yards to the north, and then using those homes as a shield as he ran back to the castle. Dane was pleased to see that he made it, but then it began to occur to him that he was hearing the sounds of a fight from the direction of the marketplace. And here he and his men were, pinned down by arrow fire and unable to help.

He wasn't just going to stand here.

Off to his left, he could see his war horse milling about, grazing on one of the many grassy, muddy areas that dotted the town. Most of the horses had run back to the castle, but not his glutton – his stallion never turned down fresh grass, which was a good thing. On the horse's back were the tools he needed to make it into the marketplace – his shield and his sword.

He had to get the horse's attention.

Emitting a low but rather shrill whistle between his teeth, he called to the beast. The animal's head came up first, sighting him, and then Dane whistled again, which brought the animal in his direction. A couple of arrows flew in the horse's direction, but they both missed, and the animal began to run towards him, startled by the sound. When the steed came alongside, Dane grabbed his shield and his broadsword.

Now, he was armed.

Slapping the animal on its fat rump, he sent the horse back in the direction of the castle as he stepped out into the open, holding the shield over his head. As he expected, multiple arrows came flying out at him, but he ran towards the marketplace, fending off the arrows with his shield.

The sounds of fighting grew louder and, as he approached, he ran straight into a Welshman with a crossbow in his hands. Delivering a crushing blow with his shield to the face, Dane dragged the unconscious Welshman back the way he'd come, handing him over to some of his men who were just coming out of their hiding places. As a few men gleefully took the unconscious prisoner back to the castle, Dane and the rest of his men continued towards the marketplace, only to run headlong into the remnants of a brutal fight.

There were dead men in the street, dead Welshmen with their long tunics and even longer cloaks. Two of Dane's soldiers were down, and he could see Dastan as the man fought off a group of Welshmen who were trying to seriously beat on him.

Unfortunately, it looked to Dane as if Dastan and Syler hadn't taken many men with them when they'd hurriedly fled the castle, because there were more Welshmen than English, and Dane charged into the fray, swinging his sword and beating back those trying to overwhelm his men. Just as he began fighting in earnest, he could see a downed knight off to his right, lying in a puddle of water, as two Welshmen tried to strip him of his weapons.

Dane was on them in an instant.

Infuriated, rage fed his actions. In a particularly brutal move, he went in for the kill right away. The Welshmen weren't wearing armor or protection, but Dane didn't care. He cut off one man's arm right away, sending the man screaming off, and with the second man, he wasn't any kinder. With a vicious upstroke on his sword, he caught the man in the chin, cutting his head off with tremendous ease. As the man's head went rolling into a gutter and his body fell away, Dane fell to his knees beside the downed knight.

It was Syler.

The man was on his face, his entire head in a muddy puddle of water. Dane could feel panic in his veins as he rolled the man out of the water and onto his back. Immediately, he could see the remains of two broken-off arrows in Syler's chest area, very close together, and he yanked the man's helm off to see if he was still alive.

Met with an unconscious knight with a bluish-tinged face, Dane quickly unbuckled the plate protection, pulling it off and yanking the arrows out with it. They were all stuck together, the arrowheads wedged into Syler's torso, but Dane ripped them all out. He could see that the arrows had pierced the man just below his heart, into the left side of his body, and he put his head against the man's chest to listen for a heartbeat or breathing.

He heard nothing.

Seized with horror, Dane rolled Syler onto his side and pounded on his back, hoping that might clear his lungs and start him breathing. He had no way of knowing how long Syler had been lying face down in that mud puddle, but he suspected it was too long. Still, he didn't want to face it. He didn't want to lose a knight, a man he'd genuinely grown to like. He didn't want to lose the camaraderie and the man's skilled sword. He pounded on the knight's back.

"Breathe, Syler," he commanded. "*Breathe!*"

Muddy water poured from Syler's mouth, but nothing more. He didn't breathe. Dane pounded again and again, not realizing that the fighting had stopped around him and his men, including Dastan, were coming up alongside, watching him as he tried to bring a dead man back to life.

"My lord," Dastan said, feeling the grief of having lost a friend as he watched. "He was down for several minutes before you arrived. I saw him go down but there was nothing I could do."

Dane heard Dastan's words but he ignored him. He continued to beat on Syler's back, shaking the man, trying anything he could think of to get him to breathe again, but he was met by silence.

"Syler, *breathe!*" he bellowed. "Do you hear me? Breathe! I command it!"

It was so very difficult to watch. Dastan had tears in his eyes. Rather than stand there and weep, however, he fell to his knees beside Syler, trying to clear his mouth of the debris the man had breathed in, trying to help Dane revive a man who could not be revived. Dane tried, for several minutes, and so did Dastan, but in the end, it did no good.

Syler de Poyer was dead.

Even after Dane realized that, he continued to pound on Syler's back but, eventually, he stopped pounding. Then, he simply sat there and hung his head.

"God," he muttered. "Oh, God... no."

Dastan gazed down at his friend and cousin through marriage, a man he'd greatly respected and admired. Heavily, he sighed.

"They were waiting for us when we rode into town," he said, his voice sounding weary and dull. "I was in the lead and Syler was back behind me, riding with the men. They hit him first with arrows, and a few others, as you have seen, but Syler fell off of his horse and straight into the puddle, and there he lay, as I could do nothing. While we were engaged, more of them waited for you to come behind us. I could hear the arrows flying at you but I could do nothing."

Dane still had his hand on Syler's back as he looked at Dastan, his face a mask of devastation and anger.

"How many were there?" he asked.

Dastan scratched his head with a bloodied hand. "Forty or fifty men, mayhap," he said. "They were Welsh."

"You are sure?"

"I am."

Dane looked down at the dead knight, feeling the stress and grief of the sight. "His death shall not be in vain," he growled. "Dastan, mount two hundred of our best men. We will follow the trail of the bastards who did this. When we find them, we shall destroy them."

"It shall be done, my lord," Dastan said, struggling to focus on what needed to be done and not the anguish he was feeling. "What would you have me do with Syler's body?"

Dane reached out, putting a gentle hand on Syler's head. It was a poignant gesture, one of kindness and regret. In his own way, he was apologizing to Syler, perhaps asking the man's forgiveness for what had happened. As the Duke of Shrewsbury, it was the first man he'd lost under his command and he took it very hard. With a final stroke to the man's dark head, he stood up.

"Cover him up and take him back to the castle," he said. "No one is to mention his death until the rest of us return. News of his passing should come from you, Dastan, since you are married to his cousin. I do not want the women hearing about this from others."

Dastan nodded, his gaze moving back to Syler and losing the battle against his grief. As Dane watched, he went to Syler and drew the man up into his arms. Kissing his forehead, he simply held him for a moment, indulging in the only display of grief he would allow himself.

"He is an only son, you know," Dastan said hoarsely. "His father will take this very hard."

That was like a dagger to Dane's heart. He put a hand on Dastan's shoulder, a hand of comfort, but he knew there was little comfort to give. After several moments of watching Dastan grieve, he patted him on the shoulder rather firmly.

"Give him over to the men, Dastan," he said. "You and I have a task to complete. We must make sure whoever is responsible for it pays with every damn bone in their body. Are you with me?"

Dastan nodded, but tears were trickling from his eyes. "Indeed, I am," he said, gently releasing Syler back onto the ground. As Dane turned away, looking for his horse, who had found another grassy patch to chomp on, Dastan quietly ordered a few of the soldiers standing around to collect Syler's body and cover him up, returning him to the castle and placing him in the cold underground vault until his body could be prepared. Dane had never heard a man weep and give orders at the same time.

But today, he did.

CHAPTER ELEVEN

AFTER A TWO-HOUR search of the lands to the west of Shrewsbury, Dane and his men returned to the castle.

The mist was just starting to lift, casting golden fingers of light down into the muddy, cold earth as the Duke of Shrewsbury and his army came thundering in through the open gatehouse, which was quickly closed again as soon as they were through. Dane reined his steed to a halt mid-bailey and was met by another small army of pages and squires, young men assigned to the stables, to take the horses away and tend to them. As his fat horse was led away, Dane removed his helm and began to pull off his gloves.

"Dane," Boden rush up beside him, having just come from the battlements. "Did you find those bastards?"

Dane was weary and frustrated. "Nay," he said. "They returned to the forests outside of the town and disappeared. We thought we found a couple of paths, but they split up and we lost the trail in Ford's Heath. After that, there were enough forests and bogs to keep them concealed. They are back in Wales by now."

Boden could see how upset his brother was, and with good reason. The entire army was greatly saddened by the death of Syler, the news of which had spread as much as Boden had tried to keep it quiet. The mood of the castle was dark and morose as Dane and his party returned and, unfortunately, returned empty-handed.

"You did what you could," Boden said quietly. "I know you tried very hard, Dane. You mustn't be disappointed in your efforts."

But that was no comfort to Dane. "I failed," he said simply. "I vowed to bring Syler's murderers to justice and I failed."

Boden glanced up, seeing William as the knight spoke to a downcast Dastan a few feet away. As he watched, William put his hands on Dastan's shoulders in a comforting gesture. Boden knew how bad everyone was feeling in the wake of Syler's death; he was feeling badly about it also, badly because he had been locked in at the castle and unable to help. Each of them was feeling like a failure in his own way. Boden finally put a hand on Dane's shoulder, a gesture of comfort.

"You may have the key to all of this in the vault," he muttered. "We still have a prisoner."

Dane's head shot up as he suddenly remembered the man he had grabbed in town. "I captured a Welshman and gave him over to the men," he said. "They brought him back here?"

"Indeed, they did."

Dane felt a surge of hope in his veins. "Excellent," he said. "While I interrogate the man, you will make sure the gates remained locked and release the women in the keep. I believe they can move about freely for now."

"I will send a soldier to release them," Boden said. "I am going with you."

Dane didn't have time to argue. His gaze moved to William and Dastan, standing in a huddle. "Dastan!" he shouted. "To me!"

Dastan rushed to him, followed by William. Boden was a little slower, having issued the command to release the keep, but he followed quickly. All four men headed to the eastern gatehouse, which was comprised of a small tower with a vault in the bedrock below it. It had been dug into the ground when the gate and wall were built two hundred years before, a dank and dingy hole in the ground that held three cramped cells. It was where Dane had instructed Syler to be taken

and stored, and it was with irony he realized one of the Welsh responsible for the man's death was also being held there.

The eastern tower, built of the same red stone that the rest of the
castle was built with, had a heavy contingent of guards at the vault
opening, a narrow doorway that contained a flight of narrow, slippery
stairs cut into the rock that led to the depths below. Dane grabbed a
torch, as did Boden, and the group proceeded down the stairs where
three more guards were waiting at the bottom, watching the prisoner.
Dane handed the torch over to one of the guards, straining to find the
cells as his eyes grew accustomed to the darkness.

The first cell was very tiny, off to his left and hardly big enough for
a man. It had heavy iron bars all around it. The second cell contained
Syler's body; they could all see it on the ground, cushioned by clean
straw, with a horse blanket thrown over it. The third cell contained a
frightened, beaten man cowering in the corner, all rolled up in a ball,
but Dane wasn't particularly focused on him.

At the moment, he was more focused on Syler.

He had to see the man for himself once last time. Stepping in to the
small cell, he knelt beside the knight's body and pulled back the horse
blanket, coming face to face with Syler's still-bluish face, only now there
was more gray to it and his eyes were half-open. With a heavy sigh,
Dane put his hand to the man's cheek in another apologetic gesture,
perhaps an apology that those responsible for his death had not yet
been brought to justice. But the gesture was short, and heartfelt, before
Dane covered the man's face again and stood up.

Now, he could focus on the prisoner in the next cell.

When the guards unlocked it, Dane pushed into the cell with Dastan and William behind him. That was all that would fit. Boden
remained at the cell door. When the prisoner remained rolled up in a
ball, ignoring the men around him, Dane lashed out a big boot and
kicked the man in the back.

"Get up," he snarled. "You will face me."

The man flinched in pain and slowly began to unroll himself. It was

William who impatiently reached out and yanked the man's cloak off his head and then pulled him up by the scruff of his dark, matted hair.

"Sit up," William barked, slapping the man in the head and then shoving him back against the wall of the cell. "You will answer him, do you hear me? Answer him or I will beat your brains out where you sit."

Dane put out a hand to still William's quick temper, and William backed away, but he was still huffing. Dane stood over the prisoner, the same young man with the crossbow that he'd clobbered in town, and folded his arms.

"*Wyt ti'n deall Saesneg?*" he asked.

Do you speak English? The Welshman lifted his head, fear written all over his face, and nodded unsteadily.

"Good," Dane said. "Do you understand that you are in a very bad position?"

The Welshman hesitated, looking at all of the serious English faces around him. "Do what you want," he said, although his voice was trembling. "I cannot tell you anything. Do what you will to me."

That brought William down on him and he delivered two nasty blows to the man's face before Dane and Dastan could pull him away. As Dane pulled the Welshman back into a sitting position, Dastan shoved William back at Boden, who yanked the young knight out of the cell. They could hear Boden angrily scolding William as Dane and Dastan closed in on the prisoner.

"I cannot keep him off of you for much longer," Dane said. "His friend is dead and he is angry. It would be best to tell me what we want to know. Who led the raid into town today?"

The Welshman had a bloody nose that was causing him a good deal of pain. He put his cloak up to his face to try and stem the flow.

"I'll not tell you!"

"If you tell me, you will live. If you do not, then one less Welshman in the world will not matter to me. I will get my information elsewhere and your death will have been in vain. I can promise you that you will not die painlessly."

The Welshman was young and it was clear that he was frightened. Perhaps an older, more seasoned warrior would have ignored Dane's demand, but the Welshman seemed to be considering it. He could see the angry redheaded knight outside of his cell being held back by another knight, and that worried him. He had a feeling they would turn the redheaded man loose on him and then he would know great pain. His fear began to build, bringing a wave of panic that he was unaccustomed to. He'd never really been in a fight, not in all his eighteen years, and now he found himself the captive of powerful English knights.

He knew nothing. He *was* nothing.

But he wanted to live.

"We killed the duke," he said defiantly. "Killing me will not bring him back!"

Dane eyed him curiously. "What makes you think you killed the duke?"

The Welshman wiped at his bloodied nose. "Because he rode from the castle surrounded by his men," he said. "He was struck down. I saw it!"

Dane looked at Dastan, who seemed to be equally puzzled. But then, it occurred to Dastan what he meant because he had been there. He had seen them take Syler out in a hail of well-placed arrows and now it occurred to him as to *why*.

Syler had been targeted.

"Is that what you thought?" he asked, incredulous. "That the duke was riding in the midst of his men into town?"

"He was!" the Welshman said, still with a defiant tone. "He's dead and now Shrewsbury will belong to Godor, as it should."

Now, the man had Dane's full attention. "Godor?" he repeated sharply. "Is ap Madoc behind this?"

The young Welshman looked at Dane with a mixture of surprise and pride. "Then you know of him already," he said. "You know of his greatness. Shrewsbury will belong to him now. You will see!"

Dane had to take a step back. He looked at Dastan as the realization of the situation washed over him. Grabbing Dastan by the arm, he pulled him out of the cell where Boden and William were standing. Facing the trio, although he was mostly looking at Dastan, he spoke softly.

"Davies ap Madoc was behind this," he hissed. "The same man who offered for Grier's hand and was denied. You heard the prisoner – now, they think they have killed the duke – because Syler was riding with the men, they assumed it was the duke with an escort and they aimed for him. Don't you see?"

The light of recognition went on in Dastan's eyes. "That's why I was not hit," he said. "Then the raid on the market was a ruse. They were trying to draw out the Duke of Shrewsbury, and they were aiming what limited arrows they had right at Syler, thinking that he was the duke when he came from the castle surrounded by soldiers. They thought he was *you*."

Dane put his hands to his head as the understanding of the situation rolled over him. He was flabbergasted and infuriated at the same time. "My God," he breathed. "The man is trying to kill me. He knows I have married Grier, or at least he knows that some man has married Grier, a man who is now the Duke of Shrewsbury. And he is trying to kill him to get to her."

"It could be that all he wants is Shrewsbury, and not Grier. She may have been only a means to an end and he has no feelings for her."

"Or he *does* have feelings for her and wants both her and the dukedom. Either way, he must get rid of me."

As that understanding settled, both William and Boden displayed a wide-eyed countenance, shocked with what had happened. They looked at Dane, who was torn between disbelief and anger. An excellent knight had taken arrows meant for him and with that thought, the anger won over.

But even as rage swamped him, thoughts of Grier filled Dane's mind. He was coming to think that it would be wise for him to discover just what manner of relationship was between his wife and ap Madoc, because if the Lords of Godor were trying to kill him in order to obtain Shrewsbury, then there might be more to this than he realized.

Grier could hold the key.

"Keep the Welshman down here," he commanded quietly. "I think it is time to ask my wife just what she knows of Davies ap Madoc and the Lords of Godor."

Dastan couldn't disagree. "I cannot tell you if there was any relationship between them," he said. "When ap Madoc's father came to offer for her hand, he made no indication that there was any relationship at all. But then again, Lord Garreth never asked him. Mayhap, it would be wise to see what Lady de Russe knows about this."

"I intend to," Dane said with a hint of suspicion in his tone. He looked to Boden and William. "Ensure our prisoner is fed and well-guarded. Willie, you will stay away from him. Do you understand?"

William pursed his lips unhappily. "If I must."

"You must. If he is injured or killed, I will send you back to your father in disgrace. Is that in any way unclear?"

Grossly unhappy, William looked away. "You do not have to threaten me."

"Answer me."

"It is clear."

Dane pointed a finger at him. "I will hold you to that." His gaze lingered on the knight a moment, looking for any signs of rebellion, before returning his attention to Dastan. "Mayhap now would be a good time to tell your wife and her cousin what has become of Syler. We cannot keep it from them for much longer. I am sure rumor of his death is quietly spreading."

Dastan nodded, dreading the duty. Dane made William and Boden leave the vault first, following them up the stairs to make sure William wasn't tempted to harass the prisoner once Dane was gone. He stood at the entry to the vault, watching William walk away while Boden spoke to the guards. Once William was far enough away, Dane thought it would be safe to leave the vault himself.

He had a wife to see.

Just as Dane and Dastan were turning for the keep, they could hear screams in the distance. Dane cocked an ear, confused and alerted.

"Did you hear that?" he asked Dastan.

The knight nodded, hearing more screams. "It sounds as if it is coming from the hall."

As they watched, servants began shooting out of the whitewashed structure that contained the kitchens, but there was even more screaming going on inside. When Dane saw William break out in a run towards the kitchen, he began to run as well. They had no idea why people were screaming and running from the kitchens, but they were certainly going to find out. Something horrific must have been happening, and after the raid that morning, they couldn't discount that somehow, someway, Welshmen had made it into the kitchens where there were knives and fire and other deadly things.

The swords came out. As William entered through the kitchen yard, followed by several armed soldiers, Dane and Dastan, and several more armed soldiers, entered from the main doorway.

And what they saw was certainly not what they had expected.

The first thing Dane saw was Grier on top of a table, covered in flour. Charlisa was against a wall with a massive spoon in her hand, screaming and swinging the spoon like a weapon, and everyone seemed to be in a panic as a flour-covered rooster went on a rampage around the floor. It was the most puzzling, and possibly most hilarious, sight that Dane had ever seen and he probably would have laughed his head off had he not just come from a very depressing and serious situation.

He wasn't in the mood to laugh, as Lady de Russe was about to find out.

CHAPTER TWELVE

"Where do you suppose our husbands have gone?" Grier asked.

She was asking the question of Charlisa, who didn't have an answer for her. After Dane had run out so quickly, Grier had spent the better part of two hours behind the bolted chamber door until one of the senior sergeants came to tell her that there had been a raid on the market, but that the raiders had fled and Shrewsbury men, including the duke, had returned after a search of the surrounding countryside.

With the castle no longer under lockdown, at least for the moment, Grier was free to go about her day, but she really didn't have any idea what that meant other than bathing and dressing, which she did with Euphemia's help.

The old servant was in fine form this morning, chatting away about things they had been discussing last night, but it was odd how differently Grier felt about the same conversation after being intimate with Dane the night before. Yesterday, she had been open in asking questions of Euphemia, but now that she had experienced the mating of a man and a woman, she felt quite private about it.

She didn't want to talk about it, even when Euphemia chattered on about how to please a husband. To Grier, what had taken place between them was deeply personal and she didn't want to share it with anyone, not even with Charlisa who had come to see how she was faring after drinking so much ale the night before.

Grier was glad to see the vivacious blond, but truth be told, she wasn't feeling all that well. The ale had given her a raging headache. However, it was her first full day at Shrewsbury as the duchess, and she was eager to get on with it. With Charlisa's encouragement, she finished dressing in the red dress made of wool, much softer than anything she'd ever known wool to be, and pinned the lovely marriage brooch on her breast. After last night, the brooch meant something to her, a gift from the man she had married. A man she was quickly growing very fond of. Fully dressed and ready to face the world, she followed Charlisa on a tour of Shrewsbury so she could learn what she needed to learn about running a castle.

It was a daunting yet exciting task.

But the truth was that it was difficult to focus on daily tasks when her husband was nowhere to be seen, and Charlisa felt the same. The outer bailey was full of men, but no knights. Still, the women continued on, and as the morning mist began to clear and the sun began to shine through, Grier and Charlisa picked up a companion in Laria, who joined them on their walk. As they moved across the inner bailey bridge and skirted the outer bailey where the men were mustering, it was that scene that had brought about Grier's question –

Where do you think our husbands have gone?

Charlisa seemed quite distressed that Dastan was not in sight. "I do not know," she said honestly. "The soldiers have said they have returned, but I do not see them. I hate it when Dastan rides to battle, but I suppose I should not complain. Since we have been married, there has hardly been any trouble at all. The worst was last month, when Lord Garreth was killed. They were gone three weeks and when they returned, it was with Lord Garreth's body and Dane was declared the new duke. And, oh! That horrible majordomo, Adalgar. Have you been told about him? He had been with Lord Garreth for many years and he wanted the dukedom for himself. When it was given to Dane, he told us that Dane was sure to fail and that they would wish for Adalgar to return."

Grier hadn't heard about the horrible majordomo but, already, she hated the man. "But Dane has not failed," she said. "He *will* not fail. He is a great knight and his father is the Duke of Warminster. He was born to serve Shrewsbury."

Charlisa looked at her, a smile on her lips. "He is kind and handsome," she said. "Just as my Dastan is kind and handsome. We are very fortunate, you and I. We have married kind and handsome men."

Grier couldn't help but smile, perhaps an embarrassed gesture. She'd noticed that Charlisa was very nearly obsessed with "handsome" husbands, as if it should be the most important thing to all of them.

Not that Grier disagreed with her.

"I suppose we are," she said. "It is odd; a week ago, little did I know this would be my fate. It seems as if this has all happened so fast and I am still trying to catch my breath."

Charlisa wasn't unsympathetic. "I can only imagine how you must feel," she said. Then, she continued rather hesitantly. "What was it like to be an oblate? Did you pray all day and all night, and hardly sleep?"

Grier shook her head, laughing softly at Charlisa's question. "Nay," she said. "We prayed at designated times, just as you do. The rest of the time, we had assigned duties. Some of us worked in the garden, some in the kitchen, and some of us sewed."

"What did you do?"

"I sewed."

"What did you sew?"

"Lace shawls that the abbey sold," she said. "We did not have much income, and the shawls brought in badly needed funds."

Charlisa leaned in to her, as if to tell her something in confidence. "I do not sew very well," she admitted. "I think I was born with ten thumbs."

Grier laughed. "I am sure it is not that bad."

But Charlisa nodded firmly and before she could answer, Laria spoke. "She is a terrible seamstress," the girl declared. "You will always know anything she makes because it looks as if a blind man pieced it together."

Charlisa pinched the girl, who yelped and rubbed her arm in the offending spot as Grier continued to giggle. "Well," Grier said thoughtfully. "You show me what I must know about running a house and hold, and I will show you how to sew properly. Agreed?"

Charlisa nodded eagerly. "Agreed."

With that, the trio headed over to the kitchens, which were in the outer bailey behind the great hall. Grier found everything about the outer bailey fascinating; the soldiers, the trades, even servants running about on their assigned tasks. There was a whole world there, a world that she now presided over, although it didn't feel quite real to her. It was a strange place, filled with strangers, but they all belonged to her and to Dane. This was to be their world together, forever, and there was joy in that realization that she never imagined possible.

Their wonderful world, together.

A week ago, she could never have dreamed that this would be her life. Two days ago, she could have never imagined she would actually be happy with this marriage, but she was. Charlisa was correct; she'd married someone handsome and kind, someone that belonged only to her, and for a woman who had been beaten and starved, isolated from the world for most of her life, she was far too trusting in her newfound happiness. She had no sense of reservation about it. Surely anyone who made her so happy was someone who deserved her adoration, respect, and loyalty.

That was the way she looked at it.

For the first time in her life, she was actually happy. She very much wanted to belong in this world that now belonged to her. And that included newfound friends that she was very curious about.

"Tell me of yourself, Lady du Reims," Grier said as they headed into the kitchen yard through a tall wooden fence. "How did you come to marry Sir Dastan?"

Charlisa lit up like a spark at the mention of her husband. "My father is a great warlord who is allied with Dastan's uncle," she said. "Dastan's family is one with great means, but my family has greater means and a greater army, so it was simply a matter of convincing Dastan that a marriage to me would be in his best interests."

"But you are happy?"

Charlisa's expression told the story. "So very happy," she says. "He has told me that he loves me. That is all I need to know."

Grier thought on the prospect of having a husband's love. It wasn't such an outlandish thing, considering her father had loved her mother. Even as a child, she had known that. The thought of having Dane's love seemed like the most unreachable of wishes, for surely a man who was forced into marriage would not love the woman he'd been tied to. Perhaps he could be fond of her, but love? It didn't seem possible, and her heart sank with that thought. Perhaps, God could give her his blessing in a husband that loved her.

It was a lonesome prayer.

"You are very fortunate," Grier said after a moment, envious of something Charlisa had. "Dastan seems like a good man."

Charlisa nodded her head fervently. "He is," she said, watching Laria as the woman went over towards the hen house. "But enough about my husband; I could speak on Dastan all day long and you would weep with boredom. Therefore, let me tell you about the kitchen yard, where we are now. You did wish to learn about Shrewsbury, so let us start here. The cook manages the yard and I will introduce you to her. She is an old woman named Alvie, and can hardly hear, but she is a master when it comes to cooking and tending the kitchens. We cannot get along without her."

From that point on, Grier listened closely to all Charlisa had to say. The woman spoke of the buttery, the butchery, the sheep herds they had that provided not only wool but meat, and the very large flock of chickens they had in an enormous coop that was watched over by two men whose sole job was to make sure the chickens didn't fall prey to any predators.

Evidently, they needn't have worried too much about protecting the chickens, because Laria was inspecting some newly-hatched chicks and a nearby rooster took unkindly to her. Suddenly, Laria was being chased by a very big rooster, screaming as she ran around the kitchen yard. Charlisa started laughing, as did Grier, watching the young girl fend off the rooster who grew angrier every time she tried to kick or swat at him. It was very humorous until Laria headed in their direction and both Grier and Charlisa realized that big rooster was coming for them. Charlisa grabbed Grier by the arm and they fled into the kitchens with Laria on their heels, who slammed the door behind them so the rooster couldn't follow.

Inside the hot, fragrant kitchen, Grier continued to giggle as Charlisa berated her frenzied young cousin.

"I have told you to stay away from the chickens," she scolded. "You know that the roosters will chase you!"

Laria wasn't too contrite in spite of the attack. "But the chicks are so sweet!"

Charlisa rolled her eyes. "You are useless," she said. Her attention returned to Grier. "I apologize, my lady. I did not intend that your first visit to the kitchen yard would end in you running for your life from an angry rooster."

But Grier wasn't bothered in the least. "Not to worry," she said. "We had to come to the kitchens, anyway, and here we are."

Charlisa nodded, distracted from her pouting cousin as she looked around the low-ceilinged structure. There was an enormous hearth with all manner of pots hanging over it on iron arms, and a big oven built right up against it. Everything was hot and steaming, and as they watched, kitchen servants bustled around completing their tasks.

There was a woman whose sole job was to make bread, and Grier watched with interest as the woman worked busily on what looked like two or three different types of loaves. There was also a woman who was responsible for the fire in the hearth, and a massive iron pot of water was tucked up towards the rear of the hearth, steaming. That was the castle's hot water supply, Grier was told.

Everyone seemed busily going about their tasks as the cook, a very big woman with a round face, round nose, and thinning white hair supervised what was going on. She had a big spoon in her hand, as she'd been stirring something that was cooking over the hearth, but when she turned and saw Charlisa and the ladies, she quickly put her spoon aside and rushed to greet them.

"M'lady," she greeted Charlisa. "What can I do for ye?"

Charlisa indicated Grier. "This is Lady de Russe, our new duchess. You will be taking your orders from her from now on." She then spoke to Grier. "My lady, this is Alvie. She has been at Shrewsbury for a very long time."

The cook looked at Grier in surprise, quickly bowing her head. "The baby," she murmured, her eyes wide at Grier. "Ye're the baby. The little lass. I knew yer mother, m'lady. God's Soul... ye look just like her."

That caught Grier off guard and very quickly, she felt her emotions bubbling up. "You... were here when my mother was alive?"

Alvie nodded. Then, she seemed to tear up, lifting her apron and blowing her nose in it. "Aye, m'lady," she said. "I was here. I loved yer mother; she was a kind and decent woman. Do ye not remember me? I used to call ye 'Lamb'. Ye used to come to my kitchen and ask for sweet cakes. Do ye not remember?"

Grier thought very hard, realizing she did remember coming to the kitchens as a child where a woman would give her sweets. "That was you?" she gasped. "I remember asking the cook for sweets and you would give me cakes of oatmeal and honey."

The old cook was nodding furiously, bobbing her head in agreement. She looked as if she was about to burst into tears as her red face became even redder.

"That was me," she said. "I was devastated when yer mother passed and yer father sent ye away. We didn't know where ye went, but that bastard of a majordomo told us ye'd gone with the church. And now ye're back!"

She seemed so happy about it, which made Grier feel some joy as well. She could hardly believe there was someone left at Shrewsbury who remembered both her and her mother from those years ago.

"I am," she said. "I have come back to stay. I have married the duke and this will be a happy place again, I promise. I do not know much about this majordomo some have spoken of, but I am glad he is gone. Did you take your orders from him, then?"

Alvie lifted her big shoulders. "Mostly from Lady du Reims, but sometimes the old fool would try and tell me what to do. But I wouldn't listen to him; nay, I wouldn't!"

Charlisa smiled as the old cook's hackles went up. "Adalgar was not a very nice man to the female servants," she said, trying to be tactful. "I did not fear him, because the duke put me in charge of the kitchens and the hall, but whenever he tried to exceed his authority, Dastan would step in and he greatly feared Dastan. It was a blessing when Dane became the duke because it forced Adalgar from the castle. He was under the delusion that he was to be the next duke."

"The idiot," Alvie sniffed. Then, she beamed at Grier. "But now that ye're here, we'll have happy times again. 'Twill be as if yer dear mother has returned. Now, Lamb, what can I prepare that is special for ye? I know! Sweetcakes!"

Grier didn't even have time to answer the woman before she was rushing off, calling to another servant lady and telling her what they needed to prepare. Grier and Charlisa watched it all, looking at each other and shrugging.

"I suppose that means she is happy to see me," Grier said, grinning. "Truthfully, I'd forgotten all about her. What a lovely discovery."

Charlisa agreed. "It is a lovely discovery," she said. But then she paused, spying Laria over near the baker, sniffing at the bread that was coming out of the oven hot and fresh. "One of the first things I must tell you about your duties is to watch out for my cousin. She cannot keep her hands off of anything."

Grier turned to look at Laria, chuckling when the baker slapped the young woman's hand as she tried to tear a piece from a fresh loaf of bread.

"She is young," she said. "She will learn to behave soon enough."

"Unless the rooster finally catches her and stabs her to death with his spurs," Charlisa said. Shaking her head at her cousin, she returned her attention to the cook and a thought occurred to her. "Have you ever cooked anything before?"

Grier shook her head. "Never," she said. "As I said, we all had assigned duties at the abbey, and my duty was to sew. Why?"

Charlisa smiled, that same dreamy smile Grier had noticed the woman had when she either looked at or spoke of her husband.

"Because I think it would be a wonderful thing to cook something for my husband," she said. "To make him something to eat with my own hands. Don't you think that would show him how much I care for him?"

Grier had no experience with anything like that, so she didn't really know, but she didn't want to sound naïve. "I am sure he would like anything you did for him," she said. "But what would you cook?"

Charlisa took Grier by the hand, pulling her over to where the cook was beginning to throw ingredients into a big wooden bowl.

"Alvie," she said, answering Grier's question by speaking to the cook. "May we make the sweetcakes? For our husbands, I mean. They are out ridding the town of the terrible raiders, so we would like to make them something special."

Alvie looked at her as if completely baffled by the question. "Ye… ye want to do this yerselves?"

Charlisa nodded firmly, looking to Grier for support, who began to bob her head up and down because she was being prompted to. Truth be told, she had no idea what to do in the kitchen, so the thought of failing to produce something pleasing for Dane was greater than the inclination to want to try.

But Charlisa had no reservations; the woman was fearless when it came to showing affection for her husband, and Grier thought that was a rather admirable quality. So what if she failed? It seemed to Grier that with Charlisa, it was all about the effort, and in that thought, Grier realized she could learn something from Charlisa when it came to her own marriage with Dane.

It *was* all about the effort.

"Aye," Grier said. "We want to do this ourselves. Surely making food with our own hands will make it taste twice as good to our husbands. Will you show us how to make these cakes?"

Alvie was still bewildered by the request, but she showed them nonetheless. In fact, she brought out a second wooden bowl and poured oats and eggs and honey into it and told the women to start mixing the dough with their hands, which they did.

Rolling up their sleeves, Grier and Charlisa stuck their hands right into the mixture and began to knead and mix, watching everything Alvie did for the dough from putting in extra honey to sprinkling ground cinnamon and cloves into the mixture. A little bit of salt went in, followed by raisins, and all the while, the women were mixing and mixing, squeezing the dough to make sure everything was incorporated.

As they worked and learned, Laria wandered over and began sticking her fingers into Charlisa's bowl, pulling forth sweet oat dough to lick. Charlisa scolded her and Alvie pulled up a spoonful of the stuff, handed it to Laria, and then swatted her on the behind to shoo her away. Laria wasn't too offended since she had sweet dough to lick off the spoon, but when that was finished, she headed back over to the baker to pilfer more bread from the woman, who gave up trying to chase her away and handed her a half of a warm loaf. Happy, Laria found a place near the door that led to the kitchen yards and shoved fresh bread into her mouth.

In all, it was one of the better mornings Grier had ever spent. Charlisa was sweet and eager, Alvie was patient and kind, and Grier thought that she could come to love her surroundings very much. There had been such uncertainty with her return home yesterday, but after the encounter between her and Dane last night, and then a morning filled with old friends and new experiences, she was coming to think that she could come to like being at Shrewsbury very much.

It was turning out to be much more than she could have hoped for.

Therefore, she mixed the dough happily, so very pleased with the direction her life was taking. When the ingredients were well mixed, Alvie helped her and Charlisa make the dough into flat little patties for baking, but when it came to actually putting them in the oven, Alvie insisted on doing it. She didn't want the women to burn themselves. They helped her put the cakes on the long, flat wooden sheet and watched her slide them into the hot oven.

Now, all they had to do was wait.

As the smell of cinnamon filled the kitchen, and smoke from the hearth began to back up against the ceiling, Charlisa followed Alvie back over to a table where the woman had been making crust for meat pies, while Grier found herself over with the baker, who was making a different type of bread. She had already made bread from wheat, but now she was mixing rye flour in with the wheat. As Grier was watching with interest, a servant opened the door from the yard, coming in with a basket of eggs.

It shouldn't have been an action that stood out in a kitchen that was busy. It was a normal action, that of opening a door, but the unfortunate reality was that Laria was standing right next to the door finishing off the warm bread the baker had given her, and the rooster that hated her was still by the door when it opened. The bird hadn't moved. When it caught sight of Laria, it ruffled its feathers and bolted through the open door, rushing at Laria and causing the girl to scream in fear.

What happened next was a chain reaction of biblical proportions.

When Laria screamed and ran, she crashed into the baker, who dropped the mass of flour she had in her hands. Flour exploded onto the rooster, onto Laria, and onto the floor as Laria ran from the rooster, and the rooster gave chase.

Covered in flour, Laria ran right into Grier, who had been watching the baker, and when she saw the angry rooster bearing down on her, she leapt up onto the baker's table, also covering herself with flour. When she slammed her hand into a bowl of water that was on the table, the water sprayed up onto her chest and neck, sealing the flour to her skin and hitting her in the face with droplets.

As Grier gasped at the mess she'd made, Laria and the rooster continued their mad dash. They crashed into Alvie as the woman tried to avoid them, and the rooster flew up and flapped its wings at Charlisa, who screamed and began slapping at it with the first thing she could find, a large metal spoon. She whacked it, but good, stunning the rooster for a moment before it picked itself up and kept running, now running because it was panicked and not because it was chasing Laria. With a wild rooster on the loose, servants were screaming and running from the kitchen, creating an uproar, while those still inside the kitchen were either up on tables or heavily armed, or both.

An angry rooster with big spurs was a fearsome sight, indeed.

"Open the door!" Grier yelled at the baker, who was closer to the yard door than the rest of them. "Open the door and he will run out!"

The baker was terrified but she did as she was told. Arming herself with a rolling pin, she rushed to the door and threw it open, only to have men charging in from the outside. In fact, men were charging in from another door as well, and very quickly, the kitchen was full of men with weapons who had heard the screaming.

When Grier happened to look up at the men flooding into the kitchen, her gaze fell on Dane, who had his sword leveled, ready for battle. Their gazes locked and Grier would never forget the look on his face.

Deadly.

The man was prepared to kill.

The rooster slipped out under the legs of the men and ran out into the yard, leaving behind a trail of destruction in its wake.

And that was the last they saw of it.

CHAPTER THIRTEEN

IN THE AFTERMATH of the fleeing rooster, the sudden silence in the kitchen was unnerving. Everyone was looking around at each other, startled by what had just occurred. No attacking Welshmen? No horrific danger? After what they'd just heard, no one could quite believe it, and when the silence was finally broken, it was by Dane.

"What in the bloody hell is happening?" he demanded.

From the look on his face, Grier knew that nothing but a clean and concise answer was going to please him. She unfurled her tucked-up legs, moving to climb down off the table.

"The rooster broke in," she said. "He was trying to attack Lady Laria, but he went after all of us."

It was a simple explanation for a circumstance that had turned the kitchen upside-down. When Dane realized that the entire country of Wales hadn't broken into the kitchen, he slowly lowered his blade, feeling somewhat weak with relief. When he lowered his weapon, everyone else did, and Dastan went over to his wife, who was standing petrified against the wall with the spoon still in her hands. Dastan disarmed her of the spoon and pulled her away from the wall.

Dane, seeing that Dastan was tending to his wife, went to Grier as she tried to climb down from the table. She was covered in flour, so much of it glued to the lovely red woolen dress from the water she had sprayed on herself. She was trying to unwind her legs from the skirt, so he reached out and simply lifted her up and off the table, setting her carefully to the ground as chunks of wet flour fell off of her. When she looked up at him, quite sheepishly, he couldn't help but chuckle at the woman.

"God's Bones," he muttered, looking her up and down. "You are quite a mess."

Grier could hear humor in his voice but she wasn't sure it was real. It was quite possible that he was so angry at her that he simply couldn't adequately express that anger, masking it instead behind feigned mirth.

"I know," she said regretfully. "It all happened so fast."

"What are you doing in the kitchens?"

She lifted a hand only to drop it back down in a futile gesture. "Charlisa was showing me Shrewsbury," she said, feeling stupid even as she said it. "We ended up in the kitchens and we asked the cook if we could make something special for you and Dastan because you were fighting a battle. We made you sweetcakes."

She was pointing at the big oven and he turned to see Alvie pulling the baked cakes from the fire. In that moment, he was rather stumped; it was a sweet and innocent gesture, something she'd done to be kind to him. When he'd come into the kitchen, this was not what he had been expecting. Now, it was a struggle against the suspicion and angst he'd had when he'd charged into the kitchen, suspicion and angst that was directed at Grier because of what the captured Welshman had told him. He needed to talk to her, to find out the truth behind her relationship with ap Madoc but, at this moment, he was feeling like an ogre about it. Could he believe in her gesture to make him sweets? Or was it a meaningless gesture because the truth was that she was secretly in love with someone else?

God, he just didn't know.

Dane very much wanted to believe that her gesture was genuine, that she was truly attempting to be kind to him. But perhaps, he was being foolish or naïve. Men didn't have feelings like women did. They weren't fools for the women they were married to or held affection for. But then he thought of his father, who deeply loved his mother, and they'd set a marvelous example for him of a happy married couple. The truth was that he wanted what they had. The past two days with Grier had shown him a surprising path to such happiness, and then last night… it had gone beyond what he'd thought it would be. A simple consummation wasn't so simple. He'd enjoyed it more than he could express.

But could he mean more to her than simply a husband? When he looked into her face, he could almost believe so.

Trouble was, he *wanted* to believe so. But with ap Madoc rearing his head, he had to get a few things straight first.

"That was kind of you," he finally said. "But there are some things I need to tend to before I can sample your cakes. Let us return to our chamber where you can change out of that dress. I have something I wish to speak with you about."

Grier went with him eagerly. She was such a mess that when he got her outside of the kitchen, he had her stand still and cover her face while he took his hands and beat at her skirt to get rid of some of the flour. Great puffs of white billowed up as he beat the red fabric, and when he was satisfied, he took her by the arm and led her back up to the keep, past his men who were now staring at the lady half-covered in white powder. Grier felt quite self-conscious.

"Your men are staring at me," she muttered as they crossed the bridge and into the inner bailey. "I wonder what they think I have been doing."

Dane laughed low. "I am sure they could not even hazard a guess," he said. "You look like a fish that has been rolled in flour and is ready to be fried."

Grier started to chuckle because he was. "It could not be helped," she said. "It was either jump on the table with the flour on it, or let that terrible rooster stab me with his spurs. You can guess which choice I made."

"I can," he said. "That should be a lesson to stay clear of that rooster. I should take that thing into battle with me."

"I am not sure a rooster would look good on your standard. They might start calling you the Chicken Duke."

"Point taken."

They were grinning at each other as they entered the keep, feeling that warmth that was sparking so easily between them. They had spent a good deal of their first few days together smiling at each other, which made this situation with ap Madoc all the more unhappy. Dane hoped with all his heart that the smiles and the warmth from her were real.

He wanted that badly.

With thoughts of Welshmen and new brides on his mind, he carefully helped Grier up the stairs because her garments were still too long and she was trying very hard not to step on the hem. Once they reached their chamber, he forced himself to push aside thoughts of ap Madoc, at least for the moment, as they entered to find Euphemia sitting by the fire, sewing up the hem of the emerald silk.

The old servant caught one look at her lady and gasped. "God's Soul!" she exclaimed. "What has happened to ye?"

Grier held out her arms as if to show the woman all of the damage. "An accident in the kitchens," she said without elaborating. "Would you be so kind as to bring me hot water so I may clean myself?"

Dane, laying his big broadsword on the nearest table, spoke up. "Bring her a bath," he told the old servant. "I think the lady needs to be doused to get all of the mess off of her."

Euphemia fled the room, closing the door behind her, as Dane went over to Grier. "Can I help you remove that mess?" he asked.

Grier eyed him. "Well," she said slowly. "I will allow it if you bolt the door. I do not need servants rushing in here while I'm only in my shift."

With a smile playing on his lips, Dane went to the door and dutifully bolted it. Then, he headed back to Grier, getting in behind her where the fastens of her dress were. As she pulled her long hair aside, which had flour and water all in the ends of it, he began to unfasten. He was almost finished when he heard her soft voice.

"There were raiders in town today, then?" she asked. "Did you catch them?"

He started to slow down as he reached the last few fastens. "Who told you there were raiders?"

"The same sergeant who told me it was safe to come out of my chamber," she said. "You said not to come out until a knight released me, but there were no knights, only a soldier. I hope you are not cross with me."

He fingered the second to the last fasten. "Of course not," he said quietly. "And, aye, there were raiders in town. I did not catch all of them, only one man. But it was a costly effort. We lost Syler."

Grier gasped, her hand flying to her mouth in shock. "Sir Syler is dead?"

"Aye."

Grier was deeply distressed. "But... but he is Lady Laria's brother," she said. "And Charlisa's cousin! Do they know?"

"They more than likely do now."

Grier fell silent a moment, feeling grief over the knight even though she didn't know him very well. "I am sorry," she murmured. "So very sorry. I shall say a prayer for him at Vespers."

Dane reached the last fasten and undid it, pulling the back of the dress apart. "I am sure his family would appreciate it," he said. "He was a good knight and he will be missed."

Grier could only shake her head in sorrow. It seemed like a costly raid, indeed. She pondered his loss as Dane went to remove what armor he was wearing, unbuckling leather strips that held on the pieces of plate.

Meanwhile, Grier pulled off her gown, stepping out of it and shoving it over against the wall so it was away from everything. There was a trail of flour along the floor where she'd pushed it along. Standing only in her shift now, she was still sadly pondering Syler's loss when she suddenly felt Dane's body up against her back.

Before she could say a word, his arms went around her torso and his mouth fixed to her neck. Grier gasped as bolts of excitement course through her veins, feeling Dane suckle on her tender neck, and instincts she never knew she had took over. Her mind may have been naïve, but her body was mature and womanly, and it had a taste of what it needed the night before. There was no hesitation, no resistance – once Dane's lips touched her slender neck, her body succumbed in an instant.

What it needed was Dane.

And he needed her as well. He'd come to their chamber with only the intention of speaking with her, but as he began to unfasten her from her gown, heated and lustful thoughts took over. He remembered her sweet body from the night before, how she seemed to be made for him and him alone. So much had happened that morning, so much he needed to reconcile but, at the moment, nothing was as important as the feel of Grier in his arms.

Perhaps, the need was as much emotional as physical.

Damn ap Madoc and his attempt to kill him. Damn the man for wanting what belonged to Dane – Grier belonged to him. Shrewsbury was secondary. Oh, so secondary. All that mattered to him at the moment was his wife, in his arms, her beautiful body responding to his. Spinning her around, Dane's mouth slanted over hers as his arms went around her tightly.

Grier submitted to the powerful kiss. She was quickly learning to crave the warmth and power that only his kiss could provide, and her arms went around his neck, holding him fast as the power of his kiss grew. He suckled her lower lip, plunging his tongue gently into her mouth as she responded timidly. She mimicked the movement of his tongue, the gentle licking, the sweet tasting. Her hands moved into his cropped hair, holding his head fast against her.

The passion was about to explode.

Dane could feel her delectable body pressing against him, pleased that she was responding to his touch. Sweeping her into his arms, he laid her upon the bed, one hand behind her head while his free hand removed her from her shift, pulling it up and over her head. Unfortunately, it tangled in her hair, and he apologized profusely, but she simply laughed at him and sat up in the bed. Together, they unwound her hair from the tangle, and eventually he pulled the entire thing off.

As Grier watched, he pulled off his sweaty tunic, leaving him clad only in his breeches. Her breathing began to quicken at the sight of his naked skin, tanned and smooth and glistening in the dim daylight. It was the first time she'd ever seen a man without his clothing on and it was a glorious sight. Dane winked at her as he moved to the edge of the bed and slipped off his breeches. Then, he was on her again in an instant.

His mouth went to her neck, suckling gently, pushing her back down on the bed. Grier closed her eyes and gave in to his onslaught as his mouth grew more insistent and his hands began to roam. One arm held her firmly around the waist as the other hand moved up her right arm, into her hair and back down onto her shoulder. He massaged her shoulder for a few moments as his mouth began to work across her jaw. He could feel her breathing growing strong and heavy beneath him, and it fed his lust. His hand moved away from her shoulder and down to her right breast.

Grier accepted his hand on her breast without resistance, feeling the gentle caress and knowing that she liked it. A sigh of pleasure escaped her lips as his caress grew firmer, kneading her gently. His other hand moved from her waist and gently cupped her left breast, and with both hands overflowing with her delicious bosom, his lips found hers.

Grier responded eagerly as his tongue delved deep into her mouth. He was squeezing her breasts gently, his fingers playing with her taut nipples. She heard soft gasps filling the air, hardly aware that they were her own. She could only submit as he continued his tender onslaught, feeling his hot, naked flesh against hers, his big body overwhelming her. When she instinctively parted her legs so that his weight would not crush her, Dane's desire moved to a higher level.

Leaving her gasping, his mouth left hers and blazed a trail down her neck and chest that ended up at her breasts. He took a peaked nipple in his mouth, suckling strongly as she writhed and bucked beneath him. Her movements were purely instinctive, a natural reaction to his body, and it only served to fuel his fervor. He was trying to go slowly with her; God knows, he was trying. But she was responding to him as if she knew what he wanted and it was driving him over the edge.

As one arm held her close, he continued to nurse at her full breasts as Grier's hands found their way into his hair. As he suckled, his free hand moved down her flat belly to the fluff of dark curls between her legs.

Now, he was where he wanted to be. He stroked her wet folds gently at first, listening to her pant, and it created a surge of hunger within him. As she writhed beneath him, he inserted his fingers into her, listening to her gasp loudly. Her knees instinctively came up, her legs parting to receive him, and Dane had all he could handle. Returning his lips to her delicious mouth, he placed his manhood at her threshold and carefully pushed his way into her.

Grier groaned as he thrust into her, emitting a softly strangled cry when he withdrew and thrust again, pushing deep inside her. She held on to him tightly, as he held tight to her, his arms wrapped around her slender body as his hips did the work. She was so slick that in little time, he was seated to the hilt.

It was the greatest pleasure he'd ever experienced.

Grier's hands were on Dane's face as he began to move within her, his careful strokes increasing in power and pace. She was so consumed with the feel and smell of him that she could think of little else. His body was creating a raging fire within her loins and she could feel his manroot moving in and out, a primal rhythm that she remembered from the night before, and one that had created the most wonderful sensations within her.

Soon, she began to mirror his actions, her hips grinding against his, sparks bursting every time their bodies would come together. The bursts of sparks grew stronger and brighter, and she began to actively search for that next contact, that next stroke, that finally brought about the explosion of thunder that rippled through her body. She cried out with the sheer joy of it as Dane thrust into her a few more times, with great pleasure, before spilling himself deep into her beautiful body.

The clap of thunder eventually faded but did not die completely. Grier lay beneath her husband, feeling his big body atop her with a satisfaction she could have never imagined. But her body was still so highly aroused that when he stroked her gently one last time, out of the sheer pleasure of being inside her, the thunder burst again and she experienced the thrill of another climax.

Dane felt her tremors and he clutched her buttocks against him, thrusting in and out of her slowly, deliciously, and feeling another release until they faded away completely. When the heavy breathing faded and the only sound filling the room was the soft crackle of the fire, Dane just lay there and stared at her.

Grier's eyes were closed, her lips parted as she dozed exhaustedly. He did not want to close his eyes, fearful of missing one moment of this rapture. He just wanted to look at her, struggling to process all of the thoughts rolling through his head. She was special to him already; whatever attraction they had between them had grown, and it was now becoming a powerful bond. To think of her having affection for another man was becoming more and more disturbing to him, and although he knew he should have asked her about ap Madoc before he took her to bed, the allure of her had been too strong.

It was still too strong.

Reaching over, he pulled her into his embrace, against his naked body.

But as he put his arms around her, his hands grasped her back and her flesh felt strange. As if she had ropes against her skin. Pulling back just as she started to open her eyes, he rolled her away from him so he could get a look at her back. What he saw caused him to sit bolt upright in bed and toss back the covers.

Grier's back was covered with scars, but not just any scars – long pieces of folded flesh, mostly between her shoulder blades, but fading off towards the bottom of her back. They weren't new scars, either; they were faded and smooth with time. When Grier realized what he was looking at, she tried desperately to pull the coverlet up to cover herself.

"Please," she begged. "Please... no..."

But Dane wouldn't let her cover the scars. Frankly, he was sickened by what he saw. "Who did this to you, Grier?" he demanded, his voice low with treat. "Tell me who did this."

She was beginning to tear up, trying to crawl away from him but he wouldn't let her. He held her down on the bed, looking at the scars.

"It does not matter," she whispered, tears popping from her eyes. "It was a long time ago."

He was trying very hard not to become enraged, but as he beheld the scars, he remembered something she'd said yesterday when she thought she was alone in the chapel. She had berated her father for sending her to St. Idloes, but there was something that stuck in his mind as he looked at her back...

The old witch who would beat young girls until they bled.

Now, he realized what had happened, part of the hellscape at St. Idloes that Grier had been subjected to. Some righteous bitch posing as a servant of God had done this to her, and there wasn't a damn thing Dane could do about it.

He was so angry that he was starting to grind his teeth.

"Please tell me who did this," he said, sounding calmer even though he didn't feel that way. "It is my right to know, as your husband."

Grier burst into soft tears. She was so ashamed that she couldn't even look at him. "When I was sent to St. Idloes at six years of age, I was frightened and unruly," she whispered. "The Mother Abbess at the time did not take kindly to my behavior. She would beat me until I stopped screaming for my mother."

Dane sighed faintly, closing his eyes against that horror. "How long did this go on?"

"I... I don't really know," she wept. "I learned very quickly that my tears brought the willow switch but, by then, the damage had been done. She beat me raw during my first weeks there and she would not let the other nuns tend me or any of the other girls she'd beaten. But one young nun helped me in secret. She cleaned my wounds and probably saved my life. She later became the Mother Abbess, Mother Mary Moria. She was one of the few who were kind to me."

Dane had been so focused on her scarred back that it took him a moment to realize that she was weeping softly. Shame and sorrow must have filled her at his notice of her scars, and he was repentant. He hadn't meant to upset her like that. Lying back down beside her, he wrapped his arms around her and held her tightly.

"I am sorry," he said. "For what you have had to endure, I am very sorry. Know that if those who did this to you were still alive, I would punish them and I do not care if they are women of the cloth. What that woman did to you was not right, Grier."

He was being so sweet and comforting, and Grier had never had anyone comfort her like that in her entire life. With Dane's arms around her, it was like she was protected from the entire world. Nothing could harm her as long as she stayed in that safe, warm haven. It was enough to ease her tears, and her hands came up, clutching at his arms as he held her.

"I know," she whispered. "It is one of the many reasons I cannot stomach my father. He did this to me."

He kissed the back of her head. "I do not blame you in the least," he murmured. "Although I had a great deal of respect for your father up until I met you, now that I am hearing how he treated you, I must admit that my respect for him is diminishing. I cannot believe such a man would be so cruel and ignorant of his own child."

With Dane's comforting presence, Grier's tears were fading. "He loved my mother," she said. "I thought he loved me until he sent me away. Mayhap he never loved me at all."

Dane gave her a gentle squeeze. "Dastan believes he could not stand the sight of you because you looked so much like your mother."

"I have been told I look like her."

"Then mayhap, it is not that your father didn't love you. I am not making excuses for the man but, mayhap, he simply couldn't stand to be reminded of the woman he'd loved and lost every time he looked at you. I can only imagine how I would feel if…"

He suddenly trailed off and Grier sensed that there was more he wanted to say but had held back for some reason. Turning her head to look at him, she could just see his chin.

"Finish what you were saying," she said. "You can only imagine how you would feel if…?"

Dane didn't want to say it. He didn't even want to think it. In fact, as he lay there with Grier in his arms, the whole situation with ap Madoc and the raid filled his mind until he could think of nothing else. He knew he couldn't rest until he clarified the situation with Grier, so he summoned his courage. It wasn't exactly a subject he wanted to bring up after having just made love to the woman, but it couldn't be helped.

He had to know.

"I was going to say that I can only imagine how I would feel if someone I loved was taken from me," he said, avoiding giving her a real answer. "I have never lost anyone I loved deeply."

Grier settled back in his arms. "Not even a parent?"

"Both of my parents are alive, thankfully, and the one who is not is of no consequence to me."

"Then you've not known great loss."

"Gratefully, I have not." He paused a moment, thinking on how to continue the conversation in the direction he needed it to go. "But I am sorry to say that Lady Laria and Lady Charlisa are knowing that pain today. Syler was a good knight and his death is a sorrowful thing for us all. We tried to trail his killers so that we could capture them and bring them to justice, but they evaded us. But I did capture one of them, and he had some interesting things to say."

Grier didn't sense anything out of the ordinary, not even the fact that he was discussing military business with her which, under normal circumstances, he would not have. But she didn't know that.

"Oh?" she said. "What did he say?"

Dane pressed his face into the back of her head for a moment, smelling her sweet, womanly scent, before continuing. Perhaps, he simply needed to fortify himself in case this conversation went terribly wrong.

Perhaps, he needed one last breath of what he could quite possibly lose.

"He said that a man named Davies ap Madoc had led the raid into Shrewsbury," he said. "That is the same man who offered for your hand in marriage, I believe."

He could feel Grier tense. Suddenly, she was rolling away from him, ending up on her stomach as she propped herself up on her elbows and looked at him. The expression on her face was wide with shock.

"How did you know that?" she gasped.

"It does not matter. Is it true?"

She hesitated a moment before nodding her head. "It is," she said. "He is Eolande's brother. When he would come to visit her on occasion, he saw me also. The next thing I realized, he is declaring his desire to marry me. He even sent his father to speak with my father about him, but my father refused."

It was a clear and honest answer. Dane sensed no subversion, which gave him immeasurable comfort, but he wasn't finished interrogating her.

"There was nothing between you two?" he asked. "You did not love him?"

She made a face, quite swiftly. "Davies? Not at all. He is a nice man, but there is nothing I could feel for him. There is nothing I *would* feel for him."

Dane considered that carefully. "Then his coming to Shrewsbury has nothing to do with some kind of bond you two share."

Grier shook her head emphatically. "Not at all," she said. "Anything he feels is purely in his own mind. I have never given him any encouragement."

Dane wasn't going to tell her how happy he was to hear that, but perhaps it was in his expression. He lay back on the pillow, staring up at the ceiling, as Grier watched him closely. Even though she didn't know Dane terribly well, at least not well enough to know his moods and behaviors, she was coming to sense something greatly troubling him.

That was obvious.

"Did... did Davies kill Syler?" she asked hesitantly. "Is that why you want to know if I have an attachment to Davies? I do not know him very well, Dane, and that is the truth. I could not tell you what he is thinking or what else he is planning to do. If I knew, I would surely tell you."

He looked over at her, reaching out to put a big hand on her head, which still had flour caked into it. There were chunks on the bed where her head had been.

"Shall I be honest with you?" he said. "I wanted to know if there was a love affair going on between you and him, enough so that he was coming to Shrewsbury to try and take you away. I wanted to know what I am dealing with. Did he kill Syler? More than likely, he did not personally kill him. But Syler was killed because ap Madoc believed he was me. He thought Syler was the new duke, and your husband, and he killed him."

Grier looked at him in horror. "He knows that we are married?"

Dane stroked her chestnut-colored hair. "When we stopped in Welshpool right after we were married, Willie inadvertently told some Welshmen that the Shrewsbury heiress had married the new duke," he said. "News travels quickly, especially when our lands are so close together. Ap Madoc must have come to Shrewsbury to exact vengeance on the man that married you. He was not aiming for Dane de Russe; he was aiming for the Duke of Shrewsbury, and I have no reason to believe that this will be the last time. I can only imagine he feels as if I have stolen something from him – you as well as the Shrewsbury titles."

Grier was beyond dismayed to hear it. "Nay," she breathed. "It… it cannot be. It cannot be! I never gave him any indication that I was receptive to anything about him. Why would he try to kill you?"

Dane could see that she was genuinely upset, which further proved to him that she was telling him the truth. He was a good judge of character, because his life as a knight depended upon that at times, and he could only sense blatant honesty from her. He hadn't meant to upset her so, but he felt it was necessary so he could get to the bottom of the situation he found himself in.

"As I said, he must feel that he was wrongfully cheated out of your hand and the Shrewsbury fortune," he said. "In any case, we must be very careful, you and I. You are not to stray outside of the castle walls for any reason. Do you understand? If ap Madoc is lurking in Shrewsbury and he were to somehow abduct you, I would have to burn down all of Wales until I found you. I would start a new war against Wales and not care in the least, so be prudent and be careful. Always tell me where you are going so that I know. That will give me peace of mind."

Grier listened to him with some surprise. What he was saying was quite strong, as if he already had feelings for her. It made her heart swell in a way she never knew it could, but in the same breath, she realized he was only saying it out of obligation. She was the Duchess of Shrewsbury and, as her husband, it would be his duty to save her should something happen. *'Tis only duty*, she thought to herself, *and nothing more.*

Somehow, that understanding hurt her tender heart.

"You need not worry," she said. "I will ensure you always know where I am. I would not worry you needlessly."

Dane could sense the depression in her words. Perhaps even disappointment. Suspecting he might know why, he sought to make himself clear. She was his wife, after all, and from what he saw, a woman of character and strength. He was willing to take the chance to share his feelings with her.

"Let me be plain," he said. "I would tear Wales apart looking for you not because I was obligated to, but because I wanted to. You belong to me now, Grier. I intend to keep you."

When she looked at him as if surprised by his words, he winked at her. That brought a grin from her.

"You... you want to?" she said, hoping she wasn't misreading him.

He nodded firmly. "I want to," he repeated. "Consequently, if some foolish wench were to abduct me, I should expect you to come after me because you wanted to, not because you were obligated to. There is a difference."

Grier was very solemn. "I would come after you and I would beat her to death," she declared. "I have never beaten anyone before, but I am a quick learner. I would learn very quickly what would cause her pain."

He liked that answer. "So you would come because you wanted to?"

She nodded, slowly, with great confidence. "I would, my lord."

Reaching out, he pulled her onto his chest, brushing a lock of that crusty hair from her eyes. "That's a good lass," he said, gazing into her lovely face. "That is what I wanted to hear."

Grier was feeling warm and tingly; she very much liked to be in his arms, their flesh touching. It made her feel giddy, as if she were about to lose her head. Just as she opened her mouth to speak, there was a knock on the door. Dane frowned deeply.

"Who comes?" he boomed.

A weak voice came from the other side of the bolted door. "Euphemia," she called. "I have a bath for my lady!"

Dane sighed heavily and looked at Grier. "I did tell her to get you a bath, after all," he said, tossing back the coverlets so he could climb out of bed. "I suppose I should be thankful she waited this long."

He rolled over Grier, playfully bouncing on her, and causing her to giggle uncontrollably. Then, he tickled her just to hear her squeal before he leapt out of bed and found his breeches. Grier caught a glimpse of his tight bare buttocks before he pulled the breeches up and secured them.

"I am coming," he called to Euphemia as he reached down and picked up his heavy, padded tunic. Heading for the door with it in his hand, he turned to see Grier still lying in bed, the coverlet now pulled back up to her neck. "Get up, love, and get your shift on. If you do not, they will know what we have been doing."

He shook his head, clucking his tongue as if they'd been very naughty, and Grier bolted up from the bed, searching quickly for her shift and finding it on the floor at the end of the bed. Dane paused by the door, waiting for her to pull it over her head, before he went to unbolt the panel. Opening the door, he ushered in a small army of servants with hot water and a tub.

Servants who were not deaf or blind. They more than likely figured out what their lord and lady had been doing, but they kept their heads down and efficiently went about their tasks as Grier smoothed the coverlet over the bed as if to cover up their activities. Dane had to shake his head at her, closing the barn door after the horse had escaped. It was like shouting to the room what they'd just been up to.

But they were idiots if they thought he'd leave his lovely young wife untouched.

Heading back over to the bed, Dane collected his mail coat, his plate, and his broadsword before heading for the door once more.

"I shall leave you to your bath, Lady de Russe," he said. "I have a few things to attend to, but I will return."

Grier followed him to the door. "Promise?" she asked softly.

He turned to look at her, seeing a warmth in her eyes that was deepening by the moment. Truth was, he had the very same warmth in his eyes when he looked at her. Whatever was happening between them was growing by leaps and bounds, and he wasn't sorry in the least.

Nor could he resist it.

"Promise," he said, bending over to kiss her on the nose. "I will return."

With that, he shut the door behind him, leaving Grier standing there as if in a daze. At the moment, she could only see, think, or feel

Dane, and she wasn't sorry in the least.

It was the most wonderful feeling in the world.

Euphemia had to call to her three times before she realized she was being addressed and, as the servants fled the chamber, Euphemia helped Grier into the tub and went about washing off the remnants of the flour that Dane hadn't kissed, caressed, or otherwise rubbed off of her nubile young body.

As Grier sat back in the tub and daydreamed, it was of a handsome young duke she was growing particularly fond of.

And of a Welsh warlord she was going to have to do something about.

CHAPTER FOURTEEN

THE MORNING AFTER the raid on the market dawned surprisingly bright and clear, with a blue sky bluer than anything Grier had ever seen. The birds were singing, the sun was shining, and all was right in her world. After another night of lovemaking and waking up in Dane's arms, surely there was nothing more beautiful than that. Grier was certain that there couldn't be a thing wrong, anywhere.

But there was one thing that was terribly wrong.

The death of Syler hung over Shrewsbury like a fog, and Grier could feel it the moment she stepped foot out of her chamber. Men seemed more subdued, and the mood in general was somber. After breaking her fast, she went on the hunt for Charlisa and found the woman in the chapel with Laria, praying over Syler's coffin. Laria was virtually inconsolable, sobbing over the brother she loved so dearly as the man's coffin sat near the altar, covered with a Shrewsbury bird of prey standard.

Heartsick for their grief, Grier prayed with the ladies for a time before leaving them to their own thoughts and prayers. They were family, after all, and she was not. She didn't want to intrude.

She tried not to feel guilty about being so happy while they were so sad.

Emerging into the day, Grier thought it would be best if she tried to assume Charlisa's chatelaine duties while the woman grieved her loss. Although she didn't know much about the day to day tasks, she figured that there was no time like the present for her to assume her rightful position.

Purely for a starting point, Grier went to the kitchens to speak to Alvie to see if the woman could help her determine what needed to be done. Alvie was quick to point out that the stores in the vaults beneath the keep needed to be inventoried for the coming winter, so that was Grier's first duty of the day. Already, the weather was turning colder, so it was time to decide what they needed to ration or replace to see them through the freezing months.

Grier caught on quickly to the process with the help of a clerk who used to serve the now-gone majordomo. Dolphus was his name, an older man with thinning hair and bad teeth, and he was the one who managed the vaults of Shrewsbury. He was also, oddly enough, the butcher. But he was a smart man, and able to read and write, so he carefully scratched out the list of what needed to be purchased or traded for before the bad weather set in and the marketplace in the town was mostly shut down.

The list gave Grier something to focus on and she felt important now, as if she were worthy of the duchess title. She had responsibilities and was, therefore, useful. When the duties in the vault were finished, Dolphus took her up to the entry level of the keep where there were four big chambers, including the duke's solar. Next to that cavernous room was the duchess' solar and private receiving room, something Grier hadn't recalled until Dolphus pointed them out. They were rooms her mother used to inhabit, rooms that Charlisa now used for her base as chatelaine of Shrewsbury.

They brought back memories.

The moment Grier entered the chambers, which needed updating and possibly a good cleaning, memories of her mother flooded her. She remembered the rooms but, in particular, she remembered the smell – the smell of pine. Her mother had loved the scent, and she would have pine needles and pine-scented oils dropped into her tallow candles, giving off that crisp, fresh smell. Pine was usually a man's scent but, to Grier, nothing reminded her of her mother more.

But they didn't smell like pine any longer, which was disappointing. Grier had so warmed to that memory. Because Charlisa has been using the chamber, it already had chairs and a writing desk, both of them elaborately carved and the wood darkly stained. Grier felt rather at home with the writing desk because, thanks to a rather strict regime at St. Idloes, she knew how to read and write, although the only things she'd ever read were bible verses and the only times she'd ever written were to copy those verses onto precious pieces of parchment if they happened to have them. More often than not, they scratched their lessons in the mud.

But at wealthy Shrewsbury, there was an abundance of parchment. It was in a writing box on the desk along with ink and quills, and as Grier looked at all of it, meant to aid the chatelaine of the castle in the accomplishment of her duties, a thought occurred to her.

It was the ink and parchment that gave Grier an idea.

The one thing in this beautiful new life that was troubling her, other than Syler's unfortunate death, was what Dane had told her the day before about Davies and his attempt to kill the duke. Increasingly, Grier knew she had to do something about it – and perhaps she was the *only* one who could do something about it – considering everything Davies was doing was because of her.

But what, exactly, she could do had evaded her until this moment.

With great thought, she'd processed the situation. She was fairly certain that Dane wouldn't let her travel to see Davies, and she was also certain that he wouldn't let her travel to St. Idloes to speak with Eolande to see if the woman knew anything about Davies' attacks. The basis for her desire to contact Davies was the very real fear that the man, at some point, might kill Dane.

She couldn't let that happen.

Three days as Dane's wife had opened up a world of such joy, of such ecstasy, that the mere thought of losing that slice of heaven brought Grier to tears. She had tasted true happiness and now she never wanted to be without it, and to be without Dane was a nightmare that she would do anything to prevent. If Davies was aiming for her husband, then she couldn't remain idle. She couldn't take the chance that Davies might hit his mark.

Therefore, the ink and parchment gave her an idea.

When Dolphus finally left her alone in the solar to go about his business, Grier sat down at the elaborate desk, pulling forth parchment and ink, sand and wax, and began to write out a missive to Eolande. Although it was true that she'd only written words where it pertained to copying biblical text for the most part, she still knew how to put the words together to form a sentence. St. Idloes was many things, but it was not ignorant in the education of their oblates, postulates, and nuns. They all knew how to read and write. Therefore, Grier put quill to paper and carefully etched out a message to Eolande asking the woman to summon Davies to St. Idloes because Grier was in want to speak with him.

And therein was another problem – how was she going to slip away from Shrewsbury to St. Idloes without Dane knowing?

Of course, it was impossible, but as Grier saw it, she had little choice. She didn't want to leave Dane; God only knew, she didn't. But she also didn't want to see him killed by a Welsh warlord. She had no idea why Davies should target Shrewsbury, or Dane – his offer of marriage had been over a year ago and she hadn't seen him since, so this resurgence of his interest in her and Shrewsbury was most unexpected. She had to get to the bottom of it and demand Davies leave her, and Dane, alone.

And Eolande was the only one who could help her.

Therefore, she crafted a missive in her rather artistic-looking handwriting, signing it only as Grier and not the Duchess of Shrewsbury. She could only hope that Eolande would help her, as she asked the woman to summon Davies and have him at St. Idloes in two days' time.

Her reasoning was simple – if she was to sneak out and leave Shrewsbury, and upset her husband, then she didn't want to drag it out. She wanted to get it done as quickly as possible.

With the missive finished, then came yet another problem – in order for any of this to work, she had to find someone to take the missive to St. Idloes, and there really wasn't anyone at Shrewsbury that she knew and completely trusted except for Dane, and the one person who had given her solid advice from the start.

Euphemia.

The old woman knew the roads and the land, certainly much better than Grier did. Having never been out of St. Idloes, Grier didn't even know how she got to Shrewsbury. Roads and directions had no meaning to her, but Euphemia, who had been living in the outside world all of her life, surely knew how to get to St. Idloes.

The plan was set.

Carefully, Grier folded the letter and heated the red wax stick over a candle, smearing on the flap of the letter to seal it. There was a seal in Charlisa's writing box, and once she pressed it into the hot wax, she could see that it was the Shrewsbury bird of prey.

Then, she summoned Euphemia.

The old servant wasn't long in coming. She knocked on the solar door as Grier was inspecting a shelf unit that was carved with babies' heads on the ends. Grier had been wandering all over the small solar, touching the walls and chairs, trying to remember where her mother might have sat or what she might have touched. But when the knock on the door came, Grier told the caller to enter and Euphemia appeared.

"Ye called for me, m'lady?" the old woman said.

Grier nodded. "Please close the door."

The servant did and politely stood next to the door, waiting patiently to hear the reason she had been summoned. Grier approached her, suddenly nervous; how could she make this sound important yet secretive? She had no experience in this kind of thing. All she knew was that she had to keep it from Dane because if he knew her intentions, surely he would stop her.

Quietly, she spoke.

"You must do something for me, Euphemia," she said.

The old woman nodded quickly. "Of course, m'lady. What can I do?"

Grier picked up the folded letter. "You can take this to St. Idloes," she said. "I would go myself, only I do not know the way and I cannot ask my husband for permission. He must not know about this, Euphemia. You must keep this secret and you are the only one I can trust."

The old woman's brow furrowed in confusion. "St. Idloes?" she repeated. "Ye... ye want me to *go* there?"

"Aye."

"But that is at least two days ride, m'lady."

Grier nodded. "I realize that," she said, feeling that Euphemia was going to refuse her. She had to make the woman understand. "But it is very important, Euphemia. My husband's life is at stake if I do not get this message to St. Idloes. That is the only way to save him. Will you not help me?"

Euphemia sensed that there was far more that she wasn't being told. She could see how distressed Grier was, so she reached out and took her by the hand.

"Come here, m'lady," she said as she led her over to a chair and gently pushed her down. "Sit down and be calm. Now, tell me why this message is so important? Why is yer husband's life in danger?"

Grier was growing upset. "There was a raid yesterday in town," she said. "The man that led that raid yesterday is trying to kill my husband. I know who he is and I must stop him, so you must take this message to St. Idloes for me. I have no one else I can ask."

Euphemia was more levelheaded than Grier, and still confused about the request, but she could see that it meant a great deal to her lady. But she was hesitant.

"How do ye want me to take it?" she asked. "Should I walk?"

Grier shook her head. "Nay," she said. "There are horses in the stable. Tell the stablemaster he has my permission to give you a horse. Tell him you must run an errand for me."

Euphemia could see that she wasn't going to be able to refuse the request. Even if she didn't want to go, she was sworn to the lady and essentially had little choice. It was her job to do whatever was asked of her but, in the same breath, she thought that the lady's request was bewildering and reckless. She wanted to stop someone from killing her husband, but surely no one could kill the man. He was a powerful knight, surrounded by other powerful knights.

And that made her hesitate.

She had seen the man and how he was with his men; they respected him. He was in full command of the army, a man who was admired by all in the short time he'd been at Shrewsbury. This woman he'd married, this naïve little waif, had only been out of the convent for three days, but the truth was that she had been in Wales for many years. Perhaps, there was more to her than a simple heiress who had become a duchess.

Perhaps, there was more to her than met the eye.

Euphemia was the suspicious sort. She'd survived all of these years being savvy and guarded. For her, it was all about money and self-protection. Coming to Shrewsbury to help the new duchess had been for the money; she knew she would receive the benefits of the position. But now, she was being asked to do something she hadn't expected and didn't like.

That was her suspicious side talking.

If she was caught with the missive, the lord would become angry at her for being in collusion with his wife. What if the woman was sending secrets to St. Idloes, secrets meant for the enemy? Euphemia couldn't be certain that wasn't the case. But looking at the lady's anxious face, she knew she had no choice, and she was frightened. Perhaps, her only choice was to flee back where she came from because, truly, she had no loyalty to the duchess. None at all. Her loyalty was to herself.

She didn't want to get caught up in any subversion against the duke.

"As ye wish," she finally said, eyeing Grier. "When do ye want me to go?"

Having no idea of the betrayal in Euphemia's mind, Grier was greatly relieved. "Today," she said. "This must go today. You must ride quickly, Euphemia. This just goes to Eolande at St. Idloes."

Euphemia nodded, averting her gaze, fearful that the lady would see what she was planning.

"I… I must gather my things, my lady," she said. "It will take me a moment to collect my cloak."

Grier nodded. "Get what you need," she said, handing Euphemia the folded letter. "Hurry, now; come back to me to tell me that you have delivered it and I shall pay you well."

That brought Euphemia around, just a little. "*How* well?"

Grier wasn't sure. She wasn't very good with monetary denominations, considering she'd never had to use them or calculate money of any kind.

"I am not sure," she said truthfully. "A few coins, at least. When you return, I will have it for you."

Euphemia simply nodded, eager to leave the solar, eager to leave Shrewsbury. The lure of "a few coins" wasn't enough to cause her to change her mind.

"Aye, m'lady," she mumbled, slipping out the door.

But Grier grasped her arm before she could get away completely. "Thank you, Euphemia," she said sincerely. "You will help me save my husband's life and I am very grateful."

Euphemia couldn't even respond. She simply wanted leave before the young duchess figured out that she wasn't going to deliver that letter, at least not to St. Idloes. But Euphemia did know who she was going to give it to.

A certain duke would be grateful for her loyalty in the end.

Rushing from the solar, Euphemia hurried to the top of the keep where the servants slept. Her meager possessions were there, and she grabbed them, all of them wrapped up in a shawl she'd brought along with her. Donning her heavy woolen cloak, the one with the big tear on the hem, she hurried from Shrewsbury's keep, praying that the duchess didn't try to stop her.

She had to get out of there.

The outer bailey of Shrewsbury was busy as it always was, and the great gatehouse was partially open as they admitted tradesmen and even farmers, bringing their wares around to the kitchens.

Euphemia had been aware of the raid the day before and she was surprised to see the gatehouse even partially open, but she was relieved. It meant that she could pass from the castle with those going in and out. No one would notice her.

But first, she had to find one of the duke's men.

The only knight she spotted with the duke's brother, a big man with a head of thick, dark hair. He was standing near the gatehouse, speaking to a soldier, and she approached him timidly.

"M'lord?" she said quietly. When he didn't respond because he didn't hear her, she raised her voice. "M'lord?"

Boden didn't realize an old woman was speaking to him until she called him a third time. Speaking to one of the senior sergeants, they were discussing putting more men on the gatehouse and he was annoyed that the conversation was interrupted. He frowned at the old servant.

"What do you want?" he asked.

Euphemia's gaze was dark beneath the cloak she wore over her head, concealing part of her face. "I am the duchess' servant, m'lord," she said. "Do you recognize me?"

Boden took a second look at the woman. "Aye," he said after a moment. "You came with us from Welshpool. Well? What is it?"

From the folds of her dirty cloak, Euphemia pulled out the carefully folded letter. "This is written by the duchess," she said. "You had better give it to the duke immediately."

Boden reached out and took the letter, eyeing it curiously. "What is it?"

Euphemia simply shook her head. "Give it to him," she said. "And be quick about it."

With that, she scooted away, losing herself in the light traffic that was passing through the gatehouse and leaving Boden standing there with a perplexed look on his face. The old woman disappeared and he looked to the letter in his hand, wondering where the old woman was going and why she'd given him this note.

Be quick about it, she'd said.

Somehow, Boden didn't like the sound of that.

His brother had been in the hall the last time he'd seen him, speaking to Dastan and William about Syler's death and the arrangements for him to be sent back to Wales. But that had been a while ago. Glancing at the keep as if to wonder what the duchess could have possibly written in a letter to her husband, Boden decided to take the old woman's advice and quickly go in search of his brother. Something told him that it was important. Finding Dane in the hall where he'd left him, he handed the man the letter and told him what the old servant had said about it.

Boden would never forget the expression on Dane's face when he read it.

As if the man had just seen the face of the devil.

CHAPTER FIFTEEN

GRIER HAD FOUND what she believed to be an old sewing box that used to belong to her mother.

On the many shelves of the ladies' solar, she came across the small box at the bottom of a shelf, buried behind small trinkets that were small carvings of animals. Little dogs and little ducks lined the shelves, blocking out the small box, and she sat on the floor in her newly-hemmed emerald gown, going through the sewing box with great reverence. Every pin, and even the faded spools of thread, had some kind of memory attached, memories that Grier had long pushed aside.

Looking at the things, she realized that she had, indeed, blocked out many of her memories about her mother. Perhaps, it had been out of self-protection, considering how she was beaten at St. Idloes when she had wept for her mother. Perhaps pushing those memories away had helped her survive the beatings. No crying meant no whipping. She began to think how truly sad it was for her to have been forced to forget her own mother, and her anger towards her father threatened to surge.

In truth, she wondered if she'd ever be able to forgive the man for what he'd done to her. In speaking with Dane the previous night, when he'd tried to explain away her father's behavior, she was coming to think that, perhaps, she should consider what her husband had said, that her father hadn't tried to be deliberately wicked to her more than he simply couldn't deal with the fact that she looked just like her mother.

Perhaps in time, she would come to believe that.

But more than thoughts of her father, thoughts of Dane filled her head. He had been so kind and gentle with her when he'd discovered the scars on her back. He hadn't shown any disgust, only concern. In fact, it seemed to strengthen his protectiveness over her, and the spools of thread ended up back in the box as Grier thought about the sweet words Dane had said to her the night before –

You belong to me now, Grier. I intend to keep you.

God, how those words made her heart swell. It was all she could do to keep her feet on the ground, knowing how Dane felt about her, and that made her want to protect him from Davies' madness all the more. She knew sending that missive to St. Idloes had been the right thing to do, for she was determined to convince Davies that any attacks against Dane would be met with her undying hatred.

In truth, she wondered if that would force him to cease. It was a foolish hope, but she had no greater leverage. If the man loved her as he said he did, then the thought of her hatred might cause him to re-think his efforts.

As she sat on the ground with the sewing box on her lap, she began to hear voices in the area outside of the solar. She could hear doors opening and closing, and one of them even slammed. She thought she heard Dane's voice, but she could not be sure. Just as she set the box aside and prepared to stand up, the solar door opened and Dane stood in the doorway, larger than life.

Grier's face lit up with a smile.

"Greetings, Husband," she said pleasantly. "See what I have found? This used to belong to my mother. It was right on this shelf and…"

The door to the solar suddenly slammed, violently, cutting her off. Startled, Grier looked into Dane's face and realized he wasn't smiling at her. There was no warmth in his pale eyes, nor was there any sign of kindness on his face. Concern filled her.

"What is the matter?" she asked. "Has something happened?"

Dane's face was pale and his jaw was ticking furiously. Suddenly, he was holding something up between them and it took Grier a moment to realize it was the letter she'd given to Euphemia.

"What is this?" Dane demanded through gritted teeth.

Grier's jaw dropped, shocked at what she was seeing. "Where did you get that?"

Dane exploded. "Answer me!"

He was bellowing, loud enough to rupture her eardrums. Fear swamped Grier, so much so that she felt faint with it. It was an effort to keep her wits about her. Carefully, she set the sewing box aside and rose to her feet, her attention never leaving Dane's enraged face.

"It is a letter to Eolande," she said, her voice trembling. "I am sorry you are angry. I did not wish to tell you because I knew you would not let me..."

He cut her off, harshly. "Because you wanted to send it in secret so I would not know." He pulled the parchment open, tearing it in his anger. "You want Eolande to summon Davies, the very man who attacked Shrewsbury. The very man I told you wants to kill me. Why do you want to see him, Grier? To feed him information about Shrewsbury? To tell him of my movements so the next time he tries to kill me, he will not fail?"

Grier was shocked at his badly misguided summation. "Of course not!" she cried. "I would never do such a thing!"

Dane's entire body was twitching with rage. "My God," he seethed, thinking that he clearly knew the truth. "And I believed everything you told me yesterday. I believed you when you told me there was nothing between the two of you. I'll give you a great compliment, woman – you are an accomplished liar because I believed everything you said."

Grier heart was in her throat, seeing the pain and anguish on his face. "But it was true, all of it! I would not lie to you!"

Dane tossed the parchment aside. In the same movement, he rushed to Grier and grabbed her by the arms, so forcefully that she yelped in pain. His big fingers dug into her tender arms, and his angry face, an inch in front of hers, was terrifying.

"But you did," he hissed. "I am wise to your ways now. Lie to me again and suffer the consequences. That raid yesterday was planned by you and ap Madoc."

"It wasn't!"

"Admit it!"

"Nay!" she screamed. He squeezed her arms tighter and she began to weep. "Dane, you are hurting me. Let me go!"

He didn't release her. He was so angry that it took all of his strength not to take it out on her, but he honestly couldn't lift a hand to her in violence. Not to her, not to any woman. He'd seen his father do it when he was a young lad and even then, he swore that he would never do the same thing.

Even if he was angry enough to kill.

"I will not let you go," he growled. "In fact, you are not going any-where, ever again. I will not take the chance that you will connect with ap Madoc and finally finish me off. What is in it for you, Grier? The wealth of Shrewsbury? Or is it that you will finally have your lover at your side?"

Grier began to fight him, trying to pull away from him. She was terrified and furious at the accusations.

"He is *not* my lover," she said, twisting in his grip. "I told you the truth last night. I care nothing for him and I never have!"

Dane shook her so hard that her head snapped, causing her to look at him with wide, shocked eyes. "Then *why* are you asking his sister to arrange a meeting?" he demanded. "Why would you do this right after a raid you deny knowing anything about? To tell him that he was unsuccessful in killing me, mayhap?"

Grier couldn't take his anger or his roughness. In a panic, she lashed out both feet, kicking at him, catching him in the knee enough to cause him to loosen his grip. When he faltered, she shoved him back by the chest and ended up breaking his grip completely. Stumbling over to the far side of the solar near the hearth, she grabbed the first thing she could, which happened to be the ash shovel. She held it up between them, wielding it in a threatening manner.

"I asked her to arrange a meeting to save your life," she cried. "I have told you the truth, my lord. Never have I lied to you. I swear to you upon my dear mother's grave that I have not lied to you. I wanted Eolande to arrange a meeting so I could tell Davies to leave you alone!"

"Syler is dead because of you."

"I did not do anything, I swear it!"

She was screaming at him by that point. Dane could have easily overpowered her and the ash shovel, but he didn't. He simply stood there, staring at his hysterical wife, so cut up inside that he could hardly breathe.

So shattered he could hardly think.

The letter, written by his wife, had asked Eolande to arrange a meeting between Grier and her brother, which Dane knew to be ap Madoc. In truth, there wasn't anything more in it than that – no real words of subversion, but the very fact that she'd tried to send the missive told him that she'd been lying to him about her relationship with ap Madoc.

Lying...

He felt as if he'd been blindsided, caught unaware, when he considered himself an astute man. He could hardly come to grips with that letter but, now, the raid yesterday made a good deal of sense. The Welshman who had offered for her hand had tried to kill him. Then Grier sent a missive asking the man's sister to arrange a meeting with her. How could he not believe the worst?

How could he not feel completely gutted?

But the truth was that he was angry at himself more than he was angry at Grier. He'd trusted a woman he hardly knew. God, they had such a lovely warmth between them, and his attraction to her was stronger than any attraction he'd ever known. She was sweet and kind and humorous... God, he loved her humor. He loved that silly little laugh she had, a laugh that had embedded itself deep into his heart.

Aye, his heart.

He loved her.

Perhaps, that was the bitterest thing of all. He couldn't remember when he hadn't loved her, and now this. Sending secret missives to a man who had once offered for her hand, but a man that Garreth had denied. Perhaps Garreth knew something Dane didn't when it came to his daughter and her relationship with the Welshman, enough to ensure ap Madoc didn't get his hands on the Shrewsbury wealth. And then he pledged Dane to his daughter, perhaps hoping Dane would protect Shrewsbury against the schemes of his daughter and her Welsh lover.

It all made so much sense now.

God's Bones, he'd been a fool.

"You will forgive me if I do not believe you," he said, suddenly quite calm where only moments before, he had been enraged. The light had gone out of his eyes when he looked at her. "Drop the shovel. I will not tell you again."

Hearing his cold words only made Grier weep harder. He could not, would not, believe her. At that moment, she didn't care what he did to her, so she tossed the shovel aside and collapsed on the floor, weeping into her hands.

"I wanted to tell Davies to stop his harassment," she sobbed. "I could not stand it if anything happened to you, my lord. It would destroy me in more ways than you could imagine, and I felt that if I could prevent it, I had to try. I was only trying to help. That was my sole motivation, I swear to God."

Her tears were creating cracks in Dane's hard façade, but he fought it. He couldn't let his guard down with her, not again. He'd already done that and it had left him open for betrayal and heartache.

Perhaps, that was what this was really about.

Heartache.

She'd hurt him.

Reaching down, he pulled her to her feet. Weakly, she tried to pull away, but he held her firm. With his weeping, shattered wife in his grip, he took her up to their chamber and put her in, locking the door from the outside and keeping the key.

The entire time, he didn't say a word to her. He didn't trust himself to, and Grier didn't try to speak with him, either. The last he saw of her, she was falling to the floor of their chamber, sobbing hysterically. It moved him; God only knew, it moved him. But he stayed strong. He wasn't going to fall for her softness and tears, not again. He'd already done that and she'd thanked him by betraying him.

Leaving Grier locked in their chamber, he went straight to the duke's solar and drank himself into a stupor.

CHAPTER SIXTEEN

St. Idloes

EOLANDE WAS IN shock. "You've *what?*" she gasped. "Davies, what did you do?"

Davies was quite calm as he faced his sister. "I told you," he said. "I killed the Duke of Shrewsbury."

It was beneath surprisingly sunny skies that the siblings faced one another, out in the same muddy area behind the chapel where male visitors were allowed. Eolande had been summoned that morning by one of the nuns who worked in the kitchen because Davies was standing at the old iron gate that led to the cloister, shouting for his sister.

Now she stood, wrapped up in a woolen shawl, facing her impatient brother and horrified with what she was hearing. She could hardly grasp it.

"So, you went to Shrewsbury, after all," Eolande said. "You said you wanted to see the man who married Grier, but you also spoke of challenging the marriage. Is that what you did? Is that how you killed him?"

Davies shook his head. "I did not challenge the marriage," he said. Then, he thrust up his chin in defiance. "We went to raid the market at Shrewsbury and when the duke rode from the castle to protect his town, we killed him. It is as simple as that."

Eolande's mouth popped open in shock, in outrage. "*Simple?*" she hissed. "You have murdered a man. And how do you know it was the duke? What certainty do you have?"

Davies would not let his sister stick holes in his victory. He was proud of it. "He rode from the castle, surrounded by his men," he said. "He rode a fine horse and wore fine armor, and he was protected by a small army. Of course it was him. Who else would it be?"

Eolande couldn't believe he was so blind. "It could have been another *Saesneg* knight," she pointed out. "They all come from wealthy homes. They all have fine horses, Davies."

"But they are not all protected by soldiers," Davies insisted before she'd even finished. "He was with many soldiers and we killed him, and I am not sorry for it. I am not sorry for the death of any *Saesneg.*"

He sounded so cold and Eolande shook her head. "You are not sorry for the death of the man who married Grier," she muttered, not surprised when he didn't deny it. "That is why you did this. All of your talk about our people starving and stealing from the *Saesneg* because we need to eat was only an excuse. You meant to kill Grier's husband all along."

Davies considered her words, thinking it made him sound like a calculating murderer, but he didn't care. He was not ashamed of his actions and, quite truthfully, she was right.

It had been his plan all along.

"I am going to Shrewsbury tomorrow," he said, avoiding addressing her accusation. "I am returning to pay a visit to Grier."

Eolande gasped. "What?" she said. "So soon?"

"Of course," he said. "And I want you to come with me."

"But why? I have no need to go to Shrewsbury. My home is here."

Davies reached out to take her cold hand. "You are dying here," he said simply. "You are nothing but bones, Eolande. They do not feed you. You have no future. Would you truly waste your life this way, like this?"

Eolande was upset by his words. Now, the focus was shifting to her and she didn't like it. "Papa sent me here for an education," she said. "It has become my home."

"And it has served its purpose," Davies stressed. "You have had your education and, now, you are slowly withering away. Come with me, Eolande. Come with me to Shrewsbury to see Grier and pay respects to her dead husband. Be present when I marry her."

Eolande was appalled. "Don't they know it was you who killed him?" she asked. "And you think to simply walk into Shrewsbury and marry Grier? You are mad!"

But Davies shook his head. "They do not know it was me," he said. "How could they? There were fifty of us. They cannot know that I was part of the raiding party."

"Then how will you explain knowing the duke was killed if you were not in the raiding party?"

That brought him pause. "I will simply say that I have heard," he said, thinking it sounded rather weak but he wasn't going to back down now. "News travels along the Marches. Do they truly think a raid, and the death of a duke, would not travel among the villages and towns nearby? Of course it would."

Eolande took a deep breath, shaking her head. "But you cannot be certain," she said. "I think what you are doing is dangerous. I fear for you."

There was the tender side of his sister, the one that made him love her so. Eolande was, if nothing else, caring and compassionate. He could see the fear in her expression.

"Do not fear for me," he said. "Be happy for me. I shall marry Grier, and you can live with us and have warmth and comfort, and all of the food you could ever want. Please, Eolande – will you not come with me?"

The way he made it sound, it was going to be difficult for Eolande to resist. Davies had all the answers, and the truth was that she was lonely since Grier left. She hated being cold and she hated being hungry but, unlike Grier, she'd never had a future waiting for her. She wasn't an heiress, and she had three brothers who would inherit the lordship of Godor. Unless she had a marriage offer, which there was no chance of at a convent, then Davies was correct – she would die here.

She didn't want to die here.

"But… but I cannot simply leave," she said after a moment.

"What is keeping you here?" he asked.

"Papa's honor," she pointed out. "He gave me over to St. Idloes for an education and, in return, I am expected to work for it. I was never to be a nun, Davies. You know that. At least, that was not the intention at the first, but now… this is all that I know. It is my home."

Davies grasped her with both hands. "But I will provide you with a better place," he insisted. "What is better than Shrewsbury Castle? You can live with Grier, and with me, and we shall be happy there."

It sounded like a wonderful life and Eolande could feel herself being swayed. To live with Grier all the rest of her life and, perhaps, even find a husband? There was nothing bad about the proposal that she could see except for the fact that her brother had just murdered the duke. If she accepted his invitation to live at Shrewsbury, somehow, she felt that would make her an accomplice in the man's death or, at the very least, signify her approval with it.

Turning, she glanced at St. Idloes behind her; the steeply pitched chapel roof, the cloister, the garden that hadn't produced anything for two years. Did she really want to remain here and starve when she could go to Shrewsbury with her brother and live in comfort?

It was not a difficult question.

She was tired of being cold and hungry.

"Davies," she said. "Your offer is generous, but you must know that I do not approve of what you've done. You killed a man who had done nothing to you other than marry the woman you wanted."

Davies lifted a dark eyebrow. "He is a *Saesneg*," he hissed at her. "How many of our *cymry* have they killed? None of them are innocent."

"Yet you want to marry one."

That stopped his rant and averted his gaze. "I do not see her that way," he said quietly. "She was in Wales when I first met her. I suppose... I suppose I have always considered her one of us."

"But she is not."

"She *will* be," he snapped, looking at her. "She will marry me and our children will be Welsh. There is no one to deny me now – no father, no duke, and no king. I shall marry her before Henry realizes what I have done and, by then, it will be too late. I will be Grier's husband and the Duke of Shrewsbury."

No matter what Eolande said, Davies would do as he wished. She had known from the beginning that his obsession was mostly with Grier. Shrewsbury had been secondary, but it was quite a prize and Davies knew it. There was nothing Eolande could say that would dissuade him from his goal, from going to Shrewsbury and claiming Grier.

Ironic, Eolande thought. Davies was perfectly willing to forget about Grier as long as she remained at St. Idloes as a nun, but the moment another man claimed her, Davies could not let it rest. If anyone was going to have Grier other than St. Idloes, then it would be him.

Now, the new Duke of Shrewsbury was dead because Davies couldn't let any man have Grier de Lara. Perhaps it was best that Eolande go with him into Shrewsbury, if only to keep him from doing anything too foolish. Having him go off alone seemed far too risky.

Her decision was made.

"When do you wish to leave?" she asked, sounding defeated.

Davies realized she was agreeing to go with him. "I told you that I want to be in Shrewsbury tomorrow," he said. "Leave with me now. Go collect your possessions. I will wait for you."

Eolande was hesitant. "I should like to say farewell. There are some that I shall miss."

Davies shook his head to that. "If you speak to anyone, they will make you stay. They will probably lock you in a room and keep you there. It is best if you do not tell anyone, Eolande. Promise me."

Eolande didn't like the idea, but she couldn't disagree with him. Mother Mary Moria could very well force her to remain, and if Eolande had to choose between the Mother Abbess and Grier, then she would choose Grier.

She wanted to see her friend.

Before the day had reached noon, Eolande joined her brother along the road to Welshpool, where his men were waiting. They were privy to Davies' plans also, and they were prepared when Davies and Eolande joined them. It was then that Eolande realized that her brother intended to enter Shrewsbury with his *teulu*, and have those men present with him at all times.

It was with a heavy heart that she understood her brother's intentions and she sincerely doubted that any of this was a good idea. But Davies seemed convinced that the duke was dead and there were no barriers between him and claiming Grier. He seemed convinced that he could enter Shrewsbury Castle and Grier would, perhaps, even welcome him. But only a day after the death of the duke and the raid on Shrewsbury, even Eolande could see that it was a foolish idea.

But Davies was blind to all else but Grier, so consumed for his want for her that he was jeopardizing his safety because of it, and Eolande knew it would be his undoing. Although she had never wielded a blade in her life, she was from a family of warriors. If she had to protect her brother by drawing a weapon, then so be it.

But damn the careless man for driving her to it.

CHAPTER SEVENTEEN

Shrewsbury Castle

GRIER DIDN'T THINK she'd slept at all.

It was dawn on the second day after the horrible scene with Dane and Grier found herself standing at the lancet window of the chamber she'd once shared with him, a chamber that had now become her prison. He'd locked her up and the only time she saw him after that was when he unlocked the door for the servants to bring her food, which she didn't eat.

Even now, the boiled mutton and other items of food from the night before sat near the door where they had been delivered, untouched. The mutton was like leather and everything else was either hard or stone-cold, making it particularly unappetizing. But it wasn't as if Grier had any inclination to touch it; she hadn't eaten anything in two days and she hadn't slept.

All she'd done was pray.

Weary and pale, she watched the sky as the sun began to rise, clutching her marriage brooch against her chest. She'd taken if off of her garment the day Dane locked her in and she hadn't let go of it. It was something Dane had given to her on the day of their wedding, along with the gold ring on her finger, and she clung to it as if that small bejeweled piece of metal was the last link to Dane.

She wasn't going to let it go.

God, how could she have been so stupid. It never occurred to her that Dane would consider her letter a sign of betrayal. Never, ever had that entered her mind. She had only been trying to help him, and for keeping it a secret, she was guilty. But that was the only thing she was guilty of – trying to help her husband by not telling him. Yet Dane thought she was sending messages to her Welsh lover, the one who had tried to kill him.

God... she was stupid.

The tears came again. It seemed to be a constant flow. She wept for the misunderstanding that was going to cost her everything, and for the shattered trust between her and her husband. She didn't blame Dane for thinking what he did; she knew it looked bad. And he must have gotten the letter from Euphemia, who was nowhere to be found. Perhaps she was locked away, too, somewhere, punished for her mistress' actions. Grier had no idea how Dane came across the letter, but she hoped Euphemia was well and hadn't been hurt in the process. The not knowing was eating her alive.

The master's chamber had several windows in it, three of which overlooked the inner bailey gatehouse as well as the outer bailey beyond. Grier could very nearly see all of the outer bailey from where she stood, and she could clearly see that men were assembling at this early morning hour.

A carriage had been brought out as well as a wagon. Perhaps it was an escort of some sort. Worse still, perhaps those two vehicles had nothing to do with the soldiers that were assembling. Perhaps, the Welsh raiders had returned. The mere thought nearly drove Grier mad with worry, so very worried that, somehow, Dane would be another target for the Welsh.

Worried that Davies had returned.

But there was nothing she could do about it. She'd tried and it had cost her everything. She had no idea what was going to happen to her now, if Dane was going to send her back to St. Idloes and forget he ever had a wife. Exhausted, unable to eat, and emotionally shattered, Grier kept the brooch clutched up against her chest because it was the only thing left from Dane.

She'd lost the man.

Turning away from the window, she wandered over to the hearth, which was dark and cold at this hour. Since Dane had locked her in, she hadn't let anyone in to tend it. She'd rather be cold. There was an iron bolt on the inside as well as the door lock, which could be locked from both sides and, as of last night after her supper was brought, she'd thrown the bolt from the inside. She didn't want anyone to come in, period. Frankly, she was content to starve to death at this point.

In truth, there was nothing to live for.

But it was dawn now and she expected her morning meal to be brought to her at any moment. Since the door was bolted, there was no way for anyone to get in. Sitting heavily before the black, sooty hearth, she was staring into the dark abyss of the fireplace when she heard a key in the lock. Someone, more than likely Dane, unlocked the door but when they went to open it, they found it bolted from the inside.

Predictably, that brought a confused pause. She heard someone try the lock again and, realizing the door was, indeed, unlocked, they tried the latch. The door didn't budge. They rattled the door slightly, a couple of times, and then stopped. There was silence for the longest time.

"Grier?" It was Dane, his voice muffled from the other side. "Unlock the door."

The sound of his voice brought tears to her eyes and she turned her head away, stifling the sobs. The door rattled again, stronger this time.

"Grier?" Dane said. "Open the door, I say."

Grier ignored him, at least for the moment. But she quickly realized that he wasn't going to go away. He'd shake the door again, and tell her to open the door, and then if she didn't, he'd probably kick the door in. Grier began to think that she should open the door if only to avoid having the door smashed and splinters all over the room. But the more she sat there and thought about it, about her situation, the more unstable and edgy she became.

Dane had locked her in like an animal. Perhaps, he expected her to act like one. Rising from the chair, and feeling woozy from lack of food, she made her way to the door.

"Go away," she said loudly. "I do not want your food, so you can return it to the kitchen. I do not need anything from you, so do me the courtesy of leaving me alone."

There were several seconds of silence on the other side of the door before she heard the reply.

"Unbolt the door, Grier," Dane said again. "I would speak with you."

The tears streamed down Grier's face as she leaned against the door, putting her hands onto as if to touch Dane on the other side. God, she missed him so badly, but she knew he only wanted to speak with her about what she'd done.

She didn't want to hear it.

"Nay," she said. "I will not unbolt it and I will not hear you tell me again how I have betrayed you. I have heard enough. I did not do it and I will go to my grave swearing that I have done nothing wrong. It is you who are a faithless soul, unwilling to believe a woman with true intentions and an even truer heart. You do not deserve me, Dane de Russe, so go away and leave me alone. I do not want to hear you and I do not want to see you. You locked me in here, and here I will stay for the rest of my life. Go away!"

She pounded on the door to punctuate the last two words, breaking down into sobs as she went back over to the chair by the hearth and collapsed in it, weeping. She half-expected him to kick the door down in his anger because she had refused his command, but he didn't. In fact, he didn't touch the door again. Grier didn't know how long she'd been sobbing when she realized there was dead silence on the other side of the door. As she'd asked, he'd gone away, and the realization of it hurt her more deeply than anything ever could.

God help her... he'd done as she'd asked.

... *gone.*

"I AM SORRY, Charlisa," Dane said. "Grier is still feeling terrible and is unable to come to bid you a farewell, but she told me to wish you a good journey. She shall see you when you return."

Standing in the cold, shadowed bailey as dawn broke, Charlisa was greatly concerned at Dane's words. Grier had been ill for a couple of days and she'd not been allowed to see the woman, per her own request according to Dane. The fact that she was still ill gave Charlisa pause.

"Then mayhap I should not leave," she said. "Dastan and Laria can take Syler home to for burial. If Lady de Russe is feeling poorly, then mayhap I am needed most here."

The escort to return Syler to Netherworld Castle, a two-day ride into Powys, was gathered in the outer bailey and preparing to depart. Netherworld Castle was an enclave of English amid the Welsh, and had been for over three hundred years. The House of de Poyer had never lost its *Saesneg* heritage and, strangely, had historically had very little trouble with its Welsh neighbors. Syler had grown up in that world, and it was to that world he would be returning.

But Dane was determined that the entire family should go, mostly because he didn't want them at Shrewsbury at the moment. They had no idea what had happened with Grier because he hadn't wanted to add to their burden. To know his wife had been part of the raid that had killed Syler would have been too much for them to deal with, and Dane simply didn't wish to burden them.

But that wasn't entirely true.

There was a greater part of him that didn't want the shame of having a traitor for a wife, so until he could decide how to deal with Grier, it was best to keep up the façade that she was simply ill and had taken to her bed. That was the story he would maintain. At the moment, he considered this a family problem, and a family problem it would remain.

"That is not necessary," he said after a moment. "I am here, as are Willie and Boden. We can accomplish whatever needs to be done, so do not worry. It is more important that you be with your family. Syler deserves that respect."

"Are you certain?"

"I am."

Charlisa looked to Dastan, who nodded his head to confirm Dane's words. It was their duty to take Syler home, so Charlisa relented. She wasn't happy about it, but she relented.

"Will you tell Lady de Russe that I will pray for her good health, then?" she said. "I am so very sorry I cannot bid her farewell in person."

Dane smiled weakly. "She is sorry, too," he said. "Godspeed, my lady. Safe travels."

With a bittersweet smile, Charlisa was forced to say her farewells to Dane and turn for the carriage as her husband moved in to help her climb into it. Dane stood back as Dastan and William helped both Charlisa and Laria into the fortified carriage, a wooden and iron cab built specifically to securely transport women and children.

It was a Shrewsbury cab, an older wagon that had spent all day yesterday with the wheelwright so he could fix the axles and shore up the wheels. It hadn't been used in a couple of decades, at least, but this morning, it was fresh and ready to traverse the bumpy roads to Wales.

Dane could only imagine that the cab, at one time, had transported Grier and her mother in days gone by. It was yet another thing to remind him of her. He watched Dastan secure the cab, silently observing as William went back to the flatbed wagon to ensure that Syler's coffin was secure. He tested the ropes one last time, which had been tested already by Dastan, Boden, and even Dane, all of them making sure Syler was secure for his final trip home.

As Dane's gaze lingered on the coffin, he couldn't help the guilt he felt, knowing how the man had died. Knowing that Grier had a hand in the man's death was something Dane didn't ever think he'd shake. He'd spent the past two days agonizing over it, alternately enraged at Grier and then wondering if he'd been unfair about it. She'd denied any involvement, swearing to God, and the truth was that Dane had some doubt. But the evidence was overwhelming, in his opinion. Even as the escort pulled out, and the fortified cab moved past him, followed by the wagon bearing Syler's coffin, all Dane could think about was Grier.

The entire situation had him in knots.

"How is your lady wife?"

The question came from Boden, who had walked up to stand beside him. Dane glanced at his brother.

"She is ill," he said.

"Have you at least sent for a physic?" Boden pressed. "It has been a couple of days, has it not? Mayhap, she needs to see a physic."

Dane simply shook his head. "She will heal."

That was all he said, but Boden knew he was lying. He knew something was wrong, although he didn't know what, exactly, it was.

Something serious was amiss.

Lady de Russe's mysterious affliction had started when Boden had handed Dane the letter that the old serving woman had given him, and he had been there when Dane had read it and then fled into the keep. In fact, he'd followed him. But once Dane had located Grier, he'd slammed the door in Boden's face and through the thick door, Boden hadn't been able to hear much of the conversation, but he had heard the tones – Dane's threatening growl and Grier's hysterical sobs.

Something was happening.

Boden had been very concerned, but he wasn't sure it was any of his business. If Dane had wanted him to know, he would have told him, so Boden reluctantly headed out of the keep, only to stop near the entry when the door to the duchess' solar flew open and Dane appeared, dragging Grier out by her wrist.

Grier had been weeping deeply as Dane continued to drag her up the stairs in a stone-cold manner that had shocked Boden. He'd never seen his brother behave so. Dane was always the congenial one, always the tactful one, so to see him treating his wife with such anger was completely out of character for him.

And no one had seen Lady de Russe since that unhappy incident.

Therefore, Boden was more solicitous than he usually was. Something was terribly wrong with Dane and he wanted to know what it was. As Dane began to walk away, William came up beside Boden.

"If the weather holds, they should make it in a less than two days," he said.

Boden's mind was still on Dane, his gaze lingering on his brother. "What are you talking about?"

"Dastan's party," William clarified. "If the weather holds, they should make good time. The roads are not too terrible this time of year."

Boden nodded, but his thoughts were clearly elsewhere. William peered at him. "What is wrong with you?" he demanded.

Boden looked at him, knowing he'd been distracted. He was torn between giving William a truthful answer or a benign lie. He settled for the truth. William may have been foolish, but he was a trustworthy fool, and a smart one.

Boden had no one else to turn to.

"I think we have a problem, Willie," he said quietly, his gaze lingering on Dane as the man made his way towards the keep.

William frowned. "What problem?"

Boden turned to him. "Swear to me this goes no further."

"I swear it."

Boden believed him, but he was still hesitant. It was difficult to put his concerns into words. He didn't want to sound like a worrisome old woman.

"Two days ago, I was at the gatehouse when I was approached by Lady de Russe's maid," he began. "You know the woman we picked up in Welshpool? The old cow with the yellow teeth? The woman handed me a letter that she said was written by the duchess. She told me to make all due haste to give it to Dane. Before I could question her further, she disappeared out of the gates and lost herself in the town. So, I went to find Dane and gave him the letter. The look on his face when he read it... Willie, I cannot describe it. I have never seen an expression like that in my entire life."

William was greatly intrigued. "What happened?"

Boden threw up a hand in exasperation. "He ran into the keep," he said. "He was hunting for Lady de Russe and when he found her, she was in one of the smaller solars. I think it is the one the chatelaine uses. As I went to follow him into the chamber, he slammed the door in my face and all I could hear was his threatening tone and Lady de Russe's sobs. The last I saw of her, Dane was dragging her up to their chamber, and no one has seen her for two days. Willie... I know Dane would never hurt the woman, but..."

William was beside himself with concern and dismay. "Of course he would not," he hissed. "But you must have some concern about it if you are so worried about all of this. Why would you ever think Dane could hurt a woman?"

Boden sighed heavily. "You would not know this, but Dane's father by blood was an abuser," he said, lowering his voice. "I have heard tale of him. Guy Stoneley was a bastard of a man. He beat Dane's mothers and aunts, from what I have been told, and did even worse things to them. He was a horrible excuse for a man, and he was alive until Dane was seven or eight years old. Until my father came into Dane's life, Guy was the only example Dane had. Although I cannot believe Dane would ever raise a hand to a woman, his father had that vicious streak in him. It is possible that Dane does, too, only he has never given in to it. What I saw... what I heard... with Lady de Russe concerns me greatly."

Now William was filled with the same apprehension riddling Boden. "What do we do?"

Boden glanced up at the keep, up at the windows of the very room where Lady de Russe was supposed to be. After a moment, he simply shook his head.

"I do not know what happened, but I do know that we cannot stand by if Lady de Russe is in need of help," he said. "I have been thinking to ask Dane what is amiss to see if I can help. Something is horribly wrong and if I can help, I want to. While I speak with Dane, mayhap you can slip into the keep and knock on the door of the master's chamber. See if Lady de Russe even answers you."

William's expression was full of anxiety. "And if she does not?"

Boden sighed heavily. "I do not know," he said. "Let me see if I can get to the bottom of this with Dane, but if I cannot, we may have to send for my father. I do not know what else to do."

William shook his head. "But your father is ill, Boden," he said. "Traveling will be very difficult for him."

"Then we send for your father," Boden said. "I will send for Uncle Matthew. And Trenton, too. Mayhap, Trenton can help if we cannot. He and Dane have always been extremely close. In any case, I intend to speak to Dane about it now. While I have him occupied, see if you can get an answer from Lady de Russe."

William nodded firmly. "I will."

"And do not let Dane know that I have told you any of this. It is best if he thinks you are ignorant."

William grinned that impish, flashy grin he was so famous for. "That will not be difficult. I am the ignorant sort."

"God only knows how true that is."

It looked as if it was about to turn into fisticuffs, as it so often did with the pair, but Boden broke down in snorts and William slapped him on the head in an affectionate gesture. Together, the two of them headed for the keep, anticipating what was to come between the Duke of Shrewsbury and his lady wife.

In truth, neither one of them was particularly eager to get at the truth.

But it had to be done.

CHAPTER EIGHTEEN

THE ALE WAS going down smoothly, as smoothly as anything Dane had ever imbibed. Ale that reminded him of Grier with every sip, every swallow, because he could only think of the night when drinking the ale in the hall had gotten her drunk.

That was when he'd seen how eager to please she was.

Grier had been trying so hard to make the men happy, to be a fitting tribute to the Shrewsbury name even if she hated the father she was representing. So much of the woman's life had been tragic, proven by the scars on her back and by her slender, starved body. Not that Dane had ever doubted those stories from her.

He wasn't sure why he couldn't bring himself to believe her now.

Perhaps, it was because this story involved another man.

Perhaps, that was the crux of it; he was jealous and he had no idea how to deal with it. He was sitting in Garreth's former solar, a solar that had always belonged to the duke since the time the keep was built. Dane sat back in his chair, looking at the paneled walls, the lavish furnishing, the precious glass in the windows. Generations of de Laras had sat in this very chair, conducting the business of Shrewsbury, building it into one of the most respected titles in England.

But the de Lara males had died out, and now it belonged to a de Russe. Dane very much wanted to be worthy of the position and he always believed he would be. But what he hadn't counted on was falling for the heiress, the very key to the entire dukedom.

He was glad that Dastan and Charlisa were gone. Dastan had been here for years and he didn't want the man to see his shame or witness his downfall. He wanted, and needed, the man's respect. He knew he wouldn't be able to keep up the charade of his wife's illness too much longer. People were going to start talking, and if she was still "ill" when Dastan and Charlisa returned, then Dane's credibility would surely be called into question.

Therefore, Dane needed to deal with this situation and deal with what his wife had done. He was thinking that he needed to send word to his father or his brother, Trenton. Perhaps, they could help him sort through all of this, for God only knew, he needed help.

A knock on the solar door roused him. He wasn't particularly interested in speaking to anyone, but before he could tell them to go away, Boden stepped into the chamber.

"Dane?" he said. "Might I have a word with you?"

Dane sighed heavily, motioning his brother in. "Come," he said. "Drink with me."

Boden came into the solar, with its fine leather chairs and expensive carpet all the way from Italy. He noticed the half-full pitcher of ale on Dane's table, reminding him that his brother had been drinking fairly heavily since the incident with his wife.

"What are you drinking?" he asked.

"Ale. What else?"

"Watered?"

"Of course not."

Boden shook his head. "It is a little early to be drinking ale that has not been watered or cut, don't you think?"

Dane's answer was to pour more into his cup, unhappy with what he perceived as criticism. "What do you want?"

Boden could already see this was going to be a difficult conversation and he braced himself. He was taller than Dane, and perhaps even stronger, but Dane was as fast as a cat and twice as deadly. He didn't want to get into a confrontation with him. Wrestling with William was one thing, but fighting Dane because he'd upset the man was entirely another. Therefore, he moved out of arm's length of Dane and into the man's line of sight. He had something to say and he was going to say it without fear of flying fists.

"Dane, I am concerned," he said.

"What about?"

"You," Boden said simply. "You and your wife. You will recall that I was the one who gave you the letter from your wife's servant, who has since disappeared. No one has seen the woman. And now your wife has not been seen since I gave you that letter and you are telling everyone she is ill. Dane, I am your brother. I love you and I am concerned with what has happened. Will you let me help you?"

Dane was staring off into the chamber, his gaze not really focusing on anything. Taking a long swig of ale, he wiped his mouth with the back of his hand.

"I appreciate your concern," he said, "but there is nothing you can do."

Boden didn't sense outright hostility, so he moved a little closer. "Dane," he hissed, trying to get his brother's rather distracted attention. "*What* has happened? Please tell me."

Dane looked up at Boden, who was looking at him with genuine concern in his eyes. Boden, who was headstrong and foolish at times, but an excellent knight. All of Dane's brothers were excellent knights, but Boden had in him something that, if brought out with experience and training, could be truly great.

That was why Dane had brought Boden to Shrewsbury – he believed in Boden's greatness – and it had been Boden who had been commanding the battlements and the outer bailey. He may have been young, for he was a full twelve years younger than Dane's forty years, but he was wise beyond those years.

He was also family. Dane was determined to keep his problem with

Grier to himself, but the ale was loosening his tongue. Perhaps if he confided in Boden, he would be keeping the issue with Grier in the family, and the man might help him see clearly in the situation. In truth, he had no one else he could turn to.

"I fear we have a traitor among us, Boden," he finally said. "I should not have trusted her."

Boden's brow furrowed. "Who?" he asked.

"Lady de Russe."

"Your wife?"

Dane nodded, looking at the table in front of him. It was cluttered with maps, parchment, an open writing box, and ink that was in danger of spilling. He shuffled a couple of things around until he came to a badly distorted piece of parchment, which he held up to his brother.

"Read it," he said simply.

Boden took it hesitantly, noticing that, when folded, it looked like the letter he'd given Dane, the one that was written by the duchess. Curious, Boden began to read, which he finished quickly because there wasn't much there. Truthfully, it didn't clarify the situation for him one bit.

"What is this?" he asked. "And who is Eolande?"

Dane was starting at his cup, deep in thought. "The sister of Davies ap Madoc, the same bastard who conducted the raid on the market-place three days ago. She is an oblate at St. Idloes."

Boden's brow furrowed. "Is *this* what your wife wrote?"

"Aye."

Boden looked back at the careful writing. "I don't understand. Why does she want to arrange a meeting with ap Madoc?"

It occurred to Dane that Boden knew nothing about ap Madoc's quest to marry Grier. Both he and Syler hadn't been present at the tavern in Welshpool when William and Dastan spoke of the subject, so he had no idea who Davies ap Madoc was, other than he was involved in the raid that took Syler's life. He sought to educate him so the man could see what he was seeing in the carefully scripted letters of that missive.

"Davies ap Madoc is part of Godor, a Welsh lordship that once belonged to Dafydd ap Gruffydd," he said. "The lords that rule over it are minor Welsh royalty. Their lands butt against the northern portion of Shrewsbury lands. Two years ago, Davies approached Garreth about a marriage to Grier but he was denied. When I asked my wife about it, she swore she had no feelings for the man, but the Welsh prisoner we interrogated told us that Davies had come to Shrewsbury not simply to raid the marketplace, but to kill the duke. According to the prisoner, Davies evidently believed he killed me when Syler fell. Is this making any sense to you so far?"

Boden hadn't heard the part about the marriage offer. He always seemed to be on the fringes when Dane was interrogating prisoners or dealing with important affairs. He was more of a follower than a leader, and lived under the assumption that if Dane wanted him to know anything, he would tell him. Now, he was telling him, and Boden was shocked, and he was starting to understand what had Dane so upset.

"Do you think that your wife has knowledge of the raid, then?" he asked, holding up the letter. "Is that why she is sending missives demanding to meet with ap Madoc?"

Dane sighed heavily, raking his fingers through his messy hair. "She swears that she has had no contact with the man for quite some time," he said. "She swears there is nothing between them and that in sending that letter to the man's sister, she wanted to meet with him to tell him to cease his harassment of me. She said that she thought she could help."

Boden watched his brother's features close. "But you do not believe her."

Dane didn't say anything for a moment. Then, he finally shook his head. "I do not know her," he said hoarsely. "The truth is that I have only been married to her for a short time. I do not *know* her. She says she only wanted to help me, but how do I know that is true? Boden, what would you think if you intercepted a message like that right after a raid that saw one of your men killed? What in God's name would *you* think?"

Boden swallowed hard. Looking down at the missive, he was genuinely trying to be objective about it. After a moment, he set the missive back on Dane's table and found the nearest chair, sinking heavily into it.

"I don't know," he finally said. "But she did not want to marry you. We all knew that."

Dane waved him off. "And I did not want to marry her, but that does not mean it was because I had a secret lover."

Boden looked at him, his dark gaze intense. "What did you do to her, Dane?"

Dane leaned back in his chair, weary and slightly tipsy. "She is locked in our chamber," he said. "I have not done anything to her. I simply locked her up until I could decide what's to be done."

"And what is to be done?"

"I do not know. I wish I did."

They fell silent for a moment, each man to his own thoughts. Boden had the advantage of not being emotionally involved in the situation; he knew that. He'd had limited contact with Lady de Russe but from what he'd seen, she didn't seem the subversive type. He had a feeling that he knew why Dane was so upset about this; he'd seen the man with his new wife. He'd seen the way he looked at her.

Like a man in love.

Matters of the heart were always the most painful.

"I know your wife even less than you do," he said after a moment. "But from what I have seen of her, she does not seem bitter or underhanded. I have heard that the kitchen servants adore her, and Lady du Reims seemed quite fond of her. The woman has been living in a convent all of these years and I do not think they teach them treachery or subversion there. If she knows ap Madoc and is trying to help you with the man, then mayhap you should believe her because, in all honesty, the letter does not seem a certainty of betrayal. The timing of it

KATHRYN LE VEQUE

is simply terrible. Mayhap, that is all your wife is really guilty of."

An unbiased view of the situation confused Dane even more, because after the rage and hurt had faded, that was exactly what he'd been thinking, too.

Was that possibly the truth?

"Then you think I have jumped to conclusions?" he asked.

Boden shrugged. "I do not know," he said truthfully. "Mayhap, you should interrogate your wife the way you interrogated the Welsh prisoner, for certainly, all I heard the day you were given the letter was a good deal of growling and weeping from behind closed doors. I cannot imagine that conversation with Lady de Russe was very productive. Did you give her a chance to explain?"

Dane shrugged. "I asked her," he said. "She... tried to explain."

"I am thinking that, mayhap, you did not really listen to her."

He was right. Dane sat up in his chair, thinking of his brother's advice and wondering why he couldn't have seen that. Leaning forward, he put his head in his hands.

"I am sure that I didn't," he mumbled. "Boden, I do not know how this has happened, but the woman has broken my heart. I thought I was quite immune to such things."

Boden wasn't surprised to hear that. It was the confirmation of what he'd suspected. "You fell in love with a woman who is your wife," he said. "That is something men hope for but seldom experience. You feel as if she has betrayed you, but I am willing to believe she has not. Dane, I have seen the way the woman looks at you. Any man should be so lucky for that. I cannot believe she has a lover somewhere, not from the way she looks at you."

Dane lifted his head, looking at him. "Then you think I was wrong?"

"I think you must calmly speak with her. Only then will you know for certain."

"I feel like such a fool."

"That is not something I usually hear from your lips."

216

Dane grinned weakly, looking at the pitcher of ale, the empty cup, and thinking he should probably sober up a bit before trying to speak with Grier. He didn't need the complication of alcohol twisting his already-heightened emotions.

"And it is not something you will hear again," he said. "Thank you, Boden. You are surprisingly wise when you are not wrestling with Willie."

Boden chuckled. "I will not let it go to my head," he said as he stood up from the chair. "If I can do anything more, I am happy to."

"You have done enough, Brother. You have my gratitude."

Boden gave him a smile before heading from the chamber, passing by Dane's chair and putting a hand on the man's shoulder. It was a strong, reassuring hand, and Dane was grateful. It gave him the confidence to do what he needed to do.

He had a wife to see.

HE'D LEFT THE door unlocked.

It was a thought that had very slowly occurred to Grier. After Dane had left her, it took some time to realize she hadn't heard the lock turn again. The sound of the big iron key in the lock was loud and distinctive, and she'd not heard it. That meant that the interior bolt she'd thrown was the only thing keeping that door locked.

If she opened the bolt, then the door, too, would open.

Wearily, Grier sat up in the chair she'd been curled in, thinking that rather than die in this chamber, she should simply return to St. Idloes.

Flee.

Remaining locked up in the keep of Shrewsbury like a prisoner for the rest of her life wasn't a better option than returning to the abbey where she'd been starved and beaten. In truth, she had a routine there, and it was the only thing she'd known, so the few days she'd spent as the Duchess of Shrewsbury would surely be forgotten, in time. It had been the glimpse of a life she was never meant to have.

She had to get away.

Looking around the well-appointed bower, she thought quickly on what she could take with her. The woolens she'd worn from the abbey were gone; after she'd vomited all over them, she had no idea what had happened to them, only that they'd been taken away. Dane had purchased four dresses for her, all beautiful and fine things, but the only one that wasn't an expensive feast for the eyes was a linen dress that she hadn't worn yet. It was plain enough, and she had to have something to wear.

She didn't want Dane thinking she'd taken the most expensive things he'd given her.

Quickly, she changed into the linen gown, which was too long for her, just like the others were. Because the shoes she'd worn from the abbey were in tatters, she did have to wear the solid leather slippers Dane had purchased for her, but that would be all. She had a shawl she'd brought with her, which had wrapped up her meager belongings of a comb and a clean shift, so she found the shawl and her shift where Euphemia had put them in the wardrobe. That was what she had come with and it was what she would leave with.

As she wrapped her possessions up in the shawl, her gaze fell on the table near the bed. The marriage brooch was sitting there, in one of the rare times she set it down, and all of her rapid movements came to a halt when she saw it.

Seeing that beautiful brooch was like a dagger to her heart.

A modest wife knows a chaste bed.

With a heavy sigh, she went to look at it. Not touch it; *look*. She wasn't going to touch it again. Dane had given it to her on the event of their marriage, but the relationship they were building was gone. Hanging on to it as if it were the last vestiges of something she had lost was foolish. The truth was that it reminded her of Dane, and she wasn't going to keep something that reminded her of the man she loved and lost through a mistake she'd made.

In fact, she slipped the gold wedding band from her finger and set it next to the wedding brooch. She knew everything was her fault, but it was made worse by the fact that Dane simply wouldn't listen to her. He'd made up his mind that she was a traitor the moment he saw the letter.

She couldn't fight a man's preconceived perception.

She was going to return to St. Idloes and never look back.

Grabbing her belongings, Grier headed to the chamber door, noticing the stone-cold food still on the tray next to it. She hadn't eaten in three days, so she grabbed the stale bread and the dried-out cheese, stuffing them into her mouth. She wasn't sure when she would eat again, so she broke the bread in two, eating one half and stuffing the second half into her belongings. The bread was so hard she nearly broke her teeth, but she had to get something into her stomach.

She had a long trip ahead of her.

Very quietly, she opened the chamber door, peering out into the corridor and half-expecting to see a guard there. But there was no one in the dark, cold corridor, and she took a few timid steps outside, looking for any sign of anyone who might try and stop her. The corridor remained still and dark, so she quickly closed the door behind her and made her way to the end of it only to hear footfalls on the staircase that led up to that level.

Someone was coming. In a panic, she thought to run back to her chamber, but she would have been seen, so she pressed into the shadows of the nearest doorjamb just in time for William to walk past her.

He didn't see her hiding in the darkness as he continued on to the master's chamber door and began to knock. Startled, and thinking he'd come for her, Grier bolted out of her hiding place and raced down the steps, hearing William as he called to her through the closed chamber door. He was calling her name. She continued to run from the keep, running outside into the cool November sunlight, rushing to the inner bailey gatehouse and ignoring the guards there.

They let her run past.

Across the bridge that spanned the moat encircling the inner bailey and the keep, she continued into the outer bailey. It was full of people, as it usually was, but Grier didn't make eye contact with anyone. She was terrified Boden or William or Dastan might see her and stop her; it was imperative she get through the gatehouse unimpeded. Once through, she was hoping she could lose herself in the town and find her way to the road to St. Idloes. She wasn't afraid to ask for directions, but she was afraid of what would happen when Dane realized she was gone.

He would probably think she'd run straight into the arms of the enemy

If he thought she was sending Davies a letter to conspire with him, then surely he would think running from the castle was a solid indication of her guilt. She wasn't entirely sure he would come for her, to be truthful, because if he was angry enough, perhaps he'd be pleased to be rid of her. On the other hand, she *was* his wife. It was possible that he viewed her as a possession, and he would want to reclaim that possession.

Grier couldn't be sure that he wouldn't come for her, so she began to re-think her destination of St. Idloes. If he came for her there, she could only imagine that Mother Mary Moria would turn her over to him. He was her husband, after all, and she was his property. She would be back where she started.

With that thought on her mind, she thought it would be best to lose herself in any number of the villages in England or Wales, and, perhaps, even find work as a seamstress. She could even work in a tavern, serving food and cleaning. She'd never done it before, but surely it couldn't be too difficult. She could learn. As she pondered what the dismal future held for her, she was nearing the gatehouse. Just a few more yards and she would be free and clear of Shrewsbury castle, and free of Dane and his anger.

It was difficult to take those few last steps, but she knew this was for the best.

... wasn't it?

Wiping at the tears that were leaking from her eyes, she nearly crashed into a man coming through the gatehouse. Startled, she looked up to see more men coming through, and one man in particular that she recognized.

And one woman, too.

Startled at the sight, she came to a halt, hardly able to believe her eyes. But in the same breath, she knew if the man she recognized had come to Shrewsbury, it would mean death for Dane. Bold as sin, he was walking in through the gates, looking for his victim.

In her last effort to protect the man, she began to scream.

After that, everything turned to panic.

CHAPTER NINETEEN

"DAVIES!" GRIER SHRIEKED. "My God... *no!*"

The sight of Davies and Eolande entering Shrewsbury threw Grier into a fit of terror. There were sentries at the gatehouse, many of them, but they didn't seem to be stopping the Welsh who were entering the gate, so she screamed at them that the enemy was on their doorstep and, dumbfounded, they looked at the woman as if she'd lost her mind. But Grier's screaming set off a series of events that would throw all of Shrewsbury into jeopardy.

The Welsh had arrived.

Davies and his men, hearing the screaming and seeing that they were being singled out, began to remove daggers. When the English saw the weapons, they drew weapons of their own. Two gate sentries were stabbed right away, but the English were swift and they were many; swords came out and they began rushing Davies and his men, who were half-in and half-out of the gatehouse. A brawl broke out as the portcullis shuddered, unable to close because there were English as well as Welsh in the way. More English soldiers poured down off of the walls, and somewhere above it all, the Shrewsbury battle horn sounded.

That shrill, mournful cry of battle.

The sound of the horn brought a tide of heavily-armed men rushing from the barracks near the stables. Up at the inner bailey gatehouse, the men on guard dropped the portcullis immediately. But William was just coming out of the keep and he ordered the portcullis raised so he could get through, and he did when it was about two feet off the ground. It was dropped again just as he slipped through and rushed to the outer bailey to see what was amiss. All over Shrewsbury, protocols were put in place as if the castle was being attacked, for surely, when the battle horn sounded, all was not well.

But Grier didn't see any of what was going on around her; all she saw was Davies, with Eolande in his grip, and Eolande was hysterical with fear. Grier's only thought was to help the woman, for she had no idea why she was with Davies, so she rushed forward to pull Eolande from Davies' grasp, but the man saw her coming.

His tactics changed.

Davies was trying to fend off a Shrewsbury soldier and protect his sister at the same time. But when he saw Grier rushing towards them, he knew what would stop this skirmish in a flash. He knew what would subdue the *Saesneg* soldiers, better or faster than anything he could ever use against them...

A woman.

As Grier came near, Davies let go of Eolande, shoved her aside, and grabbed Grier instead. In an instant, Grier found herself pulled up against Davies with a dagger pressed to her throat.

"Make another move against me and my men, and I shall kill her!" Davies bellowed. "Drop your weapons! Everyone – drop your weapons!"

As all of this was going on, William raced upon a devastating scene. He had no idea what was happening, but he could see Grier in the grip of a dark-haired man he didn't recognize with a dagger to her throat. He began bellowing to his men to cease their fighting, but he countered Davies' command that all weapons should be dropped. Men retained their weapons, forming a nervous barrier around the gatehouse so the enemy couldn't penetrate further into the castle.

The lines were now drawn.

In truth, no one really knew what was happening. Lady de Russe had started shouting and a group of men at the gatehouse produced weapons, and it had escalated from there. But now, William and some of the senior sergeants were trying to calm down the rank and file so that Lady de Russe wouldn't get a blade through her throat and bleed to death right in front of them.

"Be calm," William said, stepping away from the jostling English soldiers to catch the attention of the man who held Grier. "Be calm and listen to me. If you hurt Lady de Russe, you will not make it out of here alive, not you or any of those you brought with you. Release her unharmed and my men will make no move against you."

In Davies' grip, Grier was furious as well as terrified. She heard William's words, but she was more focused on Davies as he pressed a knife against her throat.

"Let me go," she tried to fight against him and not stab herself in the process. "How dare you return after what you did yesterday? Did you think to sneak in here and finish what you started? Did you think that I would not see you and know of your guilt?"

Davies held tight to Grier, his mind whirling. What was she talking about? *Did you think to finish what you started?* He wasn't sure what she meant, though he could guess. Somehow, someway, she knew that he had been part of the raid in the marketplace and his heart sank.

If she knew, then others knew.

This is not what he had expected when he came through the gates but, unfortunately, this was what he'd gotten himself in to. Eolande had tried to warn him, but he would not listen to a mere woman.

Could nothing ever go as he had planned?

"Be still," he told Grier sharply. "I have not come here to harm you, but you have called out your men on me. Tell them to back away."

Grier was enraged. "Of course you have come to harm me!" she spat. "You tried to kill my husband yesterday, and now you've come back to finish the job. I will not let you do it, do you hear? I will kill you myself before I allow you to harm him!"

Shocked at what she was saying, Davies didn't have a fast reply because it confirmed what he'd suspected. *She knows!* He thought desperately. As he tried to come up with something to say, Eolande came out from behind some men who were protecting her. Standing near her brother, she was a trembling mess. There were too many weapons and too many men, and she wasn't accustomed to any of it.

"Grier," she gasped. "Please tell your men not to harm Davies. Please!"

Grier couldn't see Eolande, but she certainly heard her. "Why are you here?" she asked, trying to twist her head around. "Do you know what Davies has done?"

"I know," Eolande said, tears brimming because she was so frightened. "Oh, Grier... please, tell your men to back away. Please don't let them kill my brother!"

Grier could hear the terror in Eolande's voice and she was greatly confused. All Eolande seemed concerned with was Davies, a man who had tried to murder Dane. She hadn't even answered Grier's question as to why she'd come to Shrewsbury. Had she come to help her brother, knowing Grier hadn't wanted to marry the Duke of Shrewsbury in the first place?

Grier didn't know, and anger and bewilderment made strange bedfellows in her heart as she considered the situation. The only thing missing was Dane, and she wasn't sure where he was. He was lurking about, somewhere, but she was certain he'd heard the Shrewsbury horn.

There was no mistaking it.

Now, they were all crowded at the gatehouse, two warring factions, with William trying to calm the situation. He was a lone knight against something that was far more volatile than he realized.

As Grier's eyes roamed the crowd, she finally fixed on what she had been looking for and the relief she felt was palpable. Pushing through the heavily-armed English soldiers, of which there were many, Dane's handsome features came into view. He was followed by Boden, and the two of them pushed men aside until they were standing within a few feet of Grier and Davies.

The sight of the man brought tears to Grier's eyes.

She had been in control until she saw Dane but, now, knowing the personal situation between them, and knowing she was now in the arms of the man Dane had accused her of being loyal to, she knew that whatever fragments of hope there might have been for Dane to believe her story were understandably gone now. Davies was here, and she was with him.

She knew how bad it must look.

But she couldn't give up.

Her life was on the line, in more ways than she could imagine.

DANE HAD STILL been with Boden in the Duke's solar when he heard the blast of the Shrewsbury horn.

Tipsy or not, the sound had launched Dane out of his seat and, with his brother on his heels, he flew from the keep only to be met by a closed portcullis to the inner gatehouse. Boden started screaming at the sentries, who cranked the portcullis up enough so that Dane and Boden could bolt beneath it.

On a dead run, they made their way to a large group of men and weaponry near the gatehouse. They could hear William yelling above the melee, but there was a fight of some kind going on and the portcullis of the main gatehouse was still open, though about halfway lowered. Dane couldn't imagine what was going on until he began to push through the gathered men, all of them armed, all of them edgy as hell. They were fixed on a group of men in the gatehouse entry, and that's why Dane saw it.

Grier was a hostage.

Dane had to steel himself. His first instinct was to run mad and kill the bastard with his bare hands, but the truth was that if he tried to do that, Grier would probably be dead before he could even get to her.

Therefore, he forced himself to calm, knowing he had little choice at the moment. He had to draw upon his training, upon his innate sense of composure, if he was going to get through this. He had no idea what had happened but, clearly, it was something very bad.

Heart pounding, Dane pushed through his troops before he could clearly see Grier in the grip of a shaggy-haired man.

He took a deep breath.

"Why do you hold my wife hostage?" he asked the man with the blade to Grier's neck. "Who are you?"

The man's eyes widened. "You… your *wife*?"

Dane nodded. "I am Dane de Russe, Duke of Shrewsbury," he said calmly. "The woman you are holding is my wife. How can we resolve this situation?"

After a moment's shock, the man seemed to grow more agitated. He was looking at Dane as if he could hardly believe what he'd heard.

"Nay," he finally breathed. "The duke is dead! He was killed!"

That was what the prisoner in the vault had said, so Dane proceeded carefully. There were a great many Welshmen who evidently thought he was dead and even as he asked his next question, he had an inkling of what the answer was.

"May I know your name?"

The man hesitated and, in that moment, Grier spoke. "Davies ap Madoc," she said, her voice quivering. "This is Davies ap Madoc and the woman with him is his sister, Eolande."

At the mention of her name, Eolande took another timid step towards her brother and Grier. "Please, Grier," she begged. "Tell these men to go away. Tell them go away to ease the situation!"

She was begging for Davies' life again, and that further upset Grier. Was the woman truly defending her brother, someone who was holding a knife to a woman she called a friend? Rather than stew in confused silence about it, she spoke up. She found that she couldn't remain silent any longer.

Too many things about Eolande's appearance didn't make any

sense, so for her own peace of mind, she had to know.

"*Why* are you here, Eolande?" she demanded, trying to look at her friend as Davies held her fast. "Do you know what your brother has done? He raided the town and killed a very fine knight, a man he believed to be my husband. He is a killer and now he has returned to finish the job. Did you know that?"

Eolande burst into tears. "I know," she sobbed. "I told him I did not approve of what he had done. But he did it... he did it because you married the duke, Grier."

"Shut your mouth!" Davies hissed.

"Nay!" Eolande cried. "I will not be silenced! You were not man enough to accept that Grier married another, so you came to kill a man you did not even know, to punish him for what you believed to be an offense against you. Now you hold Grier as if to kill her, and that is wrong, Davies. You cannot kill the woman because she never loved you!"

"I can do what I please!"

"You cannot force her to love you, not with all of the deaths and havoc you can create. Don't you know that?"

They were shouting back and forth, and Dane was listening to all of it, realizing a great deal as the pale, poorly-dressed, sobbing woman and the shaggy-haired man barked at each other. It was more of an explanation than he could have hoped for, because the poorly-dressed woman had no stake in this. She didn't know Dane, so she wasn't speaking to somehow vindicate Grier. Even so, she had unknowingly done precisely that. She'd put Dane on the path to understanding.

You cannot kill the woman because she never loved you.

Those were the most beautiful words he'd ever heard.

"You are the man who killed Syler de Poyer," Dane said, his gaze riveted to Davies as he interrupted the shouting going on. "I will say his name again; Syler de Poyer. He was a great knight and a fine man, and you stole his life away for something he had nothing to do with. It was me you wanted. I was told that you offered for my wife's hand and that her father denied you."

Davies was very close to losing his composure. He stared at Dane, appalled at what he was hearing. This man, this new duke who had married Grier, knew so much about him. That shook him to the bone.

"How do you know such things?" he demanded. "I do not know you. I have never heard of you, de Russe."

Dane lifted a blond eyebrow. "But I have heard of you," he said. "I heard of you through some Welshmen at a tavern after I had married my wife. I also heard of you from one of the raiders we captured yesterday, a young warrior who is even now locked up in my vault. And I also know of you from my wife, who was gracious enough to be truthful with me when I asked. Aye, I know a good deal about you, ap Madoc. Release my wife and we shall speak calmly."

I also heard about you from one of the raiders we captured yesterday. Davies' heart sank when he heard that. In truth, that hadn't occurred to him. He was furious at himself for being arrogant enough to think that all of his men from the raid had escaped Shrewsbury.

There had been fifty of them, but only forty-three had been accounted for, which wasn't unusual. Sometimes it took a few days for all of the men to show up and be counted, and Davies hadn't waited to find out, and he hadn't given the fact that he hadn't waited any thought. But he should have.

God, he should have.

Now, he was in trouble.

"You know nothing about me," he growled. "It was my offer for Grier that should have been considered. It should be me living in the castle now and not you. Who are you, anyway? You are no one. You know nothing of Wales and of Shrewsbury, and of our lives here on the Marches. *You are no one!*"

He was shouting by the time he finished, and Dane could hear the desperation in the man's voice.

"My father is the Duke of Warminster," Dane said. "I also hold the title of Lord Blackmore, of Blackmore Castle. Surely you know of it.

Who I am? The son of a duke, and now a duke myself, and I know and love these lands. They are mine. So is the woman in your grasp. Return her to me unscathed and I will show mercy. Harm her and you shall feel pain such as you cannot comprehend."

It was a threat, pure and simple. Davies knew it, but he wouldn't surrender, at least not yet. His pride prevented it.

"I hold the power, *duw*," he said, using the Welsh word for duke. "I hold the woman we both want. You will listen to me."

Dane remained calm. "I will listen."

"Nay!"

Grier suddenly piped up. She'd been listening to everything, terror in her veins, but she wasn't going to remain silent any longer. She wasn't entirely certain Davies wouldn't kill her and if he did, she didn't want to die without speaking the truth of the situation. She had to give it one more try, even if Dane wouldn't believe her.

Her heart was crying out to make things right if this was the last moment they would have.

"If I am to have my throat slit, then you will hear me, Davies ap Madoc," she said, tears forming in her eyes. "Never have I given you hope that I return your feelings. Never did I say I wished to be your bride, or that I wished to belong to you. We were never lovers and we never will be, for I would rather die than be part of anything with you. Do you understand me? I used to feel pity for you, because you felt for me the way I did not feel for you, but now I hate you. I hate you with everything that I am."

Davies could feel her heaving against him, the emotion in her body, and he was feeling increasingly ashamed. He'd come to Shrewsbury, hoping to claim her, hoping to secure a marriage with a new widow, and she was telling everyone who would listen that she hated him. She wanted no part of him. When he spoke, his voice was low, because he certainly didn't want to shout a reply. There were enough ears listening to his humiliation.

"Quiet, now," he told her. "You are distraught. I did not wish to…"

She cut him off, trying to jerk away from him and piercing her own neck with his dagger tip in the process. She gasped in pain, her hand going to her neck as the blood began to flow.

"Release me," she said in a tone between a plea and a demand. "I have never loved you, Davies. You know this. Your own sister has told you this. Eolande, can you hear me? Tell him!"

Eolande was just out of her line of sight, still trembling, still weeping. She heard her friend's plea and had no choice but to answer her.

"I have told him, Grier," she said. "He does not want to listen. He thinks he can make you love him."

"I can!" Davies boomed, realizing he had shouted and suddenly embarrassed because of it. His personal business was being shouted for all to hear and he was greatly ashamed in a situation that was completely out of his control. "You have never given me the chance."

"I *will* never give you the chance," Grier said, now trying to stomp on his feet so he would release her. "Let me go, you blackheart. Let me go this instant!"

She stomped hard enough that she hit something tender, and Davies faltered. Dane flinched, prepared to move forward and grab his wife, but Davies saw him coming and he grabbed Grier by the hair, holding the long side of the dagger against her throat. One flick of his wrist and he could drag it across her neck, opening her up to the bone. When Dane saw that, he froze.

"Stay away!" Davies cried, dragging Grier back a few feet and moving her clear of her desperate husband. "Stay away or I will kill her! If I cannot have her, then you cannot have her, either."

Dane had been listening closely to the chatter going on between Grier and Davies and Eolande, enough so that he could see one thing in particular – there was no doubt in his mind now that everything Grier had told him had been the truth. When she'd denied being ap Madoc's lover, she hadn't lied. Davies ap Madoc loved a woman who did not love him in return and, in that instant, he knew there had been no collusion.

No betrayal.

Dane felt worse than he had ever felt in his life as he realized his mistake. She tried to tell him, but he hadn't listened. He'd been stubborn and blind. Now he found himself praying that he would have the chance to tell Grier himself. He would apologize to the woman if it took the rest of his life, until she knew how much he loved her and how very sorry he was for having doubted her. A bad set of circumstances had caused him to lose faith in the only woman he'd ever loved.

God forgive him, he was a fool.

He had to save her.

From the corner of his eye, he could see William's red hair and he turned slightly, motioning the man to him. When William leaned into him, he spoke quietly.

"Get men on the battlements with crossbows aimed at ap Madoc and his men," he whispered. "They are to wait for your command."

William nodded, losing himself in the crowd of soldiers around the gatehouse and trying not to draw Davies' attention. As William headed off, Dane returned his attention to Davies, trying not to be unnerved by the sight of Grier's bloodied neck.

But it was a struggle.

"You cannot leave with her," he said calmly. "Ap Madoc, I can accept the attempt on my life. I understand your motivation. As a knight, death is part of my vocation. But the threat to my wife is something I cannot stomach. I have a feeling that even if you surrender her and I let you go, it will not be the end of it. You will come back, and back again, until either I am dead or you are dead. Is this a fair assumption?"

Davies was becoming increasingly unstable. He was ashamed, and cornered, and the woman he loved had told him in no uncertain terms that she did not return that love. That bewilderment was turning into rage.

"It is fair," he said through clenched teeth. "I will never stop."

"Then we must end this now."

"What do you mean?"

Dane dipped his head in Grier's direction. "Let her go and fight me," he said. "The winner shall get the lady and the dukedom. I do not wish to go the rest of my life looking over my shoulder for you and your archers. Fight me now and let us decide this matter, for I grow weary of this foolishness. Let us be done with it, once and for all."

Davies' gaze flicked around to all of the English standing around him. "It is not a fair fight," he said. "You have more men that I do."

Dane shook his head. "You misunderstand," he said. "I meant we shall fight each other, man to man. No armies, no *teulu*. Just you and me. Are you afraid to do it?"

That comment insulted Davies' courage and he didn't take kindly to it. Unfortunately, when he was enraged, he was reckless, as he was about to prove. Recklessness was one of Davies' most predictable traits.

"I am not afraid of any *Saesneg* bastard," he growled.

"Then accept my offer. You came to kill me, did you not? Let us see if you can."

In a flash, Davies removed the dirk on Grier's neck and shoved her at some of his men standing off to his right. Eolande was there, too, and Eolande rushed Grier before Davies' men could get to her. They threw their arms around each other and wept as Davies' men closed in around the pair.

The message was clear.

Dane knew that even as he looked at Grier, embracing Eolande. Grier was still in the control of Davies and his *teulu*, and he didn't like that in the least. But at the moment, he couldn't linger on it. She was safe so long as his men were close by, with their weapons, and they could get to her before Davies could stick a dagger into her should the situation go terribly wrong. He had to count on that. At the moment, he was more concerned about Davies himself.

He was about to have a fight to the death with the man.

And he was prepared to kill.

Dane took a moment to look Davies over; he was taller than Dane, but he was slender. That didn't mean he wasn't strong. Dane had no doubt that he could beat the man, and with Grier as the prize, he could do nothing less.

He intended to keep the woman he loved.

"Choose your weapon, ap Madoc," he said. "Anything you wish."

Davies had the dagger in his hand and he looked at it a moment before tossing it aside. Then he held up both hands.

"Fists," he said. "For what I have to do, I can do with my bare hands."

Dane thought the man was a bit overconfident, but he was pleased by the choice in weapons. He knew for a fact that he could pummel the man into the ground. But maybe that was *him* being overconfident. In any case, he was eager to get on with it, but not before he said something to his wife.

If ap Madoc got the better of him, he had to make sure it was said.

"Grier," he said.

His voice was quiet but firm. Hearing her name, Grier looked at him, her head coming up from Eolande's shoulder. She was pale, and her eyes were red-rimmed, but the love Dane felt for the woman when he looked at her was overwhelming. He'd made a terrible mistake; he knew that now. And he wasn't too proud to admit it.

He wanted her to hear it from his lips.

"I was wrong," he said. "I was wrong not to have believed you. If you cannot forgive me, I understand, but I hope you will consider it. I would be grateful."

Grier's mouth popped open in surprise and her hands flew to her mouth as if to hold back the gasp of shock. With all of the turmoil she'd gone through, the heartache and the anguish, those simple words ended it all as if her pain had never existed. Dane's words had wiped it all free until the love she felt for the man was the only thing she was aware of.

"There is nothing to forgive," she said tightly. "It was my fault. It was my clumsy attempt to help in a situation I should not have meddled in. I thought I could help, but I made a mess out of things. I hope you will forgive me, too."

Dane smiled faintly, hearing the adoration and sincerity in her voice. His heart swelled with joy. He wanted to tell her that he loved her, but there were dozens of men standing around, including one man who wanted Grier very badly. He was afraid that if he told her of his feelings for all to hear, it might incite ap Madoc somehow. But as he thought about it, he truly didn't care if the man knew or not. They were both fighting for the same women. The winner would depend on who loved her most, who was willing to fight the hardest.

Dane intended it should be him.

"Of course I forgive you," he said simply. "I love you. Remember that."

Grier looked at him with an expression that suggested she was shocked to the bone by his admission. But the light of warmth in her eyes, the one that Dane had become so familiar with, flamed into a roaring blaze as a smile of unimaginable beauty spread across her lips.

"And I love you," she said softly. "So very much."

Dane returned her smile. He heard her words, as nearly everyone else standing around them had, but he didn't care who knew it. He loved the woman and she loved him, and that was all that mattered. That knowledge gave him the strength of angels.

Turning to Davies, he could feel an unusual sense of power surge through him.

"Now," he growled, eyeing the man. "Let's get on with this."

Davies could only feel hatred as he looked at Dane. He'd heard Grier tell the man she loved him, and much as the declaration fed Dane's strength, it also fed Davies. If Dane was dead, then there would be no man for Grier to love. She would belong to Davies and he would make her love him. He *had* to make her love him. Perhaps in fighting Dane, she would see how strong he was and she would see how very much he loved her.

Delusional thoughts, but his thoughts nonetheless.

Davies was used to having his way in all things.

Wrapped in a dirty woolen cloak, with a long tunic and hose, Davies yanked off his cloak and tossed it to one of his men. When Dane saw him preparing, he did a little preparation of his own. Boden was still standing back behind him and he turned to the man.

"This should not last long," he muttered. "However, I will say this – if the worst happens and it looks as if I am losing, William has archers on the battlements. Someone must plant an arrow in ap Madoc and take out as many of his men as you can. But most importantly, get Grier away from here. Get her up to the keep and lock her in. Those bloody bastards must not have a chance to take her. Is that clear?"

Boden nodded grimly. "It is," he said. "Why can we not simply plant an arrow in ap Madoc now? The man killed Syler, Dane."

Dane lifted an eyebrow. "And that is exactly why I cannot finish him off right away," he said. "Ap Madoc is going to feel my wrath. Every blow I deliver will have Grier and Syler's name on it. I *will* have satisfaction, Boden. This is as much about me as it is about Grier or Syler. We are all involved. Do you understand that?"

Boden did. He didn't like it, but he understood. After a moment, he simply nodded, turning to lose himself in the English soldiers, quietly passing the word among them – *if it looks as if the duke will lose, grab Lady de Russe and take her to safety.* There were enough soldiers that the Welsh genuinely had no chance, but Boden understood Dane's need to teach ap Madoc a lesson. The man had tried to kill him and ended up taking out an innocent knight instead. Now, he was going to pay.

Let the schooling begin.

CHAPTER TWENTY

DANE THREW THE first punch, sending Davies flying.

Dane was well-built and muscular, but he was a lot stronger than he looked, and he threw the punch before Davies was fully prepared to take it. But Dane didn't care, nor did he give Davies a chance to recover. He went after the Welshman with a vengeance, fully intending to beat the man into a stupor and then strangle him. Since they had no weapons, it was the only way to end Davies' life, and Dane went on the offensive from the onset.

As Davies ended up on his knees, bells ringing in his ears, Dane jumped on him and threw an arm across his throat, preparing to kill the man from the beginning. He squeezed as Davies tried to dislodge him, but when that didn't work because he was starting to see stars, he grabbed a handful of dirt from the bailey beneath his hands and threw it back in Dane's face, temporarily blinding him.

As Dane launched himself backwards, off of Davies, the Welshman picked himself up and charged. Dane hadn't quite cleared his vision before Davies was on him, pummeling him in the gut and then slamming him on the back of the neck when he bent over. Dane went down and, now, Davies was on top of him.

But that didn't last long; Dane had five brothers and he knew how to fight and wrestle. Reaching behind him, he grabbed Davies by the hair and yanked hard, pulling Davies mostly off of him. Then, he rolled sideways, enough so that he was able to come up again and throw himself forward, pitching Davies to the ground. Then he threw two brutal punches, both to the face, and blood began to spray.

Now, the fight turned gory.

As Dane and Davies threw vicious punches at each other, William came down from the battlements and went to stand next to Boden. Together, the two of them watched the fight closely, hearing the increasing clamor from the men as they began to shout encouragement to their scrappy duke.

Usually, it was William and Boden wrestling or throwing punches at each other, and almost always in good fun unless one of them had seriously peeved the other party but, even then, they weren't out to kill each other. They were only trying to prove who was the strongest and, ultimately, the best fighter. But watching Dane and ap Madoc go at it, they were awed by Dane's fighting ability. Dane may have been the shortest de Russe brother, but he was by no means the weakest.

Boden began to have new respect for his older brother. And William felt the same.

"Remind me not to anger Dane any time soon," Boden muttered.

William could only nod his head, wincing when Dane threw a punch at ap Madoc's face that hit the man squarely in the nose. He swore he could hear the bones crack as blood went spraying over both men. He and Boden glanced at each other, shaking their heads with the brutality of the fight. Nearly at the same time, they looked to the opposite side of the circle of men surrounding the two combatants to see how Grier was handling it.

Terrified didn't quite cover the expression they saw.

She was clinging to the other woman, watching the fight with horror, turning her head away when the bloody spectacle became too much. As Boden and William watched her reaction, Boden leaned in to William.

"We have to get her away from those Welsh," he muttered. "I do not want to wait until the end. It is possible that they will not let her go even if Dane wins."

William nodded, for he'd been thinking the same thing. "What do you want me to do?"

Boden thought swiftly as ap Madoc delivered a blow that sent Dane stumbling backwards. "Ap Madoc's men are watching the fight," he said. "You could go over there and steal her away where she is standing. They wouldn't realize it until it was too late."

William was willing to do it. "You keep your eye on the fight," he said. "If it looks as if Dane is losing, give the signal to the archers overhead. They are awaiting your command."

Boden knew that. As William slipped away in the crowd, Boden glanced up to the battlements to see several archers positioned, their weapons aimed at the fight below. He felt much better knowing they were there, because when he returned his attention to the fight, it was clear that ap Madoc had managed to knock the wind out of Dane.

Even a man with many brothers got a licking once in a while, and Dane was getting his. Ap Madoc's blow had sent him onto his back and before he could get up, Davies was sitting on his chest, pummeling his head in the quest to knock him unconscious. The man was sitting in such a way that he was pinning one of Dane's arms, and Dane was having a difficult time avoiding the blows coming at him. Without any options, Dane had to ram a fist into ap Madoc's privates just to force the man to stop hitting him. It was a hard blow, and probably not too honorable, but it did the job; ap Madoc grunted and doubled over, giving Dane the chance he needed to push him onto his back and pounce.

On and on it went, blow after blow, and Dane had to admit he was becoming weary. Ap Madoc was, too, because he was becoming sloppy with his fists. The power behind the blows wasn't nearly what it had been at the start, and with that knowledge, Dane started planning his death blow.

In truth, he'd hoped to wear ap Madoc out, making the death blow easy, but ap Madoc had been surprisingly strong and steady. He hadn't been easy to wear down, which was where Dane had miscalculated slightly. Therefore, he was going to have to get him on the ground again in order to deliver the death blow. The more he fought with the man, the angrier he became. Ap Madoc was a man who was trying to take away everything Dane had, and he wasn't going to tolerate it any longer.

Feeling his exhaustion, Dane knew he had to move before it was too late.

The end was coming, and it was coming for ap Madoc.

———❦———

GRIER COULDN'T BEAR to watch but, on the other hand, she couldn't look away.

Her future was being decided before her very eyes.

Clinging to Eolande, the women watched as Dane and Davies threw punches at each other, rolling around in the dirt and pounding on one another until the blood began to splatter. Grier thought she might sincerely become ill as she watched even though most of the blood was Davies'.

It was all so foolish and wasteful.

It didn't have to come to this.

"Why could he not simply leave me alone?" she murmured to Eolande. "Why did he have to come, Landy? *Why?*"

Eolande was holding fast to Grier. "Pride," she said softly. "Pride and envy. As long as you remained at St. Idloes, he was willing to let you go, but the moment you became another man's possession, he went mad with rage and envy."

Grier flinched as Davies landed a serious blow to Dane's face. Looking away for a moment, she closed her eyes tightly.

"He is a fool," she hissed. "Your brother is a ridiculous fool. Does he not realize I am Dane's wife? Does he truly think he can steal me away?"

Eolande was watching her brother's blood splatter over the ground. "Are you truly happy, Grier?"

Grier nodded, turning to Eolande with an expression that conveyed the distress she was feeling. "Aye," she murmured. "I love my husband. I never thought I would. You know I did not wish to marry him. But he has been so kind and sweet... aye, I am very happy. And now this..."

She trailed off, unable to continue, and Eolande was struck by the reality of the situation. Grier had actually fallen in love with her handsome husband, for it was the first time Eolande had ever seen him. *Dane de Russe,* he'd called himself. Big and blond, he'd looked at Grier in a way that made Eolande's stomach quiver. There had been gentleness and adoration there, as bright and brilliant as when the world was new. All women needed to be looked at the way Dane de Russe looked at Grier.

And now Davies was trying to ruin everything.

Eolande's heart was breaking in more ways than she could comprehend.

"Davies came to me at St. Idloes and told me that he'd killed your husband," she said after a moment. "That is why I am here, Grier. He asked me to come with him so that when he married you, I could live here with you both. Even though you've been gone a few short days from St. Idloes, I have missed you terribly. I was very lonely without you. So, I came with him, but I also came with him to ensure he did not get into any trouble. See how I have failed."

There was a loud grunt and both women turned to see Dane literally picking up Davies and throwing him onto the ground, momentarily stunning him. As they watched, Dane came down on Davies' chest and managed to pin both arms with his knees. His hands went straight for Davies' throat and he began to squeeze.

The entire crowd of men grew silent as Dane had the Welshman by the throat. He was squeezing so hard that Davies' face was turning a deep shade of red. Realizing her brother was being strangled, Eolande began to panic.

"Do not let him kill my brother," she begged Grier, tugging on her. "Grier, please – do not let him kill Davies!"

Grier glanced at her friend, truly unable to look away from what was happening. Dane was winning and Davies was dying; it was as simple as that. But beside her, Eolande was beginning to emit hysterical pants.

It was, perhaps, the most difficult thing Grier had ever had to face.

"I cannot interfere," she said, finally tearing her gaze away to look at Eolande. "Davies has terrorized us, Landy. He killed one of my husband's knights, thinking it was my husband. You heard what was said; he has threatened to never stop until Dane is dead and I belong to him. Why *did* he come to Shrewsbury today? He thought Dane was dead, so clearly, he came to claim the widow. You know it is true."

Eolande was looking at her brother in horror. Davies' face was now turning blue. "But he is my brother!"

Grier was surprisingly unmoved. Given the choice between Davies' life and Dane's, she would choose Dane every time.

It wasn't even a difficult choice.

"He is a murderer," Grier said. "If Dane does not kill him, then he will kill Dane. Landy, I love you... but I cannot live the rest of my life fearing Davies. And I cannot let him kill Dane. He should have never returned to Shrewsbury, and now he will pay the price."

Eolande realized that her friend was not going to intervene. It was a shocking realization, which spoke of Grier's love for her new husband.

That wasn't what Eolande had expected.

Frantic, she watched as Dane continued to squeeze and Davies' face turned a deep shade of purple. Another few moments, and Davies would be dead, strangled right before her very eyes. Her brother was reckless, and arrogant, and he had done some despicable things in his life, but he was still her brother. He had been the only one out of their entire family that had ever paid any attention to her. Eolande knew Davies shouldn't have come to Shrewsbury and she'd warned him against it.

But he'd come.

And now he was dying at the hands of Grier's husband.

Something snapped in Eolande at that moment; she couldn't stand by and watch her brother die. Grier wouldn't stop it, but she would. One of Davies' men was standing next to her and she caught the flash of the dagger on his belt. Grabbing the blade, she suddenly charged out towards the fighting men, blade held high as she aimed it right for Dane's back. It was clear what she meant to do with it.

She meant to kill.

Grier was startled by the moment, realizing with horror what Eolande was planning. As she screamed and started to run after her, one of the nervous archers on the wall let loose their arrow, and it sailed right into Eolande's left shoulder, carving straight through her body and the tip coming out somewhere near her right hip.

She fell like a stone.

Dane, startled by the commotion going on behind him, ended Davies' suffering by using a twisting motion on his neck, snapping it cleanly. He was finished torturing the man. With his enemy dead, he leapt up from the body and turned to see Grier as she fell atop Eolande, who had a massive arrow embedded in her. Since Dane hadn't seen Eolande as she'd run at him with the intent to kill him, he was appalled and confused by the sight. Staggering over to his wife, he fell to his knees beside her, his hand on her head.

"Grier," he said, breathing heavily. "What happened?"

Grier was in a flood of tears as she lay over her friend. "She was going to kill you," she wept. "She knew her brother was wrong, but he was still her brother. She did not want you to kill him, but I did not believe her capable… oh, God, I did not believe her capable of this…"

With that, she collapsed over her friend, weeping painfully. Dane looked around. He could see the dirk near Eolande's right hand, now blade-first into the dirt where it had fallen. Behind him lay the body of Davies, his head twisted at an odd angle.

Struggling to his feet, Dane looked at Davies' men, who were gathered in a suspicious and fearful group, surrounded by Shrewsbury men. Weary, bloodied, and beaten, he faced the Welshmen with as much dignity as he could muster.

"He killed one of my men and coveted my wife," he said to them. "Had I not killed him, he would have killed me. I am certain most, if not all, of you were present in the raid on the marketplace, but I will not take you prisoner. Consider this my mercy. Take your lord and return home, and tell the Lords of Godor of my mercy in not punishing all of you for Davies' actions. But know this; the Duke of Shrewsbury's mercy is only given once. Cross me and I shall be unforgiving. As for your lord's sister… it was unfortunate that she chose to attack me, and we are greatly saddened by her death. I will say no more."

With that, he stepped aside as Davies' men came forward to claim their lord, bringing the cloak he'd tossed away to wrap him up in it. Dane watched for a few moments, reconciling himself to the brutal ending of a brutal battle, but he could hear Grier weeping behind him and that was of more concern to him at the moment.

His wife.

His heart was aching for her.

Grier was sobbing her heart out as she embraced her dead friend, so very brokenhearted about the chain of events. Dane knelt down beside her again, a gentle hand on her back as he sought to give her comfort.

"I am sorry," he said hoarsely. "I know she was your friend."

Grier sniffled, raising herself up to look down at Eolande's peaceful face. "She was," she wept softly. "She has been my friend since we were very young. I wish she had not charged you, but I know it was because she wanted to protect her brother. They were always close. Whether he was right or whether he was wrong was not the issue. He was her family."

Dane wasn't sure what he could say to that because the cost of Eolande's attempt to save Davies had been her life. He felt guilty when he knew he had no reason to.

"The archers were ordered to protect me," he said. "They were doing as they'd been ordered. I am only sorry your friend tried to interfere. Surely, if I had seen her, I would have simply disarmed her. I hope you know that."

Grier wiped at her eyes, her nose. Then, she looked up at him, her hazel eyes glimmering with tears.

"I know that," she said. "Although I grieve for Eolande, I understand why she did it. Had the situation been reversed, and it had been Davies squeezing the life from you, I would have run at him with a knife, too, and gladly planted it in his back. I would do anything to protect you, Dane, just as I tried to do and so badly failed. Mayhap it is selfish to say so, but the fact that you are alive and well, even though the cost has been great, is all that matters to me. *You* are all that matters to me."

That warmth was there again, that powerful warmth that Dane had felt from her since nearly the beginning. The spark that had fed their attraction to one another had turned into a roaring blaze of love so strong that nothing could destroy it. There was no other way to describe it. It was something Dane had almost lost through his own mistrust and foolishness but, now, it was back stronger than before.

Boden came around with a blanket to cover up Eolande, and Grier realized her time with the woman was over. She kissed Eolande's forehead and whispered her farewells before rising, standing beside Dane as Boden and William gently wrapped Eolande in the woolen blanket. There was nothing more they could do for her but hand her over to her own people, and they did, giving her over to Davies' *teulu*.

Grier and Dane watched as the ap Madoc men carried Davies from the gatehouse, followed by Eolande's small bundle. Grier wiped the tears from her eyes, so very grieved over the loss of her friend and, in a sense, the loss of Davies as well. She'd always known him as a rather quiet and shy man, but over the past year, something had changed in him. He wasn't the man she'd known. Now, he was united with Eolande in death. It was Davies' foolish arrogance that had brought them to this end.

Once they filtered through the gatehouse and peacefully departed, Grier's attention turned back to her husband. Turning to the man, she gazed up at him, studying his beaten face, thinking she'd never seen him look so strong or so handsome. At the end of the day, all that mattered was that he was alive, and in her arms, and the gratitude she felt went beyond measure.

"You look as if you could use some tending," she said, a weak smile on her lips.

Dane smiled in return, his bottom lip cut and swollen. "I have had worse beatings from my brothers," he said. "You needn't worry about me. I will heal."

Grier's gaze drifted over his face, reaching up to get a look at the cut on his lip. She touched him gently before dropping her hand.

"Nonetheless, I will clean your cuts," she said. Then, she hesitated. "But if you truly feel as if they are not too terrible, would you mind if I went to the chapel to pray for Eolande first? I should very much like to."

Dane shook his head. "Nay," he said hoarsely. "I will go with you. In fact, I am never going to leave your side again, Grier. Not ever."

His words brought tears to her eyes; she didn't know why, but they did. It was everything she'd always wanted to hear from the man, this noble and powerful duke who, in his humility, was the strongest man in the world in her eyes. There was no one more perfect than her Dane, and she loved him more with every breath she took.

"Nor I, yours," she whispered. "We are bound for eternity, you and I."

Dane kissed her, leaving a bloody mark from the cut on his lip, but Grier hardly cared. She threw her arms around his neck and he swept her into his arms, carrying her off towards the chapel, holding her as tightly as he had ever held anything in his life. For certainly, he'd almost lost her, in more ways than one, and he was never going to risk losing her again.

From a reluctant groom to a duke in love, Dane de Russe finally discovered what it was to be a truly happy man.

A man who had finally discovered his heart.

EPILOGUE

Two weeks later

DANE HAD HIS hand to his jaw.

"Damnation," he muttered. "I swear I still have a loose tooth."

He was sitting in the great hall of Shrewsbury on a cold December evening, trying to eat a piece of bread but feeling pain in his jaw where ap Madoc had pummeled him. Two weeks later, it still hurt. As he moved his jaw around, trying to chew around the sore tooth, Boden and William were at the end of the table, arm wrestling each other.

The pair had already gone through several rounds of wrestling, and half the room was betting on them with the same senior sergeant taking the bets and making sure neither Boden nor William cheated, which they had been known to do on occasion. But in this round, Boden won, slamming William's hand to the table and drawing a cheer from those who had bet on him. Money exchanged hands at an alarming rate.

It was a normal night in Shrewsbury's great hall after a day that had seen snow fall lightly. Even now, a fine dusting of snow covered the ground and the fires in the castle burned brightly against the chill. Sentries walked their rounds with a hint of white powder on their shoulders and heads, and in the hall, men were crammed around the tables, enjoying the roaring blaze in the hearth.

Still, it was a lovely night and a cause for some celebration.

It was Dastan and Charlisa's first night returned from Wales and from the burial of Syler. Laria had decided to remain with her family at Netherworld Castle, so the pair returned without her. Charlisa sat with Grier, chatting animatedly, while Dastan and Dane had been discussing the events of the last two weeks for most of the day. Even now, they sat at the end of the table, discussing the incident with ap Madoc down to the last detail. There hadn't been any word from the Lords of Godor about it, but Dane was concerned with retaliation, as was Dastan.

That was the subject at hand.

But there was something neither Dastan or Charlisa knew, and that was the misunderstanding between Dane and Grier that had very nearly driven them apart. Dane didn't feel it was necessary to tell them, and Grier agreed, so the issue was something that they'd kept private. However, they had discussed it exhaustively between them for the first few days after the incident, including how Dane had come into possession of Grier's letter.

Euphemia, the catalyst for the entire event, had disappeared, more than likely having gone back to her tavern in Welshpool, but neither Grier nor Dane would go after her. The woman had served her purpose for the first few days of Grier's life in the outside world, but given the fact that she'd tried to betray her mistress, no one wanted her back. There wasn't anything trustworthy about her.

In truth, the entire circumstance with the letter had been a growing experience for both Dane and Grier, as two people who hadn't known one another yet expecting trust and understanding under strenuous circumstances. Grier had learned not to keep things from her husband, and Dane had learned to trust his wife in all things.

What hadn't driven them apart had only made them stronger.

Even now, as Dane spoke to Dastan, his gaze was on Grier as she listened to Charlisa chatter. She was wearing her marriage brooch again, and her wedding ring, and it made Dane proud simply to look upon her. When Dane caught her eye, he winked and she smiled one of those adoring smiles he was becoming accustomed to. Three weeks into their marriage and neither one could remember any turmoil they'd gone through, only the joy.

Only the love.

It was something even Dastan could see as he watched Dane make eyes at his wife. He was quite happy that the very reluctant bride he'd confronted those weeks ago at St. Idloes had turned into a wife that Dane was proud to have, and he was certain Lord Garreth would have been thrilled. Perhaps the old man had known something they hadn't at the time, that the serious and dedicated knight he'd known as Lord Blackmore would, indeed, make the best sort of duke, and that the daughter he'd sent away those years ago would make a fine duchess. She was a de Lara, after all, and de Laras were the strong sort.

Grier was no exception.

But the madness of Davies ap Madoc was something Dastan was still coming to grips with. Poor Grier had been caught up in it some-how, and the fight to the death was something that Dastan still had a difficult time comprehending. Dane had taken on the Welshman who had killed Syler and he had won, the very same Welshman who had offered for Grier's hand. It was a complex situation but, given all the facts, Dastan wholeheartedly endorsed Dane's resolution of the situation. They couldn't spend the rest of their lives on-guard waiting for the next attempt against Dane's life.

The man had done what needed to be done, and Syler had been avenged. Still, Dastan wished he'd been here.

"I'm not surprised your teeth are loose," Dastan said upon hearing Dane's complaint. "But I am surprised that is the only aftereffect of the fight you described. It sounds as if it could have been much worse."

Dane smiled weakly, still moving his jaw around. "Mayhap," he said, setting his bread down and reaching for his cup of ale. "To be truthful, I am concerned for Grier. I told you that her friend, ap Madoc's sister, was killed in the chaos."

"Aye, you did. A tragedy. What possessed the woman to try and stab you?"

Dane lifted his shoulders, a rather sad gesture. "Momentary insanity," he speculated. "Who is to say? Grier said the woman was very protective over her brother, so I am sure she simply lost all control when she saw that he was losing the fight. I do not blame her; there is no anger on my part. I simply wish she had been stopped before the archer took her down. Her death was a needless one."

Dastan nodded his head faintly. "How has your lady wife dealt with it?"

Dane's eyes moved to Grier, down the table. "That is why I am concerned," he said. "She has wept over it since then. She is sad, of course, but she is also torn. She is grieved for her friend's death, yet had the woman not been stopped, she would have planted a dagger in my back, and Grier would now be grieving for me instead."

"A difficult situation, no doubt."

"Indeed."

Over at the other end of the table, William had just crushed Boden in yet another arm wrestling match and threw up his arms, gloating over his victory as some of the men cheered. Boden, unhappy that William was now taunting him, rushed the man and the two of them went down on the floor, rolling around as they tried to smash one another into the dirt and rushes. Dane and Dastan watched, shaking their heads at the antics.

"And yet," Dastan said, "some things never change."

Dane snorted as he lifted his cup. "Those two? Never. They have been doing the same thing since they were young boys."

"You would never know how much they adore one another."

Dane started to laugh, cut short when a soldier covered in a layer of snow rushed into the hall and headed for the dais. Dane thought he'd heard the sound of the Shrewsbury horn, but he couldn't be sure. He was on his feet as the soldier approached.

"My lord," the soldier greeted him, breathless. "An army has passed through town and is now upon the castle."

Dane frowned. "An army?" he repeated. "On a night like this?"

The soldier nodded. "They say they are Warminster, my lord."

Dane's eyes widened. "Are they flying banners?"

"Dark green with a black dragon upon them, my lord."

"Then open the gates!" Dane commanded. "That is my father, you fool. Open the gates immediately!"

The soldier fled and Dane whistled loudly in the direction of Boden and William, causing them to stop their wrestling.

"Boden!" Dane snapped. "Father has arrived. Get up out of that dirt and go greet him. *Run!*"

Boden was on his feet, charging out of the hall with William and a dozen other soldiers on his heels, all of them rushing out into the snowy night just as the portcullis in the great gatehouse began to grind open. As the men flew out, Dane and Dastan moved to the women down the table.

"Warminster has arrived," Dane said excitedly as he pulled out Grier's chair. "My father is here. God's Bones, 'tis a surprise. I had no idea he was coming."

Grier, who had been deep in conversation with Charlisa about her trip to Wales, had a rather shocked look on her face as Dane pulled her to her feet.

"Your father?" she said. "Didn't you tell me that he was too ill to travel?"

Dane nodded as he took her by the arm and headed towards the hall entry. "I did," he said. "But I also sent word to him almost two months ago about your father's death and our impending marriage. Clearly, he has decided to come and see for himself."

Charlisa was walking with Dastan directly behind Dane and Grier, and when she heard mention of Warminster's arrival, she rushed off to organize the servants and prepare for their new guests. Once a chatelaine, always a chatelaine. Dastan let her go, instead remaining with Dane and Grier. He'd only heard of the great Duke of Warminster and was eager to meet the man for himself.

Together, the group of them headed out into the cold night, walking through the light snow of the bailey and heading towards the gatehouse where a large party of soldiers and knights were now spilling in.

Dozens of torches lined the walls and the bailey, creating a great golden glow against the dark night. Dane was looking for his father, or brothers, and his gaze fell upon all of them in succession – his father astride his big, charcoal-colored stallion, and brothers, Cort and Gage. Boden and William were already jumping all over Gage, throwing the man to the ground in a gleeful and brutal greeting, which brought a grin to Dane's lips. But most surprisingly, he caught sight of his brother, Trenton, and of the great Matthew Wellesbourne. His heart swelled so that it brought tears to his eyes.

All of them, here.

His family.

God, it was too good to believe. The first thing he did was take Grier by the hand and run through the snow towards his father, who was just dismounting his steed with the help of his son, Cort. When Cort de Russe looked over and saw Dane approaching, his features lit up like one of the torches in the bailey. It was a brilliant smile. He rushed his brother and threw him in a hug, nearly knocking over Grier in the process.

"Dane!" Cort said happily, pulling back to kiss the man on both cheeks. "The Duke of Shrewsbury as I live and breathe. Congratulations, old man. Well-deserved!"

Dane laughed at his younger, and very handsome, brother. "Thank you," he said. He still had Grier by the hand and he pulled her against him, a big arm around her shoulders. "This is Grier, my wife. Grier, this is my brother, Cortland, but you must call him Cort. He'll punch anyone who calls him Cortland."

Grier found herself looking into the face of a young knight with copper curls and green eyes. She could faintly see the resemblance between the man and her husband.

"Welcome to Shrewsbury, Cort," she said. "I am very happy to meet you and I promise I will not call you Cortland."

Cort grinned, a smile that looked very much like his father. "A pleasure, Lady de Russe," he said. "May I say that I envy my brother his beautiful wife? He did very well for himself."

Grier flushed, red cheeks that could be seen even in the light of the torches. As Dane laughed softly at her embarrassment, his father turned away from his horse as the steed was led away and Dane found himself looking upon a much older man than he remembered.

Gaston de Russe, Duke of Warminster and the man known throughout the realm as the Dark One, had made himself known.

Dane had last seen his father over a year ago when he'd left Warminster to travel to Blackmore. His father was an enormous man; several inches over six feet, with hands the size of trenchers. He was big, strong, and intimidating. That was the Gaston de Russe that the world knew.

But the man facing him was a much older form of his father. He'd been diagnosed with a cancer in his throat last year, although Gaston had resisted that diagnosis. But, clearly, something was wrong, and as Dane looked into the man's face, he could feel his heart breaking. He looked so old and so very weary. Dane let go of Grier's hand and went to his father, throwing his arms around the man and burying his face in his neck.

Then, the tears came.

Papa...

He couldn't stand to see the man he loved most in the world so ill. It was breaking his heart. He couldn't even speak for the lump in his throat, something that Gaston must have sensed.

He held his son by marriage, but a man he could not have loved more even if he had been his son by blood. Hugging him tightly, he could feel Dane's body shake as he sobbed a few times, so very emotional at the sight of his sickly father.

"It is good to see you, Dane," Gaston said, his voice very raspy because of the condition in his throat. "Do not despair. I am still here, still alive. And I had to come and see you, even though your mother tried to lock me in a room so I could not leave."

That brought laughter through Dane's tears. He pulled his face away from his father's neck, wiping at his eyes, trying to make light of a very emotional reunion.

"I am not surprised," he said. "How is my mother?"

"Beautiful and strong."

"That is good to hear." Dane looked Gaston over again, acquainting himself with his father's state. "And you? I did not expect you to come when I sent the missive about de Lara's death and my marriage, Papa. I just wanted you to know what had happened."

Gaston smiled faintly, cupping the man's face with his big hand. "I know," he said. "But I had to come. My son, the duke. I am so proud of you, Dane. But you already know that. I have always been proud of you, even when you were young and ridiculous."

Tears stung Dane's eyes but he fought them. Instead, he smiled. "I love you, too," he said quietly. "It is such a blessing that you are here. Come, now, meet my wife."

Taking the man by the hand, he led his father over to Grier and Cort, who were standing a few feet away in conversation.

"Grier," Dane said, catching her attention. "This is my father, Gaston. He is every bit as great as I have told you."

Grier focused on Gaston, a smile on her lips, as she reached out to take his hand. "My lord," she greeted. "I have so wanted to meet you because I wanted to thank you."

Gaston's gaze drifted over the beautiful woman. "Why is that, my dear?"

Her smile broadened. "For Dane, of course," she said. "You have raised a fine son. I am so very fortunate, and I wanted to thank you for that."

Gaston liked her already. Bending down, he kissed her on the cheek, grinning at her and holding her hands tightly as Matthew and Trenton walked up.

"Dane," Matthew Wellesbourne spoke seriously. A big man with curly blond hair that had mostly gone gray, he was Gaston's best friend in the world and William's father. He pointed to his frolicking son. "I sent Willie with you so the man could grow up. What I see now does *not* impress me."

They all turned to see William, Gage, and Boden wrestling in the snow, frightening horses as they went. As Grier fought off laughter, Dane sighed heavily.

"I know you cannot tell by looking at him, Uncle Matthew, but he has, indeed, grown since he has been with me," he said. "It is something about those three together that brings out the naughty lad in each of them. They will be doing that when they are old and gray, you know."

Matthew knew that, too. In a sense, it was good to see that some things never changed, not even his wild youngest son or the younger de Russe boys. The fact that some things stayed the same was oddly comforting.

"I suppose," he said, his gaze falling on Grier. "Your lady wife, I presume?"

Dane nodded as he looked at Grier. "My dear wife," he said affectionately. "My lady, this is Matthew Wellesbourne, Earl of Hereford, and standing next to him is my brother, Trenton. Greater men you will never meet."

As Matthew went to speak to Grier and Gaston, Dane went to Trenton. Trenton, his older brother by a year, and Dane were inordinately close, and Trenton was the man Dane respected most in the world next to his father. Trenton had married the year before and had given up his position with the king in order to settle down and help Gaston manage his estates.

Now that Gaston was growing weaker, and sicker, Trenton had taken on a tremendous amount of responsibility. As the Earl of Westbury, he was the heir to the dukedom of Warminster.

A more powerful man had never lived.

Dane extended his hand to Trenton, taking it tightly. "I am surprised to see you," he admitted. "The great and mighty Westbury on my doorstep. I have missed you, Brother."

Trenton grinned; like most of the de Russe male offspring, he looked like his father to a fault. He was the man's size and strength, and nearly his personality, too. He'd had some demons in his life but, thanks to the woman he married, his life was finally running smoothly for once. For Dane, that was very good to see.

"I have missed you, also," Trenton said. "You and I usually do not spend so much time apart, but with my duties with Warminster, and your new holdings in the northern Marches, I'm afraid separation might be a new way of life for us."

Dane nodded, regretfully. "But I will always be at your side if you need me; you know that," he said. Then, he glanced at Gaston as he lowered his voice. "Why is he here? He looks terrible, Trenton. I cannot believe Mother let him come."

Trenton's gaze moved to Gaston, also. "When he received your missive about the dukedom and marriage, nothing could keep him away," he muttered. "Mother actually locked him in a chamber, trying to keep him from going. The only way she would let him travel is if all of us went with him – me, Uncle Matthew, Cort, and Gage. She would not let him go without a huge support system."

Now it made sense as to why so many of his family members had come. "How has he been?" Dane asked.

Trenton put his hand on his brother's shoulder. "Not well," he said honestly. "He spends most of his time with his grandchildren and he does not travel. That is why it took us so long to get here; we traveled slowly and stopped frequently, for his sake. But nothing would stop him, Dane; you have to know that. He is so proud of you and what you have become. I heard him tell Mother, once, that he could now die happy because Trenton and Dane had finally come into their own."

Dane closed his eyes, a brief and miserable gesture. "I hope he did not hasten that death by coming here," he said. "Come, let us go inside the hall where it is warm. He should not be out here in the cold."

Trenton agreed. They moved towards the group that was now circled around Grier, and even though she was the center of attention, which usually embarrassed her, she was carrying on a charming conversation, bringing laughter from both Gaston and Matthew. It made Dane's heart swell with gratitude to see that; his beautiful wife, now blossoming before his very eyes.

He, too, couldn't have been prouder.

"Let's not stand out here in the snow any longer," Dane said, pushing between Cort and Matthew to take Grier by the arm. "My wife will be just as entertaining in the hall, where it is warm and we are not being snowed on."

The group of them began to walk towards the hall as the Warminster escort was disbanded behind them. However, William and Boden and Gage were still roughhousing, so they left those three to their own snowy fun. In fact, Matthew was watching the trio, shaking his head at their antics.

"Is this what has been happening at Shrewsbury?" he asked Dane. "This place is so slow and unexciting that those three can spend all of their time wrestling?"

Dane looked at the man in surprise. "Shrewsbury?" he said. "*Slow*?"

Gaston put his arm around his son's shoulders. "Admit it," he said. "You've found a peaceful and completely dull command in Shrewsbury. Nothing exciting ever happens here."

Dane lifted his eyebrows, looking at his wife, who was looking at him with the same expression.

Nothing exciting ever happens in Shrewsbury.

Dane had to shake his head.

"Give me time, Papa," he said. "I will tell you just how unexciting Shrewsbury has been since I have assumed command. I think it might surprise you."

Gaston laughed softly. "I am an old man, Dane," he said. "It takes quite a bit to surprise me. Have you even used the legendary Shrewsbury battle horn yet? That thing must be rusting for lack of use."

Dane had to laugh. "You think so, do you?"

Dane was still laughing when they entered the hall, met by Charlisa and her gracious hospitality. By the end of the evening, not only was Gaston surprised by the deceptively peaceful Shrewsbury, so was everyone else. Shrewsbury wasn't the bucolic corner of Shropshire that they thought it was.

But more than the life-and-death struggle that Dane and Grier had been forced to endure, one thing was readily apparent to Gaston – the gap-toothed, skinny lad he'd first met those years ago had grown into a fine, strong man without a shadow of Guy Stoneley's manner in him. Perhaps Dane was a Stoneley by blood, but his heart and soul were purely de Russe.

And that gap-toothed, skinny young man had finally found his piece of heaven.

∝ THE END ∾

Children of the Duke and Duchess of Shrewsbury, Dane and Grier
Rory
Etienne
Adreanna
Felicity
Sophie
Sebastien
Tristen
Gregor

The de Russe Legacy:
The Falls of Erith
Lord of War: Black Angel
The Iron Knight
Beast
The Dark One: Dark Knight
The White Lord of Wellesbourne
Dark Moon
Dark Steel

AFTERWORD

I truly hope you've enjoyed Dane and Grier's story. Now, to clarify a couple of things –

As you've seen, Grier is the last of the de Lara family, the Lords of the Trinity Castles (or Lords of the Trilaterals, as they are also called). There are two branches of the de Lara family.

The first branch is the Lords of the Trilaterals, which stemmed from Luc de Lara, who came over with the Duke of Normandy (see WARWOLFE for this character). The de Laras come from Spain, and Luc de Lara was the Count of Boucau. One of the direct descendants of this branch is Sean de Lara (LORD OF THE SHADOWS). You also meet Sean's father and brother in ARCHANGEL, and the Lords of the Trilaterals are discussed a bit in that book, too.

The second branch of the de Lara family is the Earls of Carlisle (DRAGONBLADE), because Tate de Lara was adopted by the de Lara family. Being the bastard son of Edward I, the king sent his infant son to the de Laras to both shield him and take care of him, so that branch of the family is de Lara in name only – by blood, they are Plantagenet.

Therefore, Shrewsbury is not the *Dragonblade*/Earl of Carlisle branch, but the Sean de Lara branch. This book takes place three hundred years after *Lord of the Shadows*, but I think it's particularly cool that Dane is now the Lord of the Trinity Castles as well as the Duke of Shrewsbury. I think Sean de Lara would have been very proud, and comforted, knowing that his family properties and family legacy are in the hands of a competent de Russe. Since my books cover approximately 450 years (the entire stretch of the High Middle Ages), sometimes there are centuries between books, especially with descendants, and the House of de Russe is my latest (most recent) house. They kind of close up the Medieval World and take us into the Tudor World.

And with that, I hope you enjoyed the mini-family reunion at the end, brief as it was. It did my heart good to write about Gaston and Matthew one more time, and it does my heart good to see how fine and noble their children have become (except for William, Boden, and Gage, but they'll have their time, eventually!).

Much love,

ABOUT KATHRYN LE VEQUE

Medieval Just Got Real.

KATHRYN LE VEQUE is a USA TODAY Bestselling author, an Amazon All-Star author, and a #1 bestselling, award-winning, multi-published author in Medieval Historical Romance and Historical Fiction. She has been featured in the NEW YORK TIMES and on USA TODAY's HEA blog. In March 2015, Kathryn was the featured cover story for the March issue of InD'Tale Magazine, the premier Indie author magazine. She was also a quadruple nominee (a record!) for the prestigious RONE awards for 2015.

Kathryn's Medieval Romance novels have been called 'detailed', 'highly romantic', and 'character-rich'. She crafts great adventures of love, battles, passion, and romance in the High Middle Ages. More than that, she writes for both women AND men – an unusual crossover for a romance author – and Kathryn has many male readers who enjoy her stories because of the male perspective, the action, and the adventure.

On October 29, 2015, Amazon launched Kathryn's Kindle Worlds Fan Fiction site WORLD OF DE WOLFE PACK. Please visit Kindle Worlds for Kathryn Le Veque's World of de Wolfe Pack and find many action-packed adventures written by some of the top authors in their genre using Kathryn's characters from the de Wolfe Pack series. As Kindle World's FIRST Historical Romance fan fiction world, Kathryn Le Veque's World of de Wolfe Pack will contain all of the great story-telling you have come to expect.

Kathryn loves to hear from her readers. Please find Kathryn on Facebook at Kathryn Le Veque, Author, or join her on Twitter @kathrynleveque, and don't forget to visit her website and sign up for her blog at www.kathrynleveque.com.

Please follow Kathryn on Bookbub for the latest releases and sales: bookbub.com/authors/kathryn-le-veque.

Made in the USA
Monee, IL
06 March 2020